FRONTIER MAGIC · BOOK ONE

Thirteenth Child

PATRICIA C. WREDE

SCHOLASTIC INC.

NEW YORK TORONTO LONDON AUCKLAND
SYDNEY MEXICO CITY NEW DELHI HONG KONG

This book was originally published in hardcover
by Scholastic Press in 2009.

ISBN 978-0-545-03345-9

12 11 10 9 8 7 6 5 4 3 2 1   10 11 12 13 14 15/0

Printed in the U.S.A.   40
This edition first printing, May 2010

The text type was set in Griffo.
Book design by Christopher Stengel

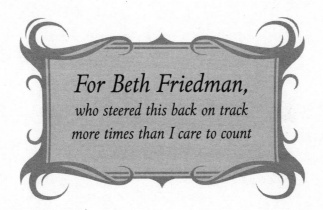

For Beth Friedman,
who steered this back on track
more times than I care to count

CHAPTER 1

EVERYBODY KNOWS THAT A SEVENTH SON IS LUCKY. THINGS COME A little easier to him, all his life long: love and money and fine weather and the unexpected turn that brings good fortune from bad circumstances. A lot of seventh sons go for magicians, because if there's one sort of work where luck is more useful than any other, it's making magic.

And everybody knows that the seventh son of a seventh son is a natural-born magician. A double-seven doesn't even need schooling to start working spells, though the magic comes on faster and safer if he gets some. When he's grown and come into his power for true and all, he can even do the Major Spells on his own, the ones that can call up a storm or quiet one, move the earth or still it, anger the ocean or calm it to glassy smoothness. People are real nice to a double-seventh son.

Nobody seems to think much about all the other sons, or the daughters. There's nearly always daughters, because hardly anybody has seven sons right in a row, boom, like that. Sometimes there are so many daughters that people give up trying for seven sons. After all, there's plenty enough work in raising eleven or twelve childings, and a thirteenth child — son or daughter — is unlucky. So everybody says.

Papa and Mama didn't pay much attention to what everybody says, I guess, because there are fourteen of us. Lan is the youngest, a double-seven, and he's half the reason we moved away from Helvan Shores when I was five. The other half of the reason was me.

I'm Eff — the seventh daughter. Lan's twin . . .

. . . and a thirteenth child.

From the day I was old enough to understand, I heard people talking to Mama and Papa about what to do with me. Aunt Tilly was the kindest. She only sighed and said it was a lucky thing I'd come first, or Lan would have been a thirteenth child with all the power of a double-seventh son. I wouldn't be near so much a danger when I went bad, Aunt Tilly said. Uncle Earn and Aunt Janna disagreed. They said Mama and Papa ought to have drowned me as soon as Lan was safely born, and it wasn't too late yet if they just had the resolution.

There were plenty of others, too, all anxious to tell Mama and Papa how I was sure to go bad, and to report every little thing I did as evidence they were right. If I spilled my soup, it was done apurpose and with evil in mind; if a ball I kicked went astray and tore up the new plantings in the kitchen garden, it was done deliberately in malice and spite. And of course their children heard the talk, just like I did, and if they didn't understand it all, they understood enough to make my life a misery.

My cousins were the worst, mainly because there were so many of them. Papa had six older brothers and three older sisters, and four of my uncles and two of my aunts had married and stayed in Helvan Shores. Sometimes I thought the whole town was related to me. But even the children who weren't relatives took their cue from my cousins.

I tried to stay out of trouble, but when I hid away from my cousins, they said I was sly and sneaking. Mama and Papa started giving me gray, worried looks when they thought I wasn't noticing. My older brothers and sisters, the ones nearest me in age, tried to protect me sometimes, but sometimes they joined in teasing me. Lan was the only one who always stuck up for me, no matter what.

When Lan and I were almost five, and because Lan was the seventh son of a seventh son, our grandfather had decided he should have a private tutor. "He's still too young to learn spells, of course, but he can learn the theory," my grandfather said, with a sidelong look at me. "Private lessons will make sure he learns goodness as well as strength and skill." Even then, I didn't need him to say anything more. I knew that what he really wanted was to make sure Lan got his magic lessons without me anywhere near, in case I might drag him down when I eventually went bad.

Mama and Papa looked troubled, but they couldn't turn down such a generous offer. I was heartbroken the day Lan started lessons. He was the only person in the world who didn't think there was something wrong with me, and now he was going to be shut away from me for hours every day. He whispered a promise to come every night and teach me what he'd learned, but that still didn't ease the hurt.

Mama found me curled up in a sniveling ball, just down the hall from the closed door of the lesson room. "Why, Eff! What are you doing?" she began, and then she saw my face and she got right down on the floor beside me and gathered me in her arms. "Honey, what's the matter?"

I just shook my head. I didn't want her to think I grudged Lan his lessons. He was special, everybody said, the same way I was wicked. He deserved those lessons — but, oh, I wanted him to be with me! Or at least close enough to call or run to when the others started in.

Even though I didn't say anything, I think Mama understood. She sat and stroked my hair for a while, and then she brought me to the kitchen and we made sugar cookies together. She didn't scold me when I spilled the milk because I was in such a hurry to show I could help. She just studied me with a thoughtful expression.

I got a lot more of those looks over the next month or so. I didn't know what to make of them. Then, about a month after Lan started his lessons, the two of us were doing his exercises in the attic one evening when Allie came puffing up the stairs. She was three years older than we were, and her blue eyes were snapping with excitement. "There you are," she said to me. "They want you in the sitting room."

"What do they want me for?" I asked.

"I don't know, but you'd better go right now. Uncle Earn is there with a policeman, and Papa is madder than blazes!"

I felt myself cringing. "I haven't done anything!"

"Then you don't have anything to worry about," Allie said, imitating the smug tones of our older brother, Hugh.

As I rose slowly to my feet, Lan's eyes narrowed. "I'm coming with you," he announced suddenly. "So it will be all right."

Allie cocked her head to one side and eyed him doubtfully. "I don't know if they want you."

"I'm still coming," Lan said.

We walked into the sitting room together, me holding on to Lan's hand tight as tight. Mama was sitting in the straight-backed chair with the carved arms; Papa was standing by the windows with his hands in his pockets. Uncle Earn was standing just inside the door next to a very uncomfortable-looking man in a blue-and-gold policeman's uniform. "There!" Uncle Earn said as we came in, stabbing his finger straight at me. "That's the child. Officer, do what you came here for!"

"And just what is that?" Papa said in the mild tone he used when he was getting ready to lay into one of the older boys about something, but he wasn't quite certain-sure he had all of the facts in the case just yet. "I've yet to hear a clear explanation from you, and until I do, this goes no further."

"You!" Uncle Earn turned a glare on Papa that would have melted fire irons. Papa just smiled gently, without a particle of yielding. "You," Uncle Earn said again, "you've kept this menace and let her live and grow with no regard to your family or the disgrace and doom she's sure to bring on us all. Maybe the luck of the seventh son will protect you, but what about the rest of us? And now —"

"Begging your pardon, sir," the policeman said, "but am I to understand that *this* is the young lady against whom you lodged your complaint?" He nodded at me, almost friendly, and I felt a tiny bit better.

"Yes!" Uncle Earn roared. "She's a thirteenth child and a witch, and she's put a curse on my house!"

"I take leave to doubt that, sir," the policeman said politely. "She can't be more than four or five, and that's too young even for natural magic."

"It is your duty to enforce the law," Uncle Earn said. "Doubts or no. And the law —"

"— applies in this regard to persons aged ten and older, that being the age the courts have set as the youngest possible to a deliberate working," the policeman said. He looked at me and winked. My mouth fell right open, and I could only stare at him as he went on. "If you wish to lodge a complaint against her guardians for lack of restraint, you'll need a writ from the courthouse first."

"That is an outrage!" Uncle Earn roared.

The policeman appeared unimpressed. "It is the law, sir, and if you'd been plainer about your business when you called me out here, you'd have saved us both some time and trouble. My duty is clear, and if you've no more to say, I'll be about it.

Evening, ma'am, sir." He tipped his hat to Mama and Papa. "Young sir, young mistress." He nodded at Lan and me. "My apologies for the interruption." He turned and left without saying anything more to Uncle Earn, who stood sputtering.

"That appears to dispose of the law," Papa observed. "Shall we settle this as a family now, Earn? What's this about a curse?"

"She's put a curse on my house," Uncle Earn repeated. "My Marna saw her out back this morning, doing a working with string and feathers. She ran off, but Marna found this." He held up a pink ribbon triumphantly.

I felt a wave of despair. Lan had given me that ribbon on our birthday, and I'd worn it constantly since then. Everyone knew it was mine, and knew how much I loved it. With that ribbon for evidence, no one would believe I hadn't done a thing, no matter what I said.

"That's a lie!" Lan burst out. His hand was clenched around mine so hard that it hurt. "Eff was playing skip-jacks on the back step, all by herself, and Marna came up behind her and yanked that ribbon right out of her hair and ran off. I saw it out of the window."

Papa looked at me. "Is that what happened, Eff?"

I nodded, feeling the beginning of hope. Then Uncle Earn stepped toward me and bellowed, "Liar! She's a born witch and a liar, and she's corrupting your precious seven-and-seven. She —"

All of a sudden, I couldn't see anything but navy blue

pleats. It took me a second to realize that Mama had moved right in front of me and Lan. It must have surprised Uncle Earn, too, because he broke off in mid-bellow. "That is quite enough, Mr. Rothmer," Mama said in an icy calm voice I'd never heard her use before, not even the time she'd seen a man whipping an overloaded horse in the street and given him what for. "No one calls my children liars in my home."

"I — I —"

"You've had your say, Mr. Rothmer," Mama told him in the same cold, calm voice. "Now I'll have mine. I've watched you and your wife come near to ruining your own children between spoiling them one minute and whipping them the next. You know my views on that, and I'll say no more of it now. But when it comes to you and Janna ruining my children as well as your own, I have more to say than you'll like hearing. And first, last, and foremost is this: It ends now."

"Sara, you're overset," Uncle Earn said. "I allow for a mother's partiality, but surely even you can see —"

"I can see plain enough that an angel straight from heaven itself would grow up crooked if she was watched and chivvied and told every morning and every night that she was sure to turn evil," Mama said. "And I can see equally plain that fussing and fawning over a child that hasn't even learned his numbers yet, as if he were a prince of power and wisdom, will only grow him into a swell-headed, stuck-up scarecrow of a man, who like as not will never know good advice when he hears it, nor think to ask for it when he needs it."

"You're mad," Uncle Earn said dismissively. "Daniel, I did not come here to be lectured by your wife."

"The door is right behind you," Papa said pleasantly.

I peeked around Mama's skirt in time to see Uncle Earn's jaw drop. "What? You don't mean . . ."

"I mean that Sara hasn't said a thing that the two of us haven't discussed and come to an agreement on already. If I hear one more word about Eff or Lan from you, or Janna, or any one of your precious children, I'll put a curse on your house myself, brother or no."

"You wouldn't dare!"

"Try me," Papa said grimly. "And if you ever attempt to set the law on my family again for nothing but a poisonous whim, you had better be prepared to defend your actions in court, for I'll have you hauled in front of a judge faster than a cat can hiss. I think that's put clearly enough even for you, Earn."

Uncle Earn just stood there, staring, for a long, long moment. Then he stiffened, glared all around, and stalked out, letting the sitting room door slam behind him.

Lan and I looked at each other, and then up at Mama. Mama looked over at Papa, and Papa said, "You stay here, Sara, while I see that things have been shut up properly after him."

Mama took me and Lan by the hand and walked us over to the straight-backed chair with the carved arms, and then took both of us in her lap at once. My head was still swimming with the surprise of it all. Not that Cousin Marna would make up tales about stealing my ribbon, nor that Uncle Earn would call a policeman to arrest me — those weren't exactly surprising. But the way the policeman winked at me! And the way Mama and Papa tore into Uncle Earn! I'd never thought such things possible. I still wasn't sure they'd happened.

Papa came back after a bit and said Uncle Earn was gone, and then he and Mama talked all serious to Lan and me about what had just happened. Mama said she and Papa couldn't do much to keep people from talking, and they could do even less about what people chose to think, but there were some things they *could* do, and we'd see for ourselves in a few more days. Papa wanted to ask me more about Cousin Marna and the other children, but Mama said firmly that it was getting late and that Lan and I should be in bed. I still had a million questions, but I couldn't get them out my tongue.

The very next day, Lan came running out into the yard, wide-eyed. "You're supposed to be with your tutor," I told him. "You better go back in before they miss you."

"I'm not having magic lessons today," he said. "Mama told me to come outside and stick with you."

Lan's tutor never came back. Years later, I learned that Papa had spoken to him about teaching both of us and had dismissed him outright when he refused. There must have been some discussion with Grandfather, too, but neither he nor Papa ever spoke of it after. At the time, Papa only told Lan and me that there would be no more private tutoring. We would have a lesson with Mama in the morning, and another with Papa in the evening, and in between Lan and I were to stick together. I think Papa must have said something to our older brothers as well, because for the next week, one or two of them always seemed to be around when the cousins came by ready to tease and make trouble. It was the best week I ever remember spending in Helvan Shores.

Then, on Monday evening, Papa held a Family Council, and everything changed.

GETTING OUR WHOLE FAMILY TOGETHER ALL AT ONE TIME ALWAYS
made me feel a little strange, because I hardly knew my oldest
brothers and sisters. Frank had been away at university since
the year I was born. Sharl and Julie had both gotten married
before I was two, and Peter had gone off East to school in
the same year. Diane had moved out the year before, to keep the
books for a candy-making business one of Papa's friends
owned. Even Charlie, who was going off to university in the
fall, was older enough that I didn't see him much. They felt
more like strange grown-ups I had to be polite to than like
family. Except for Charlie, I'd really only ever seen them on
special occasions.

A formal Family Council was special enough for anybody.
Papa hardly ever called for one; the last time, Rennie told me,
was when she and Hugh were seven and Papa and Mama found
out that their thirteenth child was going to be another set of
twins. So, trouble though it was, everyone made the effort to
come. Sharl brought cherry pie, Julie brought fritters, and
Diane brought butter fudge from the candy store. Mama

and Rennie and Nan made a dinner nearly as big as Harvest Feasting, and everyone ate until they nearly burst.

Even so, you could just tell that it wasn't an ordinary family sit-down. Everyone was twitchy, wondering what the news would be this time. But Papa didn't believe in doing business at the dinner table, so we all had to wait.

When the last of the plates had been removed and all the crumbs wiped up, everyone looked at Papa. "I told you all this was a Family Council," he began, "but this is more in the way of an announcement than a discussion. Your mother and I wanted you all to hear this from us, and this was the only way we could think of to be sure no one would be left out. I have been asked to take a position at one of the new land-grant colleges out in the North Plains Territory, and I've accepted. We'll be moving at the end of next month."

Papa said that as if it was a settled thing, but he couldn't have thought that that would be the end of it. Discussion there was, and plenty. I was surprised that most of the objecting and complaining came from the older ones. You'd think that Sharl and Julie would be satisfied running their own homes, but it seems they didn't like the notion of Mama being so far away, just in case they might have an unexpected need to run home for something. Frank and Charlie were put out by the suddenness of it; Frank especially thought Papa might have given him a hint. Hugh thought moving out West would be a great adventure, and the younger boys were just as excited, but Diane and Rennie were more than upset enough for all of them. Rennie didn't want to leave her friends, and Diane was sure that if she had to move out West, she'd never be able to come back for the music schooling she had her heart set on.

We younger ones didn't say much. Well, Jack and Robbie did, but that was mostly about how much fun it would be. Lan was quiet, but he had a gleam in his eye that meant he was of much the same opinion. Nan sat and chewed on her lower lip like she was thinking real hard, until Allie poked her and made her giggle.

Patiently, Mama and Papa laid out the whole plan. The oldest ones were grown and gone, so moving mainly affected how often we'd see each other. And while it was true that no one could drop in for a chat, it wasn't as if the North Plains Territory was a three-week trip in a horse-drawn wagon, the way it used to be. The overnight train only took two days and a night, Papa said, so we could still visit, and Mama could certainly come back for a week or two if there was a "special reason." Sharl blushed when he said that, and looked down at her waistline and told him it was a great comfort to know that.

Charlie and Diane would stay with Uncle Stephen until Charlie went off to the university in the fall and Diane finished earning her music school money. Papa gave Rennie and Hugh the choice, whether to stay as well or come West with us younger ones.

"That's easy!" Hugh declared immediately. "I'm coming. How about you, Rennie?"

"I don't know," Rennie said.

"What?" Hugh stared at her. "How can you not know? Why would you want to stay here?"

"I need to think about it," Rennie told him. She sounded cross.

"Oh, come on, Rennie!" Hugh said. "It'll be an adventure! Like the first settlers from the Old Continent."

Robbie frowned. "I don't want to live in a big forest full of monsters," he objected.

"There is no forest where we'll be going," Papa said. "There won't be any monsters, either, for it's on the east side of the Great Barrier. It won't be as comfortable and easy as Helvan Shores, but Mill City has been settled for some time."

"It's still right out on the frontier, isn't it?" Hugh said with undiminished enthusiasm. "I bet there'll be monsters! Bison, and mammoths, and those giant things with the horns on their noses, and —"

"Unicorns live in forests, dummy; everybody knows that," Nan said.

"Unicorns have horns on their *foreheads*," Hugh said with equal scorn. "I'm talking about those huge ugly things with the curly fur and the great horn on their *nose*."

"Nan!" Mama said. "You do not call your brother names. And Hugh, if you cannot remember the proper name of a woolly rhinoceros, perhaps you should spend some extra time studying your natural history from now until the day we leave. Rennie may take plenty of time to think, if she wishes.

We won't be leaving Helvan Shores for another month and a half."

Hugh groaned, and Jack piped up, asking, "What kind of school will we be going to?"

"Will it be all in one room with the same teacher, and everybody sharing books, and no pencils or paper?" Allie added anxiously.

"What is the new house like?" Nan asked, right on top of Allie's question. "Will I get my own room, or do I still have to share with Rennie?"

"Mill City is a little too large to make do with a one-room schoolhouse," Papa said. "As for the house, you'll know what it's like as soon as I do. It's being provided by the college, and we'll have to see what we find when we get there."

Mama gave him a disapproving look. "Daniel! What were you thinking? If they give us some little cracker box, we'll never fit!"

"I let them know how many of us there are," Papa reassured her. Mama still looked worried, until he added, "If the college doesn't have someone in charge with sense enough to provide a dwelling large enough to hold us all, why, it'll just show how very much they need my help, won't it?"

That made Mama laugh, and the talk settled down. The older ones still weren't totally happy with the notion, but everyone could see that they didn't have a vote. The middle ones were split between the ones like Hugh, who thought that whatever happened would be fun and an adventure, and the ones like Diane and Rennie, who seemed to feel abandoned or hurt that Mama and Papa would even consider muddling up their lives like this. And the younger ones . . . we were just confused and excited. None of us had any real notion what it would mean.

Finally, Papa called everyone to order and said, "I think we've covered the main points. Does anyone have any other questions?"

I raised my hand. "What's a *land-grant college*?"

Papa laughed. "Trust Eff to get to the heart of the matter!" he said, as if I'd asked something very clever. And then he explained.

After the Secession War ended in 1838, the Assembly wanted to do something nice for all the Northern states and territories that had stuck with them in the fight. They couldn't give out money, because there wasn't any; they'd spent it all on winning the war. But one really bright Assemblyman had an idea. There were millions of acres of Federal land all over the country that hadn't yet been homesteaded and that were bringing in no taxes or other money. Why not give some of it to the states and territories, to set up colleges? The states could sell the land, or rent it out, or build on it — whatever they wanted, as long as the money they got from it paid for colleges that taught people useful skills like agriculture and engineering and magic along with things like Latin and law.

The idea was a big hit, especially in the newest Western territories that didn't have a lot of money yet for things like colleges. The North Plains Territory was one of the first to get its grant of land, but it had taken the settlers a while to study out exactly what they wanted to do with it. In the end, they sold some and put the money aside to pay for building the college on another part, and the rest they rented out to whoever wanted to pay. They'd had a good bit of luck when the railroad came through right by the land-grant site, so they had more money than anyone expected, and no shortage of students, either, once they got going. What they were short of was professors, especially professors who could teach more than just theoretical magic.

That was why they wanted Papa. It seems he had a good reputation as a practical magician, plus they'd talked to several people who said there wasn't a teacher like him for explaining so that you could really understand and remember. They'd been after him for a whole year, and none of us except Mama had known a thing about it.

I started to get a funny feeling in my middle right about then. Neither Papa nor Mama had said anything about Uncle Earn or the policeman since that dreadful scene in the sitting room, but it wasn't something you just forgot about. And Papa had never given anyone the smallest hint that he'd ever thought of heading West. I didn't say anything at the meeting, but later, when Mama tucked me into bed, I asked her straight out.

"Is Papa making everybody move because of me?"

"What? Goodness, child, where did you get a notion like that?" Mama said.

"I thought maybe it was to keep Uncle Earn from putting me in jail," I explained.

Mama took a deep breath and let it out very slowly. Then she looked at me with a serious expression. "Uncle Earn could not have you put in jail, whether we stay in Helvan Shores or not," she said.

"But —"

Mama held up her hand, and I closed my mouth on my questions and listened real hard. "I can't deny that moving will get you and Lan away from a type of attention and comment that your father and I think is very bad for you," she said. "And I must admit that removing you from that poisonous atmosphere was one of the things we thought was a good reason to make the move."

"Then —"

This time, Mama gave me a stern look. "Eff, you should wait until someone is quite finished speaking before you jump in with your comments." She waited a moment, but I knew well enough not to open my mouth again. Once she was satisfied that I wasn't going to interrupt, she went on, "But if you and Lan had been the only reasons we had for moving — if your father hadn't been pleased and excited by the thought of trying out his ideas for teaching practical magic at a brand-new school that has no traditions to overturn, and if he hadn't liked the notion of setting his stamp on an institution that will be teaching young magicians for the next hundred years and more — then we wouldn't be going. Not even for you." She smiled. "So you should be very glad that your father does feel that way, shouldn't you?"

Well, when she put it like that, I could see that wild horses couldn't have kept Papa in Helvan Shores when there was something like this waiting. Only — "If Papa wanted to go West so much, how come it took him a whole year to make up his mind?" I asked.

"Because it's a hard thing to leave a place where you've lived most of your life, where your brothers and sisters and parents still live, where some of your children will stay behind," Mama said. "It's a hard thing to risk what you know and are sure of, just for the possibility of something better. Even when it's a pretty strong possibility, and something that's a whole lot better."

"I don't understand," I said.

Mama bent and kissed my forehead. "You don't understand now, but if you remember what I said, you'll understand someday."

She was right. I didn't understand then, but I do now.

CHAPTER 3

THE NEXT MONTH AND A HALF WAS A BUSY TIME. EVERYTHING IN THE house had to be cleaned and wrapped up and packed in crates and shipped off to the North Plains Territory. It seemed as if no one had a minute to spare for anything but cleaning and packing. Hugh tried to sneak all his schoolbooks into the very first box, so that he wouldn't have to do lessons for a month, but Papa found them and took them out again.

Then there were the aunts and uncles and cousins, who all came by at one time or another to marvel at what Papa was doing — or shake their heads over it, depending. All except Aunt Janna and Uncle Earn, that is. They didn't come next nor near the house the whole time we were getting ready to leave.

The rest of the aunts and uncles more than made up for the two of them, though. The uncles all wanted to talk with Papa about the West and business opportunities and political questions. The aunts wanted to talk to Mama about living so much nearer to the frontier. Some of the aunts tried to commiserate with Mama, as if she must dislike the idea of moving

West. Mama soon straightened *that* out, but that only set them all to wondering how she could dream of doing such a thing. And the cousins were so interested in telling us what to expect that they even forgot about teasing me.

"I heard there are great beasts, the size of a house, that can stamp you flat as paper!" Cousin Bernie said.

"Those are mammoths," Robbie told him. He'd been doing extra reading on the North Plains ever since he found out we'd be living there, and he enjoyed showing off his new knowledge to the rest of us. "They used to be all over North Columbia, but when the first settlers came from the Old Continent, they killed all the ones in the East. Well, almost all. Peter said he saw a man once who'd caught one and tamed it and rode it like a horse."

"You can't ride a thing as big as a house!" Cousin Bernie said with magnificent scorn.

"They do it with elephants in India," Hugh said. "They don't ride them the way you'd ride a horse; they strap a sort of carriage seat to the elephant's back, and four or five people can sit in it at once and ride."

"I bet a mammoth could carry ten people!" Robbie said with enthusiasm.

"Maybe twenty!" Bernie said, abandoning his objections in favor of such an interesting alternative. "Maybe you can catch one, Robbie!"

"It would have to be a small one," Robbie said thoughtfully. "Young, I mean. So you'd have time to train it up."

"Catching even a small one would be hard," Jack put in. "Since they're so big."

"You could do it if you dug a big pit, and it fell in," Bernie said.

"How would you get it out again?" Robbie objected. "They're awful heavy. You'd have to get someone with lots of magic to do it. Maybe more than one."

"Have you got a better idea?" Bernie said.

I could see the boys were going to spend the rest of Cousin Bernie's visit arguing about mammoth traps, so I left and went upstairs. Mama and Aunt Tilly were visiting in the parlor, and I didn't want to have to sit straight and be quiet while they went on about what to take for housekeeping and what to leave behind.

Things went on like that for the whole month, and then, suddenly, all our belongings were gone and it was time for us to leave as well. Mama helped me pack a trunk all my own, and pasted a silhouette of me on it that she'd cut out of black paper, so that everyone would know it for mine. Then there was an enormous party, with Grandfather and all the aunts and uncles and cousins, even Uncle Earn and Aunt Janna, though they came late and left early.

We boarded the train the next morning. The trip was the kind of thing you remember forever. There were so many of us, even without Diane and Charlie and Peter and Frank and Sharl and Julie, that we took up almost half a car. The train company had separate boarding areas for men and women, so

Papa took Hugh and Jack and Robbie and Lan one way, and Mama took Rennie, Nan, Allie, and me the other.

The train station was loud and confusing. Mama set Rennie and Hugh to help mind the younger ones, because they were the oldest. Of course Rennie complained that Jack and Nan should be helping, too, and Mama pointed out that Jack and Nan weren't old enough for childminding, and Jack, especially, was as likely to get into trouble as the childings he'd be watching. Rennie pouted and said she wished she'd stayed with Uncle Stephen after all. Papa told her it was too late for that and to behave. After that, she just sulked quietly.

I didn't mind Rennie. I spent most of the trip looking out the window, watching the land change. First, there were plowed fields and small villages, then big rolling mountains that the train had to wind through like a snake because it couldn't just climb up and down like a mule or a horse. Then there were midland cities, bigger than Helvan Shores, almost as big as the great ports on the East Coast, but bare of trees and full of dust.

Whenever the train stopped at a station, we would get off and run up and down the platform to stretch our legs. Hugh wanted to explore, but Mama wouldn't let him. She said there wasn't enough time, and the train wouldn't wait for him if he got lost and was slow coming back. Even at the meal stops, when all the long-riding passengers were let off for an hour to eat in the little dining room at the train station, Mama insisted that he stay close.

In between stops, Papa told us about the North Plains Territory. Mill City was right at the edge of the Great Prairie, on the Mammoth River. To the east were forests of oak and maple and pine, and the farms that men were carving out of them despite the haunts and greatwolves and Columbian boars that lived in them still. To the west were the plains, the wild country where great herds of mammoths and bison trampled everything in their path, woolly rhinoceroses with horns on their noses as long as a grown man's arm made the earth shake when they charged, and steam dragons and spectral bears hunted anything that moved.

On the far side of the plains were mountains, sharp and high, that no one had seen but a few explorers. Papa said that at least ten expeditions had tried to find a way through them to the Pacific Ocean, but only three men had ever come back alive, and they were stark out of their heads. There was a monument in the capital to Lewis and Clark, who headed the first group that went missing, back in 1804. It was more than wild country; it was unknown.

I loved listening to Papa's stories, but it made me wonder what Mill City would be like, being right at the edge of the wild like that. I could see the country changing around us as the train carried us farther west. The stops were farther apart, and when we got off the train to run, the platforms were shorter. Then the train plunged into the woods, and we watched the trees stream past the windows, ancient and dark and frightening despite the sunlit slash the railroad company had cleared through their midst to run the trains. I stared out the window at it for an hour, and fell asleep still staring.

Lan shook me awake when we reached Mill City. I'd begun to worry that it would be another tiny place like the towns we'd passed through, but it wasn't. It wasn't like Helvan Shores, either. Everything looked new and raw — the square warehouses near the station, the dusty dirt roads, the station itself. Even the people and wagons looked like they'd only just been finished; neat enough, but without the kind of polish folks had back home. And over to the side, past piles of logs and crates, just visible between the rows of big, flat railroad cars, was the dark, foamy water of the Mammoth River. On the far side, the western side, there was just grass and a few trees.

Mr. Farley, the dean of the college, had come to meet us with three wagons and several large men to help with our trunks. Mama rounded up all us children and told us in a no-nonsense tone to stay *right there* until we were ready to leave. Not even Hugh so much as thought about disobeying.

We stood and watched the wagons and the people passing by. Rennie and Hugh and Jack started arguing about something, but I didn't pay attention. I was still half-'mazed with sleep and the strangeness of this new place. Then, just as Papa and Mama came back to collect us, I saw a woman walking in our direction, and I felt a jolt go through me. It was as if I recognized her, even though I'd never seen her before.

She was a tall black woman wearing a high-crowned hat trimmed with cherries. A white lace neck scarf fell across the top of her close-fitting blue jacket. Her lips were full, and her crinkly black hair made an enormous bun at the nape of her neck, but what I remember best were her eyes. They were wide-set and bright with intelligence, and I felt another shock when her gaze locked onto mine.

She held my eye for only an instant, then nodded politely and passed on to the grown-ups. But I knew she was still aware of me.

"Morning, Mr. Farley," she said in a deep, clear voice. "Is this your new professor?"

"Ah, yes," Mr. Farley said, looking nervously at my parents. "Ah —"

"Do please introduce us," Mama said to Mr. Farley.

"I — yes, of course," Mr. Farley stammered. "Mr. and Mrs. Rothmer, allow me to introduce Miss Maryann Ochiba. Miss Ochiba, Mr. and Mrs. Rothmer."

"Pleased to meet you," Miss Ochiba said. She and Mama looked at each other long and hard, and then they each gave a little nod, as if they'd had a whole conversation and both had come away satisfied. "These will be your children," Miss Ochiba went on as if there'd been no slightest pause. "They've been saying you have a good-sized family."

"Any size that's wanted is good," Mama said, and then told her our names.

"I teach in the day school," Miss Ochiba said when she was done greeting each of us. "Will your children be attending there?"

Mr. Farley looked alarmed. "Oh, I don't think any decisions have been made just yet. The Rothmers have only just arrived."

"Perhaps you'll come to tea some afternoon so we can talk it over," Miss Ochiba said to Mama. "Day school doesn't start for another three weeks, so I have my afternoons free."

Mr. Farley opened his mouth to say something else, but Mama beat him to it. "I should be delighted," she said. "Send the day and time around tomorrow."

Miss Ochiba smiled suddenly. "I'll do that, Mrs. Rothmer. Nice meeting you." And she sailed off down the street.

Mr. Farley gave a big sigh and called some directions back at the men who were pulling out in the two wagons loaded with our trunks. We all piled into the back of the last wagon, with Mama and Papa and Mr. Farley up front. Rennie started to complain about not having a seat, but after one look from Mama she just flopped down in the wagon and took out her temper in glaring at Hugh and Jack. The boys didn't notice. They were too busy hanging over the side rails and pointing, though Hugh did remember to keep a grip on the seat of Lan's britches so he wouldn't fall out.

I let them push me up to the front, right behind the seats, where you couldn't see very well. I was curious about Mill City, maybe as much as they were, but I was also a mite scared.

I didn't expect things to be much different, no matter what Mama thought. As soon as people found out I was a thirteenth child, I was sure they'd make my life every bit as miserable as ever they could. But without my cousins, it wouldn't be as easy. Marna and Lynnie and Simon and the others had known just exactly what little things to do to drive me wild and which things were most hurtful to say. Things that people who weren't family wouldn't think of. Maybe here, people wouldn't catch on so quick.

So I was pleased enough to stay out of sight, even if it meant I didn't see much. Besides, I could hear Mama and Papa and Mr. Farley talking, and that was at least as interesting as Mill City.

"We have a bit of a drive ahead of us," Mr. Farley said as the wagon started to move. "The college is being built about three miles away, as the crow flies, but there's a loop of the river in the way, and the new bridge isn't finished yet. So we have to go around."

"It will give us a chance to see more of the town," Mama said. "And it is a lovely day for a drive." Just as if we hadn't all been sick to death of riding after two days on the train.

"Mrs. Grey and my wife will be waiting for us," Mr. Farley said. "They were concerned that the train would come in late and you'd have a hard time getting your children fed and settled before dark."

"That's very neighborly of them," Mama said.

"Folks here look out for one another," Mr. Farley told her.

"We have to. That is — it's not that the city isn't safe, being on the east bank and all, but we've got into the habit."

"Just so." Papa's voice was a little dry. "When is my appointment with Mr. Grey? I would like to present my credentials as soon as possible."

"Well, he'd planned to meet your train himself," Mr. Farley said. "He's very pleased at having a proper educated East Coast magician on staff at last. But one of the outer-ring farm settlements was having a little problem, and he was the only one able to go and see about it."

"I understood that Mr. Grey was a magician," Papa said. "Is he also an agricultural expert, then?"

"Oh, no — that is, no more than any of the rest of us outside the agricultural department," Mr. Farley said hastily. "But magicians are in short supply here, and since magic is the only thing that will hold back the wildlife, we take turns maintaining the barriers for folks west of the river. Well, except when there's a major breach; then it has to be the best man we have." He paused. "I fear from the description we received that Gannertown will lose most of this year's crop."

"I — see," Papa said, in the tone that meant he was going to give whatever he'd just heard a good hard think before he said anything else about it.

"Mr. Farley," Mama put in, "I do hate to interrupt, but would you mind telling me what that very interesting building over there is? The one with the gold pillars on either side of the door."

"That's the North Plains Territory Homestead Claim and Settlement Office," Mr. Farley replied. "The hotel for settlers making claims is that big square building, and the courthouse is across the street, with the clock tower. Farther down, just there, you can see the Farmers' Bank; that's really the town center. We have two general stores . . ."

Since I couldn't see what Mr. Farley was pointing at, I stopped listening, and after a while I dozed off. The next thing I knew, Papa was lifting me down in front of an enormous stone house with a wide porch and a dirt yard. A small, worried-looking woman came out to greet Mama, while the boys ran in all directions.

We had reached our new home at last.

CHAPTER 4

THE HOUSE THAT THE COLLEGE HAD PROVIDED FOR US WAS LARGE enough to satisfy even Nan (we each got a room of our very own). The Board of Directors had bought it from a lumber baron who'd made a fortune in the timberlands to the north and then gone back East to flaunt his fortune in front of the folks there. They'd intended to use it for classrooms until they got their new buildings built, and putting us into it instead left them a mite short of space. So for the first three years, Papa's classes met in the front parlor, and Professor Graham's classes met in the sitting room next to it.

Professor Graham was the college's other professor of magic. One of the families who owned the big grain mills had sent him East to school on the understanding that he was to bring his knowledge back to the territory, and though he'd been quick enough to agree when he left, you could see plain as plain that he wasn't pleased now that he was back. He lorded it over everyone, on account of his schooling, and at first he couldn't make up his mind whether Papa was his competition or his ally. He was considerably put out when he discovered that Papa wasn't much interested in being either.

I was too young then to pay heed to Professor Graham or his notions, and I probably would have known nothing about them if it hadn't been for his son, William. William was just one year younger than Lan and me, a thin, sandy-haired miniature of his father. William's mother was an invalid, so his father had the raising of him, which meant more rules than you could shake a stick at. We were the first friends he'd ever really had, because his father didn't want him mixing with less-educated folk, and none of the other college families had children his age.

He almost didn't get to mix with us, either, after Professor Graham found out that Mama and Papa were sending us to the day school instead of giving us special tutoring at home. But in the end the professor decided that William would be a good influence on us, and let him stop by to play when he wasn't studying.

William took his influencing seriously, though he was mainly parroting the things his father said. He'd go on about the responsibilities of magic and the importance of proper learning at the slightest excuse, usually whenever Lan or Robbie came up with an idea for a prank he didn't approve of.

Once in a while, I even took his side. Truth to tell, I thought it was funny to see Lan and Robbie come in for something like the lectures I'd had all my life. Then, too, I felt sorry for William, stuck in the house with the professor and a sick mother most days and with no friends but us.

My brothers and sisters and I all made friends at school right away. The upper school was even larger than the one back in Helvan Shores, which was a relief to Hugh and Rennie and Nan. Jack didn't care, and Allie and Robbie were still down in the day school with Lan and me. Lan and I were in the same class, along with nine others. They were fascinated by us because we were twins, and of course no one knew that I was a thirteenth child or that Lan was a double-seventh son. I would have hung back, since I knew that sooner or later the other children would find out about me, but Lan dove right in and dragged me along with him. And the topic of family size and birth order just never came up.

For the next three years, Lan and I had basic schooling — reading, writing, arithmetic, history, and natural history. We weren't taught any magic theory until we turned nine and went into the fourth grade; that was the way all the schools handled it then. Still, being around the house with the college students in and out for classes meant that we all picked up a bit, even though William was the only one who got lessons. Professor Graham had advanced ideas about training children in magic, and he was a little put out that Papa wasn't eager to run educational experiments on us.

The first class of the Northern Plains Riverbank College graduated just before Lan and I turned nine. There were seventeen students who finished, out of the twenty-two who'd started. Our whole family had to get dressed up and go to the ceremony, because six of the seventeen were taking degrees in magic, three with Papa as their sponsor. I could have done without the honor. All I remember of the graduation itself was that it was long and hot and boring, and that even though it was still early in the spring, the bugs were out with a vengeance, buzzing around our sweaty necks and landing to sting any bare bit of skin they could find.

After the ceremony, things brightened up. We joined the crowd on the lawn, where punch and cakes had been set out on long tables draped in white. Half of Mill City seemed to be there, and most of them didn't know any of us, so as soon as we could, we slipped away from our parents and started through the lines over and over. Robbie was especially good at wheedling an extra piece of cake from the ladies who were serving, so he got nearly twice as much as the rest of us.

I was coming away from the tables with my third piece of cake, feeling very daring, when a voice behind me said, "Well, if it isn't young Eff! Didn't I see you a few minutes back with a plateful of sweets? What happened, one of your brothers knock it over?"

I turned and found Henry Masters, one of Papa's students, smiling down at me. He looked different in his black gown, with the flat-topped hat shading his brown eyes. His smile, though, was exactly the same as ever.

The smile reassured me, and I said, "Robbie bet me I couldn't get them to give me another piece without getting caught. You won't tell, will you?"

"Never," Henry said solemnly. "Cross my heart."

"Ah, Henry!" Professor Graham came up behind Henry and put an arm around his shoulders. "Passing on good advice to young Francine here?" Professor Graham always called me Francine, even though I'd asked him very politely once to call me Eff like everyone else.

"Actually, she was giving me some," Henry said, and winked at me. "She recommends the cake."

"Yes, very good," the professor said in that tone that means someone hasn't really heard a word you said. "So what are your plans now, young man? Going back East to continue your studies?"

"No, sir," Henry said politely.

"No?" Professor Graham frowned. "Surely you realize what a name you could make for yourself, with your talent!"

"I'm afraid I'm more interested in paying my debt to the Farmers' Society," Henry said. He sounded like he was apologizing for something, but he had his shoulders set like a man readying for a fistfight.

The professor's frown deepened. "You're not considering going out with one of those crazy settler groups, are you? Think, man! Three years of advanced training in New Amsterdam or Washington, and you'd be in a position to pay them back with double the interest!"

"The Farmers' Society doesn't need money," Henry said, still polite as polite, but starting to get an edge on the underside of his voice. "They need magicians. Without magic to hold off the wildlife, those settlers are gambling with death every year, and sooner or later they'll lose. That's why they paid my college tuition."

"The Farmers' Society is much too eager to push people out into dangerous territory, in my opinion," Professor Graham said, as if that settled the matter.

"With all due respect, sir —" Henry began, but he never finished his sentence, because just then Harmony Quillen ducked out of the crowd and took his arm.

"There you are, Henry!" she said. "I've been looking all over for you." She smiled at Professor Graham. "You will loan him to me, won't you, Professor? Milo and I are having an argument over the riding horses that Susan is training, and I need Henry to back me up."

"But of course, my dear," Professor Graham said with a smile. Henry made a polite good-bye and went off with Harmony. The professor stood for a moment, watching them, and his frown returned. I decided that it'd be best if I took myself off before he remembered I was there.

I meant to ask Papa later about the Farmers' Society and why Professor Graham was so displeased with Henry, but I got a stomachache from eating too much cake and it went right out of my head. I didn't think of it again until almost a month later, when we went to the train station to see Mama off.

Mama was going back east to Helvan Shores for two months, because Sharl and Julie had *both* finally gotten around to having babies, and they wanted Mama's help with their firstings. I didn't understand it, myself — after all, Sharl and Julie were the oldest girls, so they'd had a chance to practice all the baby care on us younger ones. I thought that when I got old enough to be having babies, I'd need help for sure, because there weren't any younger ones for me to practice on. But then I thought that maybe Sharl and Julie were worried that they'd forgotten things in the last nine years, and that was why they were so insistent that Mama come back to help.

Not that they needed to do much insisting. Mama was so pleased that she agreed right off, and if she could have, she'd have brought all the rest of us back along with her. But there wasn't anywhere for all of us to stay; even between them, Sharl and Julie couldn't put all of us up, and Papa pointed out that the idea was to make less work for the two of them, not more. So Mama was going alone, and we all went down to the train to say good-bye.

The train station was even busier than usual, because the waterways were open and the first loads of logs had floated down the river on the spring floodwaters. Some of them were milled right in Mill City, and some floated farther on down the Mammoth River, but most of them got piled onto flatcars and shipped east to the mills there, to be made into houses and furniture and wagons and boats and all the other things people used. The area around the train smelled of damp and fresh-cut wood as well as coal and steam and grease, and the yards were full of men and logs and flatcars.

The other reason the station was busy was one I didn't know until Henry Masters saw us on the platform and came over to give us greeting. "Professor Rothmer!" he said to Papa. "You're not leaving us, are you?"

"No, we're just seeing Mrs. Rothmer off on a visit to the family back East," Papa said. "Are you heading out, too?"

Henry laughed and sketched a little bow to Mama. "I am, but not eastward. My settlement has been assigned, and I'm here to pick up our homestead allotment equipment."

"Where are they sending you?" Mama asked with an uneasy frown.

"To a completely new segment, about a hundred miles to the southwest." Henry sounded excited. "We're starting with twenty families, right at the edge of the settlement zone."

"Oh, Henry!" Mama said. "On the edge? And so far away from the safety barrier!"

"Who's your backup?" Papa asked.

"There'll be a circuit-rider every two months, and they'll send another magician with the next group to join us. It's not as bad as it sounds; the first year, I only have to cover the central settlement itself. Getting the spells up may be a scramble, but after that I'll have plenty of time to stretch them to cover tilled land."

"Wow!" Jack couldn't keep silent any longer. "You're going to homestead out West? Will you get to see mammoths and dragons and everything?"

Henry laughed. "I hope not! My job is to keep the mammoths and dragons and everything *away* from the settlers, and it'll be much easier if they aren't around."

"It's a big responsibility," Papa said slowly. "And I don't mean only the settlers."

"I know that, sir," Henry said. "I'll do you proud."

Mama sniffed. "Daniel has enough to be proud of already," she said. "If it comes to choosing, we'll be prouder if you come back safe."

Before Henry could answer, the train's whistle blew loud and long, and the conductor came down the platform to warn everyone to board. Mama started hugging everyone all over again, just as if she hadn't given us good-bye hugs twice already, and Henry wished her good journey as she got on the train at last. Then we all moved up the platform to where we could see her sitting by the window, and we waved until the train pulled out.

I missed Mama from the very first minute. We all did. I think Papa missed her worst of all, though of course he didn't say anything to us. The boys didn't say anything, either, but you could tell they felt the same as the rest of us by the way everyone just happened to be right around the front porch every day about the time Papa brought the mail home.

It was a good thing Mama left when she did, because she

hadn't been back East for even a week before Julie had her baby. Papa opened the letter right there at the Post Office, and came home with a big smile on his face, so that we knew the news even before he got in the door. "Your sister Julie has had a little girl," he told us.

"Hurrah! I'm an uncle!" Jack said, and everyone started talking at once.

Everyone except me, that is. I was feeling a little peculiar. I hadn't thought about being uncles and aunts until Jack spoke up. Then Nan said, "And Papa is a grandfather!" and I felt even more peculiar. All sorts of memories came rushing back, and I shivered. I didn't want to be like my aunts, not even like Aunt Tilly, and I didn't want my sisters to be like them, either. I didn't want my brothers to be like my uncles. And I most especially didn't want Papa to be like our grandfather.

Then I thought that maybe it took a long time and a lot of nieces and nephews to get as mean as all the aunts and uncles had been to me. After all, there were twelve ahead of me just in our family, and all my older cousins, too. I swallowed hard. Maybe it was my fault. Maybe all the aunts and uncles had been fine until a thirteenth child came along. If that was it, then as long as none of my siblings had thirteen childings, they'd be safe. It would be a long time before anybody got close to having thirteen babies. I'd have plenty of time to convince them to stop before then.

"What are you thinking about so hard, Eff?" my father said in my ear.

I was so startled that I said, "Being an aunt." *

Papa laughed, and I saw that he didn't understand what I meant.

"It's a big responsibility," I said, but he only laughed harder. I didn't really want to explain in so many words what I'd been thinking.

Papa still didn't understand. He lifted me up right off my feet and hugged me, and then he went through the whole family hugging everyone. He read Mama's letter out loud to all of us, and we had roast chicken for dinner that night even though it wasn't Sunday.

Mama wrote every few days, though her letters were very short because she was so busy. Three and a half weeks later, she wrote that Sharl had had a baby boy, and we went through the whole thing again. I was happy to have the roast chicken, but I wasn't sure about the fuss that went along with it. After all, we wouldn't be seeing either of those babies for a long, long time.

The rest of the summer got steadily worse and worse. Mostly, that was because Mama had to stay in Helvan Shores longer than she'd expected. Sharl took sick the week after her baby was born, and for a while it looked like she might die. Mama's letters got shorter and shorter, though she tried to send something every day or two so we wouldn't be so worried.

I wasn't worried, exactly. My first thought, when we got Mama's letter, was that if Sharl died then maybe I wouldn't be counted as a thirteenth child anymore. Then I saw how upset everyone else was, especially the older ones and Papa, and I wondered if I was really as evil as Uncle Earn said, to have such thoughts. I was glad I hadn't said anything out loud.

I stayed out of the way as much as I could for the next two weeks, so that I wouldn't have to pretend to feel bad when I didn't. I couldn't tell anyone, not even Lan. When the news came that Sharl was out of danger, I felt like a sham. Nobody noticed. We all sent letters to Mama and Sharl, and then settled down to wait for Mama to come home. But from then on, I knew that Uncle Earn had been right about me. I was a real thirteenth child at heart, and if I didn't look out extra-sharp, I'd end up doing horrible things to somebody one day.

CHAPTER 5

THE REST OF MY NINTH-YEAR SUMMER WAS NO BETTER THAN ITS beginning. Some of that was because of Rennie. Since she was the oldest girl still at home, she took over running the house while Mama was away. Before Mama had left, I'd overheard her telling Mrs. Callahan, who came twice a week to help out with the cleaning, that she hoped that once Rennie saw the work it took to manage a household, she'd be in less of a hurry to have one of her own.

It didn't work out the way Mama planned. As soon as Rennie got over missing Mama and feeling all worried about Sharl, she started bossing the rest of us mercilessly, like she wanted to prove that she could handle the householding better than Mama. She even tried to boss Mrs. Callahan, but only once. The rest of us learned pretty quick to do our real chores — the ones Mama had left for us — and then take off the first chance we got.

The boys mostly went out to the experimental farm that the college ran to educate the agricultural students. It was only about four miles away, next to a little creek that the students used for some of their irrigation projects, and they could swim and fish. Jack and Hugh built a rat trap and set it out by the fields. They wanted to have rat fights with the other boys, but Papa found out before they'd caught enough rats. They didn't get in as much trouble as you might expect, because Professor Wallace, who was in charge of the agricultural school and the farm, also found out about it. He thought counting all the different sorts of rats would be very useful, and said he'd pay them a nickel a rat if they kept track of exactly where they'd caught each one. For the rest of the summer, they caught rats, and they made three dollars and thirty-five cents apiece.

Lan didn't spend much time out by the farm. In the three years we'd been in Mill City, he'd made a lot of friends, and nearly every morning one of them would come by our house to see if he wanted to play ball or collect wood for the miniature fort they were building. He always went. I tried to go along the first couple of times, the way I always had before, but the other boys made it plain as day that they didn't want any girls along. I could see it made Lan uncomfortable to stick up for me, though he did it, so I stopped trying.

It was the first time I'd spent much time apart from Lan, and I passed most of it on my own. I knew most of the girls from the day school, but I wasn't really comfortable with them. I was sure that if they knew I was a thirteenth child, they'd behave just like everyone back in Helvan Shores. Besides, if I did really, truly make friends with someone, and they didn't mind when they found out I was a thirteenth child, I might drag them down when I went bad.

So I spent most of that summer on the roof of our porch. There was a window at the end of one hall that you could crawl out, next to a little niche where the storeroom stuck out. If I backed into the niche, I was invisible from the window and really hard to see from the ground unless you knew just what to look for. Rennie never found me, and I could sit and think, or read, or write in the little diary-book that my sister Diane sent me for my ninth birthday.

Things perked up around August when Mama came home, and then it was fall and Lan and I started the fourth grade. That was how they listed us, at least — Lan and I were both in fifth-grade history and natural science, and they decided to put me all the way up into sixth grade for reading and composition. Schools out in the territories weren't so strict about keeping people all in one grade, the way they did back in Helvan Shores. We had one girl in our fifth-grade natural science class who was only seven, and there were a couple of older boys who were back with us in arithmetic.

Everyone was excited about fourth grade. Our very first class was with Miss Ochiba, who taught most of the classes in magic at the day school. For fourth grade, that meant theory and background; we wouldn't be doing actual spells until we were ten. The magic classes were the one area where nobody was ever put ahead in school, though if you were slow about learning you might be kept back. Hardly anyone was slow —

magic was too important. Out past the Great Barrier, it could save your life, even if you weren't a full magician with the strength and knowledge to cast one of the Major Spells.

Usually, the fourth grade was split into three classes, but for the basic magic class we were all packed together into the big classroom at the end of the school. The boys were on one side of the room, and the girls on the other, so I couldn't take a seat next to Lan. I picked a spot near the front, next to Debbie Buchowski, where I could see the big blackboard without craning my neck to look around somebody's head.

The blackboard in Miss Ochiba's classroom was half hidden behind a big painting in a carved frame. The painting showed a forest of towering pines, coming down to the shore of a lake. Right at the edge, you could just see a group of people and tents down along the water, and three raw stumps where some trees had been cut.

"Hey, Kristen, do you know what that's for?" one of the boys called, pointing at the picture.

"No," the blond girl in front of me yelled back. "And if I did, I wouldn't tell you." She turned to the girl next to her and said in a lower voice, "My sister took this class last year, and he thinks she told me all about it."

"Didn't she?" the second girl asked. "Didn't you *ask*?"

"Of course I asked," Kristen replied. "But she said Miss Ochiba never does class twice the same, so there'd be no point to talking."

"I heard that she never takes attendance or looks at the class list, but she always knows who's skipped," the girl on the other side of Kristen said.

"Hsst! Here she comes."

The general ruckus ebbed just a bit as Miss Ochiba took her seat at the table in front and opened a little blue book. She paid no mind to us one way or the other, so after a minute or two the noise picked up again. I was starting to wonder if she was going to let us go on for the whole time, when the school bell tolled the last time to mark the start of the day.

Miss Ochiba closed the book with a snap and stood up. The noise started to die down, but not fast enough for Miss Ochiba. She gave it a second or two, then raised her left hand and said in a soft voice, "Silence."

The noise stopped. I could see Jack Murray's mouth moving over on the other side of the room, but no sound was coming out. His eyes went wide as ever they could stretch, and so did everyone else's. We all turned back to the front, but there wasn't a rustle or a scrape or a squeak to mark it. The only sound in the whole world was Miss Ochiba's soft voice saying, "In the future, I expect your silence and complete attention at the bell, without the necessity of enforcement. I trust I am clear?"

We all nodded, and for almost the whole rest of the year, silence just slammed down on that classroom the minute the school bell rang for the last time, without Miss Ochiba having to even raise her eyes.

"Very good." Miss Ochiba lowered her hand and the little rustling and scraping and coughing sounds came back. "Let us begin." She stepped to one side and pointed at the painting that was hanging in front of the blackboard. "Who can tell me what this is?"

Several hands went up. "Thom," she said.

"That's the timberlands up north, by Three Forks," he said. "My father works there," he added, as if he thought he'd better explain how he came to know such a thing.

Miss Ochiba nodded. "That it is," she said. "Thank you, Thom. What else is it? Kristen?"

"It's a lumber camp," Kristen said. "You can see the tents, and the place where they've been cutting down trees."

"Very observant," Miss Ochiba said. "Thank you, Kristen. What else is it?"

Miss Ochiba didn't have very many hands to pick from this time. "Susan?"

"It's a forest? And . . . and a lake, or maybe a river?"

"Excellent. Thank you, Susan." Miss Ochiba paused. "What else is it? Anyone?"

The silence was as profound as it had been when Miss Ochiba had called the class to order. We all stared at the picture, wondering what else it was a picture of. There didn't seem to be anything left that hadn't been mentioned. I felt a prickle down my back, and all of a sudden I knew the answer — or at least *an* answer. I waited for someone else to see it, but nobody raised a hand, not even Lan. Miss Ochiba just stood there, waiting, as if she could wait and say nothing for hours, for the whole rest of the day.

Finally, I lifted my hand from the desk. "Yes, Eff?" Miss Ochiba said.

"I-it's a picture," I said. "A painting."

Miss Ochiba nodded. "Yes. Thank you, Eff." She looked around and everyone tensed, wondering if we would have to think of something else. "This is a painting; a picture of a lumber camp; a picture of the northern timberlands; a place where a forest meets a lake. All these things are true, and they are all true at the same time. What you see depends on how you look. And it is one more thing." She turned and waved her hand past the picture, and it shimmered and disappeared, as if folding itself up too small to see. "It is an illusion." There was a quiet sigh from the class.

"This is the most important lesson you must learn about magic," Miss Ochiba went on. "There are many ways of seeing. Each has an element of truth, but none is the whole truth. If you limit yourselves to one way of seeing, one truth, you will limit your power. You will also place limits on the kinds of spells you can cast, as well as their strength. To be a good magician, you must see in many ways. You must be flexible. You must be willing to learn from different sources. And you must always remember that the truths you see are incomplete."

Miss Ochiba paused. We all stared blankly for a minute, and then heads started bending and chalk scraped on slates as everyone took a note. Miss Ochiba smiled and went on. "We will begin the year by taking a general look at the three great theoretical systems of magic: the Avrupan, the Hijero–Cathayan, and the Aphrikan. We will then review some of the great magicians of history, from Socrates to the present day, their contributions to the development of modern magic theory, and the spells and techniques they invented or discovered.

"First, last, and always, however, I expect you to learn to see. Therefore —" Miss Ochiba picked up a piece of chalk from the desk in front of her and tossed it to one of the boys in the front row. "How many different ways can you see this? What is it?"

We spent the rest of the class looking at ordinary things and thinking up all the other things they were, that you wouldn't just up and pick straight-out. Miss Ochiba's blackboard chalk was a mineral and a cylinder; Debbie Buchowski's blue sweater was a birthday present; Jamie Fremont's lucky piece was a Cathayan coin, a souvenir.

When we got home that day, William was waiting impatiently on the front porch. "Hey, Lan!" he yelled. "Where've you been? I got Father to give me the afternoon, and now it's almost gone."

"School," Lan yelled back, and added "dummy" under his breath. Then he ran for the porch, with Robbie right behind him. I trudged along after, knowing that they'd talk with me for a moment or two before they went off to their fort, if only out of neighborliness. When I came up to them, they were arguing about Miss Ochiba's class.

William was at his most annoying, all superior and know-everything; Robbie was bouncing around like the lid on a kettle getting ready to boil over; and Lan was looking as cross as ever I'd seen him. William seemed to think he was better than the rest of us because he was getting private teaching at home, and had been memorizing basic spells for nearly a year already, though he was the youngest of us all and couldn't actually cast any of them yet. He didn't think much of Miss Ochiba's different ways of seeing, and he didn't think much of learning Hijero–Cathayan and Aphrikan magical theory and history, either.

"After all, we're Avrupans," he said. "And our magic works better than anyone else's. That other stuff is just a waste of time."

"The United States isn't in Avrupa," Lan corrected him. "We're Columbians."

William waved that away. "We all came from Avrupa to begin with. From Albion, or Gaul, or Prussia, or somewhere. That's what's important."

"Says you!" Robbie said. "Why should we learn about Avrupa, when we went and had a revolution to get away from them?"

"That was almost a hundred years ago!" William said. "Avrupan magic is the best, and we should learn the best."

"How can you know it's the best, if you don't learn about anything else?" I said.

All three boys turned and looked at me. "Everybody knows already," William said. "Like knowing water is wet, or rocks are hard, or which way is up."

"Magic makes its own rules," Lan retorted.

William looked shocked. "That's from Plato! How do you know that?"

"It's something Papa says," I put in quickly. It was actually something from one of the lessons Lan had with that tutor, back in Helvan Shores, but if we started in on that, sure as anything William would end up asking awkward questions, and the whole thing about Lan being the seventh son of a seventh son might come out.

Lan grinned suddenly. "Hey, school's out! It's dumb to waste time arguing about it. Let's go finish the fort before somebody comes around with chores." As they ran off, he looked back and winked at me, so I knew he'd understood.

The boys vanished into the bushes behind the house. Looking after them, I wondered suddenly what William was, that wasn't what you'd first see in him. The notion kept me thinking for the rest of the day, and on after supper when the boys came back, and for many days after. It felt like an important question, but I couldn't think why, and I couldn't seem to get an answer for it. Eventually, other things pushed it out of the front of my mind — schoolwork, and chores, and Kristen

Olvar asking me to join her sewing club, and planning for Harvest Feast, among other things. But they couldn't push the question out of my head altogether. It sat waiting in the dark back of my mind, waiting for me to have time to come back to it. And eventually, I did.

CHAPTER 6

MISS OCHIBA'S CLASS WAS THE HIGHLIGHT OF THE REST OF THE school year. Some of the history was familiar — we'd learned about the Greeks and the Roman Empire the year before — but it all seemed different when we looked at their magic and not just at all the battles and emperors. The parts about Aphrika and Cathay were mostly new, and I found them fascinating, no matter what William said.

But the best part was what Miss Ochiba called "seeing." We never knew what day it would happen, or what we'd be asked to do, only that it would involve finding different ways to look at familiar things. We spent one class coming up with different uses for a fork, and another thinking up different ways to get a basket of eggs across a creek without breaking any of them. And one day, we spent the whole class making puns.

That was what did it, in the end — the puns. Lan and Robbie had been arguing with William off and on all year about Miss Ochiba and the right way to learn magic, and up until that day, they'd looked like winning in the end. There were two of them, and Robbie was old enough to be learning the beginning spells. He got real good at distracting everybody in the middle of an argument by demonstrating how to make a stick float in the air. William was stubborn, but he was slowly wearing down.

Until the puns. Lan and the other boys loved that class, and they kept on punning long after. Making puns became a game, and then a secret code. And William was no good at it. It drove him near crazy, listening to the others go on and not being able to join in. Then when he was tongue-tied and ready to burst with it, the boys would start in all over again.

"Hey, William, cat got your tongue?"

"Maybe he's *horse*."

"If you're sick, maybe you should try *lion* down."

"He can't be feeling that bad; he's not *dragon* around."

"That sounds more like *ewe*."

"Oh, that pun really *sphinx*."

I don't think the boys meant any harm; they were just looking for an excuse to start in on a new chain of puns. But it always seemed to come out like picking on William, and that made William go all stubborn and ornery every time. So instead of blowing over, the argument just kept on growing like a snowbank, all winter long.

And then one day in the early spring, when the little blue starflowers were just coming up around the edges of the coarse patches of snow that still stuck fast wherever large tree trunks or boulders blocked the sun, Robbie came tearing up to the house all muddy and red-faced. I was sweeping the porch because I wanted to be outside in the sun and it was still too cool to just sit, so I saw him coming.

"Eff!" he yelled. "Get Papa, quick! It's Lan —" He stopped at the steps, wheezing and too out of breath to talk.

I dropped the broom and ran inside. Papa was teaching a class, and we weren't supposed to interrupt for anything, no matter what, but I didn't care, not if Lan was in the kind of trouble that would make Robbie look so wild-eyed. I just burst in yelling, "Papa! Papa! Something's happened to Lan!"

Papa and his five students looked up from a diagram that was spread out on the table in front of them. Papa's eyes met mine, and then he came right over. "What is it that's happened?"

"I don't know!" I sobbed. "Robbie's out front — he says to come quick!"

Papa nodded and brushed past me. The students exchanged glances, and all five of them followed. The last one, a big, soft-spoken man named Gil Mannering, stopped next to me and said, "Lan's your twin, isn't he?"

I nodded. I couldn't remember anyone putting it like that before; usually, everybody said I was Lan's twin.

"You won't be wanting to wait to find out what's wrong, then," he said, half to himself. "Come along."

I didn't wait for any more permission than that. I just followed along.

When we got out to the porch, Papa was trying to get

57

Robbie settled down enough to make some sense. Robbie just tugged Papa toward the creek. "You have to come quick, Papa! Before he drops him. It's too high. Hurry!"

Sense or not, that was enough to start everyone running. I fell behind pretty quick, but Gil saw and came back for me. He didn't say anything, just scooped me up and carried me off like a sack of flour.

Robbie led the way toward the fort the boys had built in the windbreak, and then past it a little way to the creek. The creek was swollen right to the top of its banks with meltwater and running fast. Here and there, you could see eddies and foam where the big rocks were, that we used for stepping-stones in the summer when the water was low. Over the sound of the rushing water, we heard voices, and then we arrived.

Two of the boys from our class at school were standing by the creek, staring upward. A third was dragging a fallen branch out from the bushes toward the bank. Lan stood a little apart, his face white as paper. His hands were clenched into fists, and he was holding them out in front of him like he was trying to raise up a bucket that was too heavy for him. He was staring upward at William, who was floating in the air over the creek, a good twenty feet from the ground, limp as Nan's old rag doll and moaning softly. Every time Lan's hands shook, William rose a little higher.

One of the college students laughed. Papa glared at him, then said quietly, "I'm here, Lan."

"Papa!" Lan gasped. "I can't hold him up much longer, and I can't get him down."

"You're doing very well," Papa said calmly. His hands were busy in his pockets, pulling out string and keys and papers. "Just hang on another minute. Mr. Mannering, put a net under that boy right now, and hold it until we have him down. Mr. Jordan, I want a control ward as soon as you can have one up. Mr. Stepka, you handle the shield — I don't want any backsplash hitting these other children."

Papa kept talking, telling each of his students what to do while he laid out the spell that he'd be casting. Normally, I'd have been more than a little interested. Papa didn't often work magic when the family was near to see. But right then, I was watching Lan and William.

Everyone else could see that Lan was tiring fast, and that when he ran out of energy, William would drop straight into the swift, treacherous water below. Everyone else could see how hard Lan was trying to keep William up just as long as he could, so that Papa and the others would have a chance to bring him down safely. That's what they saw, but Lan was my twin, and I saw something else.

Lan was madder than a wet cat. That was where he'd found the energy to lift William twenty feet high and hold him there; he was feeding the magic with his anger. He'd used up a good part of his mad by then, but he was still mad enough that the angry part of him didn't really *want* William to come down safe. He wasn't just fighting to hold William up. He was fighting himself, too.

I wondered for just a second what William had said or done to make Lan so mad, but there wasn't time to think about that. I looked up at William, and then down at the banks of the creek. There were plenty of people on our side to catch him, if he moved over a little and didn't come down too fast; the whole street and half the college seemed to have collected in the few minutes we'd been there. I sidled over to Lan.

"It's just old William," I said softly, not like I was talking to anyone, especially not looking at Lan. "He doesn't mean half he says, and the other half, he doesn't know any better. It's just old William. I bet he's learned enough of a lesson."

I felt something hot and angry wash across my skin, like the heat from a bonfire. I stayed where I was. "It's just William," I repeated.

Lan sighed, and William started to sink. Slowly. Someone on the bank yelled, and Papa shouted some words over the students' muttering. William glowed blue, as if a soap bubble had suddenly appeared around him. Lan gasped and collapsed in a panting heap. William's bubble swooped down to the bank, quickly but under control. The bubble vanished. The boys cheered as William dropped the last few inches onto the grass, safe and sound.

Naturally everyone started demanding explanations. First in line was Professor Graham, William's father, who'd arrived in time to see the last few minutes. As soon as he was sure William had come to no harm, he demanded to know who was responsible.

"Lan Rothmer, Professor," one of Papa's students told him.

"Nonsense," Professor Graham snapped. "He's had no training, and he's not even ten yet. He can't possibly have done such a working." He looked at the older boys who'd been on the creek bank when we all arrived. "Now, which of you cast that spell?"

Papa had been checking Lan over, the same way Professor Graham had been checking William, but he heard what the professor said and looked up. "It was Lan, all right, and you have my profoundest apologies, Professor Graham."

Professor Graham's head whipped around and his eyes narrowed. "How?"

Papa looked down at Lan with a rueful expression. "Lan's a natural magician. I've been thinking that something would break loose soon, but I hadn't expected anything quite so dramatic. Nor so dangerous."

"A natural — you mean you're a seventh son?"

Papa nodded.

"And *he's* a seventh son?"

Papa nodded again.

Professor Graham blew out a long breath. "I don't understand why you didn't mention this before, Professor Rothmer. The training of a natural magician, especially one with such potential power —"

"— is a topic on which everyone seems willing to express an opinion," Papa said a trifle sharply. "Sara and I consider it more important to train the man. Apropos of which —" He nudged Lan.

Lan stepped forward. He still looked pale, but he wasn't shaking anymore. He wasn't angry, either. He was scared. "Please, sir, it was me," he said, and swallowed hard. "We were arguing, and — and I lost my temper, and it just happened. I'm sorry." He put his chin up and looked at William, who was sitting on the ground, shivering. "I'm sorry, William. I — I didn't mean for it to happen."

"I see," Professor Graham said slowly, but he was looking at Papa. After a moment, he switched the look to Lan. "I will accept your apology, young man. And your explanation. I trust, however, that there will not be a repeat of the incident."

Lan gulped. "I — I'll try, sir. I mean, I'll try not to. But I didn't do it on purpose, and I'm not sure I know how to keep from doing it." He looked a little sick as he spoke, and there was a murmur from the other boys on the riverbank. Some of them gave Lan wary looks, and Lan looked even sicker when he saw them.

"Teaching you how to keep from doing it is my job," Papa said briskly. "And, no doubt, Professor Graham's, if he will be kind enough to assist."

Professor Graham looked startled, then nodded. "It will be my pleasure."

"Now that your abilities have broken loose, it shouldn't

take long for you to learn to control them," Papa said. "And after such a spectacular beginning, I doubt you'll be capable of even lighting a lantern for at least a week. By the time you've recovered enough for another such performance, you'll know how to avoid it." He spoke to Lan, but loudly enough for everyone to hear, and a sigh ran through the crowd as people relaxed.

Professor Graham's eyes narrowed again briefly. Then he said, "Let's get these two home. And no argument from you," he added to William, who hadn't even begun to say anything. "If you aren't exhausted, you ought to be. Come — your mother will be worried."

Papa smiled slightly. "And so will yours," he said to Lan, and took his hand. He and Professor Graham and Lan and William moved off toward the houses, with most of the grown-ups trailing along behind.

One of the boys who'd been with Lan and Robbie came over to me — Dick Corman, who'd been dragging the branch down the bank when we showed up. "You're Lan's twin," he said.

I nodded.

"Is he really a double-seven?"

I nodded again. There was no point in denying it. Maybe there'd been a few people in the crowd who hadn't put together what Papa and Professor Graham had said, but it wouldn't be long before the ones who had figured it out enlightened them. By the end of tomorrow, everyone at school would know.

"Wow," Dick said, looking after Papa and Lan. He looked back at me. "Does that mean you're a natural, too? Because you're his twin?"

I stared at him. "I don't know," I said after a minute. "Nobody's ever said."

"Maybe they don't know," Dick said, looking back toward the dwindling crowd. "They like to pretend they know everything there is to know about magic, but they don't really, or why would they always be talking about research?"

I tucked that away in my head to think about later, and changed the subject before he started asking too many more questions. "What were you doing with that branch when we came up?"

To my surprise, he flushed. "I didn't think Robbie would get back in time. I thought if William dropped in the creek, maybe he could grab hold of the branch and we could pull him out." He looked at the dark swirling current. "I guess I wasn't thinking too clearly."

"At least you were trying to do something," I said. "Everybody else was just standing there." I paused. "What did William say to get Lan so mad?"

Dick started to say something, then stopped and looked in the direction where Papa and everyone had gone.

"What did he *say*?" I asked again.

"William lost his temper first," Dick said slowly. "Over the puns. He said they didn't have anything to do with real magic. And then he dared Robbie to float something bigger than that little stick he practices with all the time."

"He dared *Robbie?*" I said.

Dick nodded. "And *then* he said that when he turns ten, he'll be floating plates and bricks and all sorts of things, because he already knows the spells. Lan told him not to talk twaddle, and William told Lan that with the training he was getting in school, he'd never even be good enough to be a drudge magician — that none of your family had any real magical talent, and that your father must know it or he wouldn't be sending all of you to the day school."

"Oh," I said. Even hearing about it secondhand made me just as mad as Lan had been. No wonder he'd yanked William right up to the treetops like that. For a minute, I was sorry I'd tried to calm Lan down.

I told Dick thanks and trudged on home, thinking hard the whole way. I wasn't sure if I should tell Papa what I'd learned, or not. It felt important. But I could also feel a nasty part of me that wanted to tell Papa the whole story in order to get William into trouble, a part that wanted its own revenge on William for what he'd dared to say about Papa and Lan. *The evil part of me*, I thought. By the time I got back to the house, I'd decided not to give in to it, so I didn't say anything to Papa at all.

CHAPTER 7

THAT SPRING LEADING UP TO MY TENTH BIRTHDAY, WE HAD MORE rain than a mammoth has hair. It rained in slow, steady, day-long streams and in sudden rushes like someone dumping a bucket out. The streets that weren't paved went ankle-deep in mud or worse, so that taking out a carriage or wagon became something that took care and planning. The few days of sun we had were nothing like enough to dry things out.

Then, just as school was letting out at last, it dried up and got hot. The churned-up mud took a week to bake nearly as hard as bricks, full of deep cracks that were wide enough to stick your whole finger in. The leaves on the trees curled up, and the grass dried out hard and sharp as pins. Over it all hung the sun and the dust. Not a breath of air stirred.

Naturally, the boys spent all their time down at the creek. Lan went with them whenever he could get away from his extra magic lessons. Everyone else stayed on the porch, because even Papa's best spells couldn't cool the house off enough for comfort in the daytime. Everyone except me, that is.

I spent my time on the roof, in the hiding place I'd found

the summer before. If I didn't move much, it wasn't any hotter there than on the porch, and no one could interrupt me to do chores or errands.

The day Professor Graham came by, I was on the roof and Mama and Papa were on the porch, having the same conversation they'd had nearly every day since the hot spell started. Mama complained about the heat and the dust and the extra work it made, and Papa said she should think of the settlers, trying to farm when first they couldn't plant for the rain, and now anything they had gotten in was drying up and blowing away. Mama said if she felt for anyone, it was the settlers' wives, who had even more dust to deal with than there was in the city. They could go on like that for hours, play-arguing. They'd already been at it long enough to chase Rennie and Nan and Allie off to find someone to visit.

I wasn't really listening, just enough so I'd notice if either of them said anything about me. I recognized Professor Graham's voice when he turned up, and something in it when he and Papa exchanged greetings made me close up my book and pay close attention.

Papa must have heard it, too, because he didn't waste much time on socializing. "What brings you over, Professor?" he asked as soon as everyone had finished with their hellos.

"There's been another incursion," Professor Graham said, sounding grim. "Near Braxton, this time. Ten families, wiped out."

"Braxton!" Mama gasped. "So close!"

"It's a good fifty miles west of the river, Sara," Papa said mildly.

"Yes, and there's no reason to think the Great Barrier is weakening," Professor Graham put in hastily. "But the lesser spells the settlements have been using just aren't up to the job of holding back the wildlife."

"Not in a year like this one, anyway," Papa said. "Any word on what it was?"

"An assorted mob," Professor Graham said. "A herd of mammoths overran the magician's barrier and trampled the fences. They'd been stampeded by a mixed pack of Columbian sphinxes and saber cats, and there were scavengers following after — jackals and terror birds, from the sound of it. There were only four survivors."

"Oh, Daniel," Mama said.

There was a short silence. I thought about what Professor Graham had said. We'd studied the animals of the North Plains Territory in natural history in school. They were divided into two sorts, the ordinary and the magical. The ordinary ones were things like mammoths and dire wolves and saber cats and terror birds, and the magical ones were steam dragons and Columbian sphinxes and spectral bears and swarming weasels, and all of them were deadly dangerous, magical or not. And those were just the plains animals; there were other things just as bad in the northern forests, and no Great Barrier magic to keep them off, either. It was suicide to go west of the Mammoth River, or north of its headwaters, without a magician to keep you safe; everybody knew that. But it hadn't occurred to me until right then that you could have a magician and still not be safe.

"Thank you for telling us," Papa said.

"Don't thank me until you've heard it all," the professor warned. "The new head of the Settlement Office is disturbed by all these recent incidents. They've requested that the college send you, me, and Jeffries out to study the settlements, with a view to improving their magical protections."

"And?" Papa said.

"And that damn fool thinks we should bring along the seventh son of a seventh son," Professor Graham said.

"What?" Papa sounded outraged.

"No." Mama's voice was quiet and very firm. When she spoke like that, you knew that there was no point in arguing.

"Sara, we may not have a choice," Papa said reluctantly. "This is a land-grant college. The Homestead and Settlement Office has the right to request our assistance; that was part of the agreement."

"No," Mama repeated. "Lan is not an employee of this college, nor of the Settlement Office, nor of anyone else in Mill City. He's a ten-year-old boy." There was a rustling sound, and then footsteps against the porch floorboards. "I'd appreciate it if you'd take me into town right now, Daniel. I will not have my son pushed into matters far beyond his age and understanding, and I intend to make that very clear to the officials of the North Plains Territory Homestead Claim and Settlement Office."

"I told them that," Professor Graham said. "They won't listen."

"They will listen to me," Mama said. She sounded perfectly composed and angry as anything, both at the same time. "Because if they do not, Lan and I will be on the next train east. Living here has been very good for him. I'm not having all the good undone because the settlement board is panicking."

"You can't do that!" Professor Graham said, startled.

"I most certainly can," Mama said. "I'm his mother, and I'm not an employee of this college, nor of the Settlement Office, either."

"Rothmer —"

"I'll reserve the train tickets while she's at the Settlement Office," Papa said. "Do you want to take anyone else, Sara? It might save some face at the Settlement Office if we make the trip look like a family visit."

"At the moment, I really don't care how foolish the Settlement Office looks," Mama said. "But we can discuss it on the ride into town, if you think there's need."

And that was that. Just as soon as they could get the buggy hitched up, Papa and Mama and Professor Graham were off to town. They stayed away the whole rest of the day, and I would have given my best Sunday dress and a year's growth to have been able to see what happened when Mama arrived at the Settlement Office. I almost went and asked Rennie if she'd do a scrying spell to see, but I'd have had to tell her why, and

Rennie couldn't keep a secret to save her life. Besides, I wasn't entirely sure she could work a scry spell. She never paid much attention to her magic lessons, that I ever saw, and even if she'd learned scrying, there was a good chance she'd forgotten how since she graduated from the upper school.

Mama and Papa were home in time for dinner, and they didn't say one thing about the Settlement Office or Lan. I thought about telling Lan, at least, what I'd heard, but in the end I didn't. It was plain that Mama and Papa didn't want him knowing, nor me, either. I couldn't unhear what I'd heard, but I could pretend I hadn't heard it.

Three days later, Papa and Professor Graham and Professor Jeffries left to study the settlements.

They were gone most of the summer. We got letters every week, regular as dawn and dusk, and Mama read them out to us after dinner. Sometimes people from the college stopped by to ask how we were and how Papa was getting on — students and professors, mostly, though Dean Farley visited twice. Nobody ever came from the Homestead and Settlement Office.

Meantime, Mill City filled up with people. Some were from the settlements, farm families who'd decided to come in where it was certain-sure to be safe and where they could earn some money, since their crops for the year were gone. Some were from the East, new folks looking to get land from the Settlement Office. But there wasn't much land left on the east side of the Mammoth River, and the Settlement Office was having enough trouble taking care of the hamlets and tiny-towns they already had on the west side of the river. They weren't starting up any new ones right then. So the Easterners mostly ended up angry and frustrated.

Papa came home in mid-August. He and Professor Jeffries just rode up one day, all unexpected, and found Mama having tea with some students on the front porch. Papa and Professor Jeffries were dusty and sunburned, but Mama hugged both of them anyway, and so did the rest of us. Then Mama made them sit right down and have tea, too, though they were covered with dirt and she'd never in a million years have let any of the boys do such a thing.

The next day, Papa went down to the North Plains Territory Homestead Claim and Settlement Office. He came home cross as two sticks and locked himself in his study. Three days later, he sent out copies of his report on the settlements — not just to the Settlement Office, but to Uncle Martin in New Amsterdam, Mr. Loring in Washington (who was head of the Frontier Management Department that was in charge of all the country's Homestead and Settlement offices), three or four senators and a dozen assemblymen who represented border states all along the Mammoth River, and the heads of the two biggest settler groups, even though one of them was halfway down the Mammoth River in the Middle Plains and had nothing to do with us.

From then until school started, our house was busy as a train stop, with people coming and going and talking seriously with Papa about his report. Dean Farley came three times, and once the school's president, Mr. Grey, came with Professor Graham. The professor shook his head and told Papa he was a brave man, but Mr. Grey said that Papa had only done what any man of conscience ought, and that the Settlement Office must realize at last that the college was not going to be manipulated or coerced. Later on, I asked Hugh what Mr. Grey meant, and he said that Mr. Grey was glad of the chance to show the Settlement Office that they couldn't boss the college around, but because he was president of the college, he couldn't say so in plain words without maybe offending them.

The day before school started, I was out back with Rennie, weeding the kitchen garden, when two peculiar-looking men came up. They wore simple homespun coats over bright shirts, and squared-off hats with feathers stuck in the hatband. The older one was tall and skinny and dark-haired, with a square-trimmed beard and three hawk feathers in his hatband. The younger one was medium-tall, blond and broad-shouldered and not much older than my brother Charlie. He only had one feather in his hat, a long, shiny black one from a crow's wing. As soon as she laid eyes on him, Rennie straightened up and patted at her hair.

"Pardon me, ladies," the older man said, and Rennie straightened up further yet and almost smirked. "Could you tell me where I would find Professor Rothmer?"

"Papa's in his study," I said.

73

Rennie frowned at me, then smiled her best smile at the two men. "My father is inside. If you'd like to come around front to the porch, Eff can run and tell him you're here."

"That will be most satisfactory," the older man said.

Rennie made a shooing motion at me behind her back. I made a face at her, being careful that the visitors couldn't see me. I knew well enough what was proper without her bossing me just to show off in front of company. But the very minute I was out of sight I ran as fast as I could to Papa's study to tell him we had more visitors.

I was quick enough that Papa and the two men arrived at the front of the house almost at the same time. Papa checked, just for an instant, and when he got a good look at the two of them, his face got the little smile on it that meant something interesting was about to happen. Rennie didn't notice; she was too busy making a face back at me as she went past me into the house.

"Professor Rothmer?" the older man said.

Papa nodded. "That I am, sir."

"Toller Lewis," the man said, extending his hand. "President of the Long Lake City branch of the Society of Progressive Rationalists. And this is my nephew, Brant Wilson. We've come to see you on a matter of business, so to speak."

The corners of Papa's mouth got deeper, as if his smile was getting stronger without getting any wider. He took Mr. Lewis's hand and shook it. "What business would the Society of Progressive Rationalists have with a practicing magician and a professor of magic?"

Mr. Lewis shifted his feet and opened his mouth, but then he closed it again without saying anything. Brant looked over at him and then turned to Papa and answered, "I'd like to attend your class on Theory and Application of the Great Barrier Spell this fall, with your permission."

Papa looked startled. The Society of Progressive Rationalists didn't hold with magic and magicians. I'd seen one of their pamphlets once — it had said that magic was a snare and a crutch, and men would only realize their full potential if they stopped using it and depended on their brains and strong arms instead. That made no sense to me; after all, magic takes plenty of brains. And why would anybody want to work three times harder than they needed, just to say they hadn't used magic to build a house or make a coat or dig a well? The Rationalists didn't hold with religion, either, so they weren't real popular in most places.

"Are you quite sure you haven't confused me with Professor Swanson? Engineering seems more in your line," Papa said.

"No, sir," Brant said firmly. "I want to take your class on the Great Barrier Spell. Also Professor Jeffries's class on the wildlife beyond the Mammoth River. You see, we're hoping to be allowed a settlement next year."

"If you're hoping to learn enough magic to protect your people from the wildlife in one or two classes, I'm afraid —"

"Certainly not!" Mr. Lewis burst out.

Brant made a little settling-down motion with his hand, and his uncle pressed his lips together. "I don't want to learn how to do magic, sir; I want to learn what you are doing *with* it, in as much detail as possible, so we can find our own ways of protecting a settlement." He gave his uncle a sidelong glance and added, "It's only the use of magic that's forbidden, after all, not the study of it."

"If it were anyone else, I wouldn't allow it," Mr. Lewis grumbled. "But you're stubborn enough to run off and try it without permission, so I expect you'll be stubborn enough to resist the temptation to use what you learn."

The corners of Papa's mouth had just about disappeared back into his face, but he didn't laugh at either of them. "I don't think you have anything to worry about in that regard," he said to the older man. "Your nephew hasn't had the training to cast the sort of advanced spells we'll be working on, even if he wanted to. I'm more concerned with this settlement scheme of yours. Founding unprotected settlements has been tried before, you know. And they've failed every time."

"We are well aware of the risks," Mr. Lewis said.

"Nevertheless, I doubt the Settlement Office will approve your proposal."

"But just think, sir, what a tremendous step it will be, if we can show that it's possible to set up and maintain an outpost without magic!" Brant said, leaning forward. "It would open the whole vast plain west of the Mammoth to settlement."

"Very true," Papa said, "if you could be sure of doing it. But the Settlement Office may take more convincing than you think. They're very sensitive on the subject of settlement protection at the moment."

"Thanks to you, sir," Mr. Lewis said approvingly. "Yes, I've seen that report you wrote, and we hope to make use of some of the nonmagical suggestions. Your design for a central compound, for instance —"

He broke off as the door swung open again and Rennie came through, carrying a tray with four glasses, a pitcher of water, and a plate of the biscuits Mrs. Callahan had made for supper. "I thought maybe you'd like some refreshment while you talk," she said brightly.

Papa nodded approval. He motioned to Mr. Lewis and Brant to sit down. Rennie set the tray on the little twig table, then took a chair and started pouring water and handing it around. I backed quietly into the house and left. I could see she'd forgotten to bring any napkins or biscuit plates, and I knew as soon as she realized, she'd look for me to get them if I was still there.

So I never did hear the rest of the conversation, and Rennie was cross with me all evening. But when the college classes started three weeks later, Brant Wilson was one of my father's students, squared-off hat and crow's feather and all.

CHAPTER 8

ONCE SCHOOL STARTED, EVERYTHING SEEMED TO CALM DOWN, FROM the weather to the settlers to the Settlement Office itself. Our daily visitors went back to being students coming for classes or to ask Papa special questions. Hugh packed his trunk and left for the same university back East that Charlie and Peter had studied at, after explaining carefully to Dean Farley that he didn't mean it as any reflection on the Northern Plains Riverbank College, but he thought he'd prefer a school where he didn't have to take half his classes from his own father.

Rennie was still at home, though she'd graduated upper school and should have started work or been studying for college. But Rennie didn't want more schooling, and she couldn't seem to find a job that suited her in Mill City, however hard she looked. I thought it was probably because nobody would let her start right in bossing people, without taking a turn being bossed first, but I kept my opinion to myself.

It wasn't long before I was glad I hadn't said anything, because a month after school started, Corrie Bergston came to class with a hacking cough, and nearly everyone caught it, including me and Lan. Rennie split the nursing with Mama, and I didn't like to think how miserable a time I'd have had if I'd given her reason to be cross with me. I was miserable enough as it was.

Lan wheezed for a week, like everyone else, and then the coughing slacked off and he went back to school. I wasn't so lucky. The cough turned to a putrid sore throat, and then to something else that made me hot and achy all over for weeks. Mama had the doctor in, and then another doctor, and then pretty nearly every professor at the college who might have some practical use to them, and the minister on top of them all. Most of the time, I was too tired and achy to care about anything except making them go away, but after a while it sank in through the fog in my head that I must be really sick for all those people to keep coming with nasty-tasting potions and spells.

One of the times I felt clear enough to think, I finally asked Mama what was wrong with me.

"You have rheumatic fever, Eff," she said. "It's a very dangerous disease, but you're past the worst of it now, if we're careful."

"If we're careful?"

"Rheumatic fever lingers in the body, even after you start feeling better," Mama explained. "You'll have to lie here quietly for a long time if you don't want to have a recurrence."

"You mean I could be sick all over again?" I asked.

Mama nodded. "All over again, and worse than ever," she told me. Her voice wobbled, so I knew it was serious. "You might die, or the fever could weaken your heart, despite all our spells and potions. So you see how important it is for you to stay quiet."

I nodded. Mama looked like she wanted to say something more, but I lay back and pretended that I wanted to go to sleep. She tucked up the coverlet and kissed me before she left. I lay awake for a long while when she was gone, thinking as best I could.

My head was still fairly muddled, but I'd got the part about dying, all right. It seemed wrong to me that all the doctors and magicians should put so much work into trying to keep me alive, when if they'd known I was a thirteenth child and bound to turn evil in a few years, they wouldn't have lifted a finger. Only then I thought maybe they wouldn't mind about me being thirteenth, after all. Mill City was different from Helvan Shores. In the five years we'd been here, nobody'd made any fuss about me being a thirteenth child. If anybody had noticed, it seemed they didn't much care. Nobody had made any fuss about Lan being a double-seven, either, except for the Settlement Office. If I stayed away from the Settlement Office, maybe it would be all right.

Not that I had any call to go anywhere near the Settlement Office, or anywhere else, that year. Mama meant it when she said I had to stay quiet. I spent most of that year in bed, and missed all of school. For a while, Lan brought lessons home and I tried to catch up, but Mama wouldn't let me put in a full day working, for fear the fever would go to my brain, so I finally had to quit. I was really sorry. Once you get over the novelty of the thing, it's almighty boring, lying in bed all day for months. Even lessons would have been better.

My older brothers and sisters tried to cheer me up, but except for Rennie they were all in school most of the day, and had chores and homework to do after. They didn't have much time to spend entertaining an invalid. A few of my classmates came a time or two, but I didn't know most of the girls very well and the boys were embarrassed to be visiting a girl, especially after they saw I didn't have any interesting scars.

The only things that made those months bearable were Rennie and Lan, and the visits I had from William and Papa's students. Rennie sat and read to me for hours every morning, and never complained a bit — at least, not where I could hear.

William was the surprising one. He'd started going to the day school in the fall; I guess Professor Graham decided that if day school was good enough training for the seventh son of a seventh son, it was good enough for William. He'd been nervous at first, until he found that the boys in his class had heard all about the set-to he'd had with Lan back in the spring, and thought he'd been brave to stand up against a double-seventh son, even if he hadn't known that he was doing it at the time.

After school started, William stopped by every single day on his way home and told me what happened in class and what his father would think of it. It got a little wearing, sometimes, but I could see he was really trying, and it was nice to see a face that wasn't one I'd seen every day of my whole life. Also, once he'd gotten through telling me about school, he'd talk about other things, or play checkers. I didn't find out until years later just how worried he'd been that I was going to end up a permanent invalid like his mother.

Lan came by himself, evenings, and did his studying in my room. I was glad for the company, and I liked seeing him practice the spells he was learning. It took me two weeks to figure out that glow spells and fire-burst illusions weren't the usual things a first-year magician learns, even if he was a double-seventh son.

Papa found out what Lan had been doing a few days later, and read him a tremendous scold over working new spells without proper supervision, never mind the reason. Then he taught Lan a couple of really good ones, and started sending some of his own students up to do advanced illusions. It got to be kind of a contest among them. Even Brant Wilson came, though he had no magic and couldn't do illusions. Instead, he told me about the Society of Progressive Rationalists and the settlement they were planning.

"Why do you wear that feather in your hat?" I asked him one time.

"Eff," Rennie said reprovingly. She'd been reading to me, and had gone off to get some hot cider for us when Brant arrived.

"It's a reasonable question," Brant said to her. "We're

taught that no reasonable question should be considered impolite."

"I imagine that gets hard to keep up when you're talking to other folks, though," Rennie said. "Especially if you're the one doing the asking."

Brant sighed. "Sometimes we do cause offense, but it's always unintended."

"Were you offended?" I asked. "Just now, when I asked about the feather?"

He laughed. "Not at all. We wear feathers for a lot of reasons. They show that we belong to the Society of Progressive Rationalists. We use them as badges of office, too. And they remind us of how much we might do, of how high we can fly under our own power, without magic."

"You can't either fly," I said. "Not without magic. You're just making that up."

Rennie frowned at me. "Eff! Mind your manners! Being sick is no excuse for rudeness."

Brant laughed again. "It's all right, Miss Rothmer. It's a turn of phrase, Eff, that's all. A metaphor. I'm not used to taking spells into consideration all the time. I can see this year is going to be an education in more ways than one."

I stuck my tongue out at Rennie when he looked at her, real fast so he wouldn't see it. Her face was a study, trying to be polite and interested to Brant and scoldy to me, both at the same time. Brant even noticed, and darted a quick look back at me, but by then I was just looking doubtful again.

"I didn't mean to say that we can actually fly like birds without magic," Brant told me. "But our ideas and imaginations can soar, if we don't cripple them by looking to spells to do everything for us. The man who designed the new engine for the railroads is a Rationalist. While everyone else was trying to use magic to improve it, he used his mind and his knowledge, and the result is an engine that works better and is more reliable. And you don't need to have magic to use it. That's the sort of thing we need more of, if —"

A knock at the door interrupted him. Rennie rose and opened it. "William!" she said. "Is it so late already?"

"Hello, Miss Rothmer," William said. "Excuse me; I didn't know Eff had another visitor."

"This is Brant Wilson," I said. "William Graham. He's Professor Graham's son. Brant's from the Society of Progressive Rationalists," I added to William.

William frowned for a second; then his face cleared. "Oh! That's the people who don't believe in magic." Then he looked at Brant and went purple as a cooked beet.

"Not exactly," Brant said. "We believe magic exists; we just don't believe in *doing* magic, or using things made by magic."

"That's all right, then," William said, nodding. "It'd be pretty stupid to think magic doesn't exist, when people do spells all the time. Why are you poking me?" he added, looking at Rennie.

Rennie turned red and looked cross, but before she could

snap at him I said, "She doesn't think you were polite, but since you're not part of our family, she can't say so straight out without being impolite herself."

"Eff!" Rennie sounded like she couldn't decide whether to laugh or read me the biggest scold I'd had in months. "Honestly, I don't know what to do with you."

"You don't have to do anything," I said. "I'm Mama's problem, for that. And I don't see that it's so important. Brant doesn't mind, and William's practically family now."

William looked surprised and gratified. Rennie rolled her eyes and looked at Brant. Brant laughed. I could see that William was getting ready to ask some more questions, and I didn't want Rennie mad at him. "Brant and the Rationalists want to start a settlement," I said, to give him something else to think on.

"But I thought you said you didn't do magic," William said.

"We don't," Brant told him. "We plan to start a settlement without using any magic."

William's eyes widened. "You can't put a settlement on the west side of the river without using magic! How would you keep off the mammoths and the sphinxes and — and everything else?"

"We have some ideas," Brant said. "A double trench and a palisade would stop the larger creatures — Samiel thinks the right defenses could halt even a mammoth stampede, if they're properly designed. The smaller animals aren't much of a danger to a village, only to lone travelers. The real difficulty will be protecting the crops. Barricading enough acreage for ten families to farm, or even five, just isn't practical."

"Five?" William's eyebrows scrunched together, the way they always did when he was puzzled by something. "But ten families is the minimum for a settlement."

"Yes, but they don't all have to be farming," Brant said. "We'd actually planned to start with fifteen families, because we want to be as self-sufficient as possible. It's sometimes difficult to find goods that haven't been —" he hesitated "— touched by magic, so we already make most things ourselves. We don't want our settlers having to buy things that they could make themselves, if they had time."

"What sorts of things?" Rennie asked, leaning forward with interest.

"All sorts," Brant said. He waved an arm expansively. "Nails and horseshoes and cloth and furniture — we have a blacksmith who's going, and his wife's a weaver. Leather for saddles and harnesses and boots. Candles and soap, plows and kitchen pots, combs and clothespins." His eyes were glowing and he seemed to have forgotten we were even in the room. "We *can* do it," he finished fiercely, though nobody had said he couldn't.

"Sounds to me like you'd need a whole city for all that," I said.

"We'll have to haul in a few things, at first," Brant admitted. "But the planning committee has prepared very carefully, and they're being even more careful about selecting the people who are to go. The settlement *will* work."

"Are you going with them?" Rennie asked.

"I hope to," Brant replied. "It's why I'm studying here. The planning committee has plenty of people to pick from who can farm and weave and smith, but they'll need someone who knows something about the territory and the animals, and what things have been tried and whether they've worked or not. Even your magicians can't manage everything; a lot of the settlements have unmagical protections, too."

William gave Brant a long, skeptical look. "It doesn't sound like much fun to me," he said finally.

"Not fun, exactly," Brant said with a smile. "But just think of it — building a whole new community, the first one ever without magic! It will prove to everyone that we don't need magicians to settle the plains, and the government will *have* to open the territories for settlement. It will make history!"

"It won't be the first one ever," William said in a grumpy tone. "Lots of places on the Old Continent got along without magicians after the Roman Empire fell apart. Anyway, you can't do it unless the Settlement Office lets you, and I bet they won't."

Rennie glared at William, but Brant just looked determined. "It may take time, but we will convince them," he said firmly. "This is too important to let some shortsighted officials get in the way."

"I don't want to talk about the Settlement Office," I said.

"They're just — boring. Tell me about something else." Tears stung my eyes. Just saying the name of the place was hard; I didn't want to hear anything more about it. William and Brant gave me surprised looks. Rennie clucked and stood up.

"She's overtired and getting cross," Rennie told them. She turned to me. "Time for a nap. It's not so long since you were feverish, and Mama will slay me outright if you take sick again."

I objected a little, for form's sake, but I didn't really mean it. Rennie was right; I was tired. And if napping cut the visit short, it at least put a stop to the talk of the Settlement Office and what it would or wouldn't do.

By spring they were letting me out of bed for a little, and I only had to take the fever-prevention potions once a day. I was as weak and clumsy as a new puppy, and Mama fussed and fretted over me, and ordered me back to bed twice, until Papa asked her what she expected when I hadn't used my legs all those long months. After that, Mama didn't fuss so much, and after a few weeks Papa started me doing training exercises. Gradually, my legs got stronger, though Mama still wouldn't let me run or do too much hard work. I was glad enough to be let off hoeing the garden and pumping water for the kitchen, but I wasn't sure that getting landed with all the sewing and piecework was a good trade.

Shortly after the snow melted, when the Settlement Office announced who'd be going off to start new homesteads, we found out that Papa and William had been right: The Society of Progressive Rationalists wasn't on the approved list. They didn't give up, though. The folks who'd come to Mill City in hopes of moving west stayed on, hoping they could persuade the Settlement Office to change its mind. Brant wasn't even that discouraged. He said they'd expected setbacks, and it was just an opportunity to show people in Mill City how to get along without magic.

The other big thing that happened that spring was the start of the McNeil Expedition. The report that Papa had written all those months ago had said in no uncertain terms that somebody needed to do a proper study of the animals and magical creatures that were causing so much trouble for the settlements. Somebody back East had paid attention, because Dr. Allen McNeil came out on the first train after the last snow melted to do just that. He wasn't a medical doctor, just educated all the way up as far as you can get.

Papa said Dr. McNeil was a famous naturalist and magician, and he was going to spend a whole year out on the wild plains beyond the river, examining animals and watching the way they lived. He was taking a small group along to help. Five of them were students from the college, and one of the students was Brant.

CHAPTER
9

NOBODY WAS QUITE SURE HOW BRANT WILSON HAD TALKED DR. McNeil into letting him go west to study the wildlife, but he'd done it, and he was elated by the chance. Our whole family went down to see them off at the Settler's Pier, where all the people who were heading west to the settlements went to be ferried across the Mammoth River in big, flat-bottom boats. I didn't know 'til I got there that it was going to be a big send-off, with Mr. Harrison, the new head of the North Plains Territory Homestead Claim and Settlement Office, making a speech. If I'd known that, I'd have played sick and stayed home. As it was, I hid behind Papa in the crowd and didn't hear a word the man said. I did take a real good look at Mr. Harrison himself, though, so I'd know him and could dodge away if I saw him on the street.

The doctors said I was still delicate and had to stay quiet, so the summer was nearly as boring as the winter had been. I didn't even have visits from Papa's students, once the college finished up for the summer. Luckily, everyone decided that I was well enough to go back to the day school in the fall, or I think I'd have just about gone crazy.

The year I'd spent being sick put another big wedge between me and Lan. I'd always known that when he started coming into his power, he'd blaze ahead of me in his magic lessons, but I'd thought we'd at least be together in our regular classes. Instead, he was a year ahead in everything, and I was back with the tagalongs a year younger than either of us. The few girls I'd begun to know were not that interested in talking with someone a year behind them, and when they did try, we didn't have much to talk about. I didn't know what had been happening in their classes, and they weren't interested in what was going on in mine.

Most of the teachers made things worse, trying to make them better. They stood me up in front of the room on the first day and talked about the rheumatic fever and me missing a whole year of school, and how everyone should be extra kind and welcoming now that I was back. By the time they finished, there wasn't one single one of my new classmates who dared say hello, either because they feared to catch whatever I'd had or because they feared a teacher would see and decide they hadn't been kind or welcoming enough.

If it hadn't been for Miss Ochiba and William, I'd have gone staring mad in the first month. When I got to Miss Ochiba's magic class, she read my name in order, along with everyone else's, just as if I'd always been there. I'd almost have believed she hadn't noticed I'd missed a whole year, if she hadn't stopped me at the door after class and said, "It is good to see you back, Miss Rothmer. I expect that you will catch up very rapidly in your magic lessons, if you choose to do so."

"Uh, thank you, Miss Ochiba," I stammered.

She gave me a penetrating look, then raised her voice just a little and looked over my shoulder. "Do remember that I wish to be informed of any extra lessons your families may decide to add to your training."

"Yes, Miss Ochiba," I murmured, and I heard another voice in back of me muttering the same thing. I slipped out the door and blew a sigh of relief, and William ran into me from behind.

"Sorry, Eff," William said. At ten, he was short and he'd put on just enough weight to be called wiry instead of skinny. He glanced back, but the classroom door was closed. He heaved an even bigger sigh than I had. "She meant that last for me, you know."

"I think she meant it for both of us," I said. "Otherwise she wouldn't have said it so we both heard. Miss Ochiba always knows exactly what she's doing, that way."

"I suppose." William looked back at the door again, then down at his feet. "You want me to tell her that your father isn't like mine? Giving extra magic lessons and things, I mean. Well, except with Lan, but he's —" He broke off and glanced at me and then back down.

"He's special," I finished for him as we walked toward our

regular classroom. "He's the seventh son of a seventh son, and I'm —" I caught myself just in time to keep from saying I was an unlucky thirteenth, and changed it to "— just his twin sister."

"You're special, too," William said fiercely. "You're just quiet about it."

I looked at him in surprise, but he didn't add anything more and I couldn't ask what he meant because we'd arrived at our next class and Miss Jensen was waiting impatiently for us to take our seats so she could start on the math lesson for the day.

I thought about what William had said, and what Miss Ochiba had said, off and on for the rest of the day, and then some more that evening. William was right, but not the way he thought he was. Being a thirteenth child was just as important as being a double-seventh son, only in the opposite direction. And nobody had told Miss Ochiba what I was.

It took me two full days more to work up the courage to talk to Miss Ochiba, though I could plainly see that if I didn't do it, nobody else would. Lan wouldn't give me away, and Robbie and Allie wouldn't think of it. Nan and Jack were in the upper school, with no reason to come back and talk to the day-school teachers, and Papa and Mama were still too mad at Uncle Earn, even after all that time, to stop and think that he might have been right. But it was a hard, hard thing to pause after Miss Ochiba's class and ask her if I could stop in to talk for a minute at the end of the day, privately.

What got me to actually do it, instead of dithering for another week, was the thought that not warning Miss Ochiba would be just the sort of thing I'd do if I were starting to go bad. That scared me, almost as much as the Settlement Office. Uncle Earn had never said *when* I was supposed to go bad, and I'd always kind of assumed that it wouldn't happen until I finished school and got to be grown up enough to make some real trouble. But I didn't know for sure and certain, and if it went and happened earlier . . . I could see that I'd have to be extra careful, so it didn't sneak up on me before I could warn people.

I worried and fretted about that talk all day and got two bad marks for inattention in reading and history. I thought about taking it back, or saying I wasn't feeling well and needed to go straight home. But that would just be putting it off, because I knew Miss Ochiba wouldn't forget.

So when school was over for the day, I went into the big room where Miss Ochiba taught her magic classes. Miss Ochiba was just locking up the big cupboard where she kept all the ingredients for the spells she taught, and there were two older boys and one girl from the last class still fiddling with little brooms and dust cloths at the big tables across the back. The girl giggled and whispered to the boy next to her when she saw me.

"I will be with you in a moment, Miss Rothmer," Miss Ochiba said as I hesitated in the doorway. "Take a seat on the left, if you please."

The girl at the worktable had seen me come in. She glanced from me to Miss Ochiba's back. Her eyes widened, and she nudged the boy next to her and whispered some more. Miss Ochiba turned and gave the girl a long look. A moment later, the top of the table made a popping sound, and a bright green cloud puffed up, right into the girl's face. A smaller cloud puffed in front of one of the boys; the other one jumped back, though nothing seemed to be happening to his part of the table.

"Well done, Mr. Legrande," Miss Ochiba said. "Miss Wilkerson, Mr. Cohen, I trust that after this you will remember that cleaning up after a spell requires as much care and attention as casting it."

The smoke began to clear, and I saw that the girl's hair and face and the whole front of her calico dress were colored bright green. The boy was blue from his nose down. They looked at each other in horror, while the second boy gave a bark of laughter, then darted a scared look at Miss Ochiba.

"Just so, Mr. Legrande," Miss Ochiba said. "I believe you are all finished for the day. You may go."

The boy who hadn't turned color gave her a wide-eyed look and bolted out of the room. The other boy hesitated, and the girl burst into tears. "I can't leave like this!" she wailed. "Miss Ochiba, how long will this last?"

"One day," Miss Ochiba replied.

"A day! How am I going to get home without anyone

seeing me? What am I going to tell my parents? Miss Ochiba, can't you do something? This is humiliating!"

"Humility is as good for the soul as it is for the memory," Miss Ochiba said, and her lips twitched as if she was trying not to smile. She handed each of the two unnaturally-colored students a note. "Give that to your parents. I shall expect you in class tomorrow, coloration and all."

"No!" the girl said. "I can't — I won't! Everyone will laugh at me."

"You are neither the first nor, I fear, the last to need such a reminder. Be thankful I intervened; the usual result of that particular mistake is a set of tentacles that are extremely painful to remove."

The blue boy looked suddenly very thoughtful. The girl didn't seem to hear. "*Please*, Miss Ochiba!"

"Twenty-four hours," Miss Ochiba replied implacably, and shooed the two of them out the door.

"Now, Miss Rothmer," she said, crossing back to the table where I sat. "I believe you wished to speak with me. I hope this unfortunate incident has not put you off."

"N-no, Miss Ochiba," I said. After watching those three students, I had the feeling Miss Ochiba could handle just about anything, even a thirteenth child. I wasn't sure I'd like it much, but that was beside the point. But now that I was here, I didn't know quite how to begin. I'd kept silent on the subject for eight years, ever since we moved to Mill City, and the habit was just about as strong as the fear that lay behind it.

And that old fear was as strong as it had ever been. On top of it, I was afraid of how Miss Ochiba would see me once she knew.

My head was near certain that talking to Miss Ochiba was the right thing to do, but my heart wanted to turn around and run. I managed to keep my feet from moving, but I couldn't get my mouth started. I just sat there, feeling scared and tongue-tied.

"Was it something regarding your magic lessons?" Miss Ochiba prompted after a minute.

"Yes. I mean, no, not exactly. I —" I twisted my fingers together and looked down at my hands. "You know Lan's a seventh son. Well, there are seven of us girls, too."

Miss Ochiba studied me, frowning slightly. I waited for her to do the addition, but her expression didn't change. Finally I said, "I'm a thirteenth child, Miss Ochiba."

"So I gather," Miss Ochiba said, tapping one finger lightly against the tabletop.

"I-I thought you ought to know," I said. "Since you're doing the magic teaching. Uncle Earn said —" I stopped, because Miss Ochiba's eyes had narrowed and she was nodding. "You know Uncle Earn?"

"Not in the least, nor do I wish to," Miss Ochiba said. "I take it that your uncle is a primitive Pythagorean, and has inflicted his unfortunate views on you?"

"Uh —" We'd studied about Pythagoras in our magic-history classes, two years before, but I didn't remember it as well as I should have. "Pythagoras started number magic?" I said.

Miss Ochiba beamed. "Very good, Miss Rothmer." Her voice took on the lecturing tone she used in class. "Pythagoras laid the numerical foundation for both mathematics and magic. Unfortunately, like many of the ancient Greeks, his work was not always as rigorous as it might have been."

"You mean he was wrong about thirteenth children being evil and unlucky?" I said.

"Say rather that his comprehension was woefully incomplete," Miss Ochiba replied. "Which is no serious fault in Pythagoras, who lived over two thousand years ago and did not have the benefit of later work to improve his understanding, but is inexcusable in anyone with a modern education."

My heart sank. Even if I didn't remember much about Pythagoras, I knew that "woefully incomplete" didn't mean "wrong."

"So it's really true," I blurted.

Miss Ochiba made a clucking noise. "Miss Rothmer, you appear to be a sensible young woman. Consider. Yes, in Avrupan numerancy the number thirteen is associated with a variety of ills, and yes, you are without question a thirteenth child. But you are also a seventh daughter, and the number seven has as much or more association with positive power and good luck as the number thirteen has with bad." Her eyes narrowed suddenly and she looked at me with an extra-thoughtful expression. "Is your mother by chance a seventh daughter?"

I had to think for a minute which of my aunts were Mama's sisters and which were sisters-in-law. "No, ma'am. Mama has two sisters and two brothers."

"Then you are not a double-seventh daughter," Miss Ochiba said. "But you are the first of twins, a position second only to being the eldest in a family for imparting self-mastery and general authority. Taking a wider view, I presume that with your father's family being so large you have some number of cousins; so long as you have even one who is older than you, you cannot be your paternal grandfather's thirteenth grandchild. Are there cousins on your mother's side of the family? More than one, older than you are?"

I nodded.

"Then you cannot be your maternal grandfather's thirteenth grandchild, either. I daresay you were not born on the thirteenth day of the month, and as there are only twelve months, you cannot have been born in the thirteenth month of any year. You are not old enough to have been born in the thirteenth year of this century. All these numbers, and more, have meanings and importance, according to Avrupan numerancy theory."

My head was whirling, but not enough to miss noticing that she'd made a point of mentioning Avrupa twice. I frowned. "Miss Ochiba, are you saying that all those numbers don't mean anything in other kinds of magic?"

Miss Ochiba smiled. "Some of them don't mean anything; others don't mean the same things. Hijero–Cathayan number magic is quite different from Avrupan, and the Aphrikan tradition hardly deals with numbers at all."

"Different how?" I asked suspiciously.

"The Hijero–Cathayans view life as a process of change," Miss Ochiba replied. "A small child is not the same as a young man or woman, and a youth is not the same as a parent or an elder, though they may have been born on the same day and have similar places in their respective families. Since the day of birth does not change, the Hijero–Cathayans change the meaning of the number. A thirteenth child —" She stopped and looked at me, then went to a small cupboard at the back of the room. She took down a short, fat book bound in faded red leather and leafed through it for a moment.

"What does it say?"

"'Thirteen is of fire and heaven, thus of the sun,'" Miss Ochiba read. "'The changes are also of the sun. At dawn, the fire is cool and distant, growing stronger and more passionate as the sun climbs the sky. At noon, the heat is greatest, for good or ill. The afternoon holds strength until the sun falls into twilight. Travel up or travel down; remember balance. Two feet on the ground are unshaken; two feet on the rungs of a ladder are unsteady whether they move up or down.'"

"What?" I said.

Miss Ochiba read it again. I still didn't understand it, but it didn't sound too bad, especially the part about "for good *or* ill." I said so, and Miss Ochiba smiled again. "The Cathayans think that both people and magic are too complex to be summed up clearly in a few words, so the fewer words they use, the more ambiguous they are."

I thought about that for a minute. "What about Aphrikan magic?"

"That is too difficult to explain in one short afternoon," Miss Ochiba said, "and I have lessons to prepare. If you will come again tomorrow, however, I shall be happy to teach you as much as you wish to know, within my own knowledge."

"Yes, please, Miss Ochiba," I said.

And that was how I started getting my own extra magic lessons.

CHAPTER

10

FOR THE REST OF THAT YEAR, AND A GOOD MANY YEARS THEREAFTER, I stopped by Miss Ochiba's classroom when school was over. For the first few days, it was only me, but then William and Lan noticed that I wasn't coming directly home after school, and came around to see what was up. Then Miss Ochiba asked some of the other students who'd shown an interest, and all of a sudden we were an extra class.

Lan only came for the first few weeks. What with his regular schooling and the extra lessons he was already getting from Papa and Professor Graham, it was just too much time for him to spare. William kept coming, same as me, which was a surprise. I hadn't thought he'd care for extra work, especially after all the bad things he'd said about learning Aphrikan magic.

But Miss Ochiba could make almost anything interesting, and she knew a lot about Aphrikan magic. Both of her parents had been conjurefolk. Her mother had been brought to Columbia on one of the slave ships, back before the Secession War, and her father was one of the anti-slavery advocates from the Aphrikan colonies in South Columbia. He'd come north with enough funds to buy a whole shipload of slaves free, then settled down in Pennsylvania with Miss Ochiba's mother to help the abolitionists in the North. So Miss Ochiba grew up learning first-rate Aphrikan magic from her parents at home while she was learning Avrupan magic at school.

By Christmas, we'd learned the first basic spells in the day class — snuffing candles, stopping a rolling ball without touching it, silencing a specially made squeaky machine — and were beginning to work on things that required more energy and concentration, like lighting the candles and getting the balls rolling in the first place. In our after-school Aphrikan class, we were still doing foundation work, which is like a cross between trying to watch everything around you very closely and trying to meditate quietly inside your head, both at the same time. It was very difficult. Miss Ochiba insisted that we keep trying until we could do it to her satisfaction, but she never said what would satisfy her.

We found out unexpectedly, about three weeks after Christmas. It was a bitter day, clear and sunny, but so cold the snow squeaked underfoot and the air outside hurt to breathe. Most everyone hightailed it for home as soon as the regular classes were finished, because everybody knew it would get colder the later it got, and there'd probably be a nasty wind. That was why there were only four of us in the after-school class that day — Alexei Sokolov, Kristen Olvar, William, and me. I should have gone straight home with Lan, because on extra-cold days Mama still worried about the rheumatic fever coming back, but I hated missing my extra class, no matter what the reason.

Miss Ochiba had us put our chairs in a half circle, and we started in, sitting very still, trying to see everything and not think about anything, to hear Miss Ochiba's instructions and follow them without really listening. We'd been working for ten or fifteen minutes when my head whipped around toward the window, without me intending it to. An instant later, I realized that everyone else had done the same thing at exactly the same moment.

Something moved across the sky at the upper corner of the window. It looked like a small, dense cloud, but we all knew it wasn't a cloud. The sun sparkled and flashed from the heart of the "cloud," and it left a thin white tail behind it for the crosswind to rip to shreds.

"Miss Ochiba," Alexei said, "what is that?"

"A steam dragon," Miss Ochiba said calmly. "You cannot see it clearly because the cold air condenses the outer part of the steam around it."

"But —" said William.

"Hush," said Miss Ochiba. "Listen."

In the quiet, we heard the first alarm bell start, and then another, tolling one-two-three-pause, one-two-three-pause. I'd heard the bells a time or two before, but never in the rhythm of the wildlife alarm before.

Kristen shivered, still staring out the window. "How did it get past the Great Barrier?" she whispered.

"It flew over," William said in a that's-obvious tone. "Just like the ducks do. The barrier doesn't go up much higher than the clock tower on the town hall. It —"

My stomach dropped as the white sparkly cloud suddenly dove toward the ground. Miss Ochiba moved in front of the window, but not before the cloud was stripped away by the dragon's speed and we all got a glimpse of its silver-snake body trailing steam all the way down. The nearest alarm bell lost its rhythm and went into an urgent jangle. I felt something hard and bitter cold run down my side, like the flat of a knife blade left out of doors in winter. I shook my head, and everything around me seemed to whirl around once and then drop into its usual place.

Alexei licked his lips. "Miss Ochiba, what was that?" he asked, and from his tone we all knew that this time he didn't mean the steam dragon.

"That was your sense of the world, unfolding," Miss Ochiba replied. "Excellent work, all of you."

"'Sense of the world?'" William said doubtfully. "Because we saw the steam dragon?"

Miss Ochiba's lips curved in the faintest of smiles. "No, Mr. Graham. Because all of you knew the small cloud you saw was really a steam dragon, because all of you knew that each of your friends was also aware that it was a steam dragon, and because all of you knew those things before the dragon came into sight."

I saw right off that Miss Ochiba was right. We'd all turned toward the window without thinking, before we could have seen anything outside. Kristen and William even had their backs partly toward the window, and they'd whipped right around with the rest of us.

Kristen and Alexei were nodding, like they were thinking the same as me, but William had a stubborn frown on his face. Miss Ochiba's smile grew a little more. "You will have plenty of opportunity to test your world sense," she said to William. "Foundation work is not something you master in one or two tries. You four will move on to circle work, but only three days each week. The other two days, you will continue to do foundation work with the rest of our group. And," she added with a significant look at Alexei, "you will progress much faster if you also practice on your own, even when you are not working on it here."

Everyone at school knew that Alexei did as little extra work as ever he could. It was a nine days' wonder when he joined Miss Ochiba's after-school class, and I'd heard that some of the older boys had a bet on how long he'd keep coming. But now he only looked thoughtful. "If I practice, can I learn to feel a steam dragon coming from farther away?" he said.

"Yes," Miss Ochiba said. "I can safely promise that with additional practice, you will increase the distance at which you can sense steam dragons and other creatures. How great an increase will depend on a number of factors, including your native ability, so the skill may not be as useful in the end as you hope."

"Even a little . . ." Alexei said under his breath. Then he nodded, once, as if he was making an agreement with her. "I'll do it."

"The bells have stopped," Kristen said.

We all looked at the window, except for Miss Ochiba, but there was nothing to see but sky. "They'll ring the emergency-over in a moment," Miss Ochiba said. "I think this will be enough for today, so you may leave as soon as they do."

William and Alexei immediately started for the coat hooks. William looked back over his shoulder at me. "Come on!" he said. "I'm not going to miss seeing a real steam dragon, just 'cause you're slow."

"Oh!" Kristen said, and shuddered. "You're not actually going after that thing, are you?"

"Why not?" Alexei demanded. "It can't have come down very far away, and it's not like it'll still be alive. Not once they ring emergency-over."

"This may be our only chance to get a good look at a real steam dragon," William added. "Eff, are you coming?"

Truth to tell, I was a lot more of Kristen's mind than William's or Alexei's. Just seeing the steam dragon from the window had given me the shivers. But William was the closest thing to a friend I'd ever had, and I didn't want him looking at me the way he was looking at Kristen right then. "Hold your horses," I said. "An extra minute or two won't matter. That thing was big — they're not going to cart it off in a hurry."

"Eff!"

"Go on without me, then," I said, knowing perfectly well he wouldn't. "I still want to ask Miss Ochiba some things."

Miss Ochiba stopped tidying her desk and looked at me expectantly. I swallowed hard. I hadn't meant to say that straight out until I'd thought a little more. But now I was stuck, so I said, "When the steam dragon came down, I felt real peculiar for a minute. Why was that?"

"Peculiar in exactly what way?" Miss Ochiba asked.

I described the sinking in my stomach and the cold-knife sensation, while Alexei and William left off struggling with their coats and sidled close enough to hear.

Miss Ochiba pursed her lips. "The sensations you felt are quite normal," she said after a moment. "That is, they are part of your developing world sense. When you begin to know things in this way, your mind tries to fit the new knowledge into old, familiar patterns."

"Like smelling something funny?" William broke in. "Or hearing a strange noise?"

"Exactly," Miss Ochiba said. "But the world sense is very . . . individual. The exact sensations — and their meanings — are not the same for every practitioner, and it will be better if you all learn for yourselves how to interpret them. It will no doubt feel 'peculiar' at first, but it becomes more natural with time and practice."

"Time and practice, time and practice," Alexei grumbled. "Isn't there anything magical we can just *do*?"

"Sure," Kristen said. "You can mess up."

William snickered. Alexei turned angrily, but Kristen said, "Listen! The bells have changed."

That sent us all scrambling for our coats, and then out the door. The boys went straight toward the area where the steam dragon had fallen, and I trailed along behind. It wasn't too hard to find. Practically everyone else on the street was heading the same way, especially as we got closer.

A good-sized crowd had collected by the time we found the place, so we never actually got near the dragon. Still, even from the back we could see the bottom half of it draped over the feed store, like a silver fire hose twice as big around as I was. A big strip of snow had melted off the roof on either side, and I heard one of the men say it was a good thing the dragon had come in winter or the buildings would have caught fire.

I didn't stay long. It was too cold to stand around watching the backs of people's coats, and I'd already seen more of the dragon than I'd wanted. I couldn't get away from it, though, because even when I got home, it was all anyone could talk about. When the alarm started, Nan and Allie had been almost home, and Robbie and Jack had already arrived. Robbie was in a temper because Mama hadn't let him go out to look after the alarm was over. I didn't tell him I'd actually seen the dragon, even though it was just from a distance. I thought it would only make him cross.

Keeping quiet didn't help, though, because when Papa and Lan got home, Robbie found out that Papa and Professor Graham had been among the magicians who'd brought the steam dragon down. He started complaining right off, but what really made him pitch a fit was that Lan had been allowed to go along, on account of his double-seven training. Even though Lan hadn't actually done anything but watch, Robbie was furious. He kept saying that he was two years older than Lan and it wasn't fair, until Mama sent him to his room for the rest of the evening. He was grumpy for days afterward.

In the end, everyone who wanted to get a good look at the steam dragon had all the chance they wanted, because it took the best part of a week to move its body from the place where it had fallen. Some of the men got it coiled up and mostly out of the street and off the roof before it froze too solid to move, but then the argument started.

Mr. Stolz, who owned the feed store, said that the dragon belonged to him because it had landed mostly on his property. He wanted to sell the body to a circus. The Settlement Office wanted to have it stuffed and mounted and put on display for people who wanted to be settlers, to give them some idea what they'd be in for. The North Plains Territory governor wanted to send it to Washington. And the Northern Plains Riverbank College wanted it to study.

In the end, the college won, since it was the college magicians who'd brought the dragon down before it did more than eat a horse and dent Mr. Stolz's roof. Also, President Grey convinced everyone that letting the magicians study up on a brand-new, fresh steam dragon would be the best thing for all of them. The Settlement Office went along with it right away, because they thought the magicians might find better ways to deal with the dragons, or at least tell when they were coming in time to get livestock indoors. The hardest one to convince was Mr. Stolz. He'd really wanted that circus money to fix his roof with, but in the end, even he gave in.

So they got four teams of horses and a special flatbed wagon and most of the students and professors and handymen, and moved the frozen steam dragon over to the wildlife experiments building. It was too big to fit inside, so for a while there were crowds of people outside staring at the dragon and the professors working on it. After a bit, though, folks got tired of watching the naturalists climbing around with their measuring sticks and slide rules, and things got quiet again.

After the naturalists finished, the magicians started in. All the college students — and Lan — were in the thick of it. Over half of the magic students were planning to go for settlement magicians or do fieldwork on the wildlife when they graduated, so they were even more excited about having a brand-new steam dragon to study than the professors were.

The college made regular announcements in the paper of what they'd found out, mostly to reassure people. The steam dragon had been a female, probably blown east by a freak storm. None of the settlements west of the barrier had reported attacks or other sightings, so we weren't likely to be seeing flocks of them come spring. There was some unpleasantness when the weather warmed up and the dragon began to thaw out.

"It's because we didn't expect it to go bad and smelly all at once like this," Lan told Robbie and William and me. "We thought we'd have a couple of weeks when the inside would still be frozen, even though the outside was thawing out. But Papa says that it has enough magic, even dead, to warm up fast all over."

"Yuck," Robbie said with considerable relish. "I bet it'll stink up the whole college. Maybe even half the city. Hey, Eff, your bedroom is on that side of the house. Better not open your window 'til you've had a good sniff of the wind!"

"Don't be dumb," Lan told him. "Papa and Professor Graham already have teams of students doing preservation spells on different sections of the body."

"My father said they couldn't have the whole neighborhood complaining about the smell," William confirmed.

"I wish they'd let me help more," Lan said crossly. "They wouldn't need such big teams if they let me do one of the preservation spells."

"Are you doing preservation spells already?" I said, impressed.

"Well, no," Lan admitted. "But I bet I could if Papa would

let me. I sneaked a look at the next study book, and they don't look that hard."

"You aren't thinking of trying them on your own, are you?" I said.

"Of course not," Lan said loftily. "I know better than that." He grinned. "Besides, Papa'd know in a minute that it was me. That's the problem with being a double-seven — nobody else's magic feels the same, so it's too easy to get caught."

I didn't find that particularly reassuring, but in the end, it wasn't Lan who got in trouble over the steam dragon — it was Robbie. Late in the spring, when the snakes came out, he went down to the meadow and caught himself a dozen garter snakes. He dipped them in gray milk paint and then told the boys in his class they were baby steam dragons, hatched from eggs the dead steam dragon had laid before the magicians got it. He sold all but two of them for a quarter each before Mrs. Bertelstein came calling on Papa, all indignant because he'd dare let his own son spread such dangerous creatures all over town. She was even more indignant when Papa called Robbie in and made him admit what they really were. Robbie had to pay back all the money, and explain and apologize to all the parents, and on top of that he had extra chores for weeks.

Papa wasn't so upset by the fake steam dragons as he made out — I heard him telling Dean Farley about it later, and laughing. Mama was upset, though. After Mrs. Bertelstein's visit, Mama was the one who had to smooth down the neighbors and the other mothers, and while she was plenty good at smoothing, she didn't much care for having to do it. A week after it all came out about the painted garter snakes, Mama gave Robbie a talking-to. None of the rest of us heard what she said — Mama never yelled, even when she was mad as fire — and Robbie wouldn't talk about it to anyone afterward, but it must have been something to hear, because Robbie shaped up and didn't so much as pull the girls' pigtails in the school yard for nearly a month.

ONCE MAMA'S TALKING-TO STARTED TO WEAR OFF, ROBBIE WAS pretty impressed with all the fuss his fake dragon babies had caused. Mrs. Bertelstein wasn't the only one who'd believed the painted garter snakes were really baby dragons, so a lot of rumors got started. The college and the Settlement Office had to issue announcements, and Papa and the other professors had to spend a lot of time talking to the Mothers' League and the police and the Firemen's Association and a lot of other people. Most of the other boys admired Robbie's cleverness, too, except for the ones who'd bought the painted snakes. And William.

William was almost as cross with Robbie over the fake dragons as Mama had been. I thought at first that it was because of all the extra work his father had to do on account of the snakes. Professor Graham had to go around to almost as many reassuring meetings as Papa, so he wasn't home much for a while. I knew that having his father gone so much bothered William, but when I tried apologizing to him for my brother's behavior, he got cross with me instead.

"*You* haven't done anything wrong," he said.

"But he's my brother."

"That doesn't make you responsible for everything he does," William shot back. "Why are you always apologizing for things that aren't your fault?"

I stared at him, speechless. William had been my friend for so long by then that I'd clean forgotten that I'd never told him about me being an unlucky thirteen.

"Come to think of it, that big steam dragon last winter is the first thing I can think of that you didn't find some reason to blame yourself for when something went wrong." William gave me a long frown. "Have you got a curse or something?"

"N-not exactly," I said, and then the bell rang for class and we couldn't talk any longer.

I thought about that conversation for a couple of days. Mostly, I thought about how I'd never warned William I was a thirteenth child, and whether I ought to now. But it didn't seem like something I needed to do right away, the way it had when I was stewing over whether to tell Miss Ochiba. Partly that was because I was afraid that William wouldn't be my friend anymore if he knew I was an unlucky thirteen, and partly it was because I was beginning to think that maybe Uncle Earn had been wrong about what being a thirteenth child meant.

Until William pointed it out, I hadn't noticed that the steam dragon had come and gone without me ever worrying that it'd come on account of me being an unlucky thirteen. It hadn't even occurred to me that the steam dragon might have been my fault somehow. Now that I came to think about it, it still didn't seem to me that a steam dragon turning up like that could have been my fault. I was quite sure that Uncle Earn would have blamed me for it if he'd been around to see, but for once I was just as sure that he'd have been wrong. Just thinking that felt so peculiar that I almost forgot to worry over what to tell William.

Luckily, William didn't ask again about me being cursed. Even after thinking about it for a week, I wouldn't have known what to say. And then it was the end of the school year, and time for the placing tests, and I forgot about it. I might have remembered again if the news about Dr. McNeil's naturalizing expedition hadn't come right at the end of school and thrown everyone into a tizzy.

Nobody'd heard any word from the expedition since they'd passed the last settlement boundary back in September. All the people who had friends or relatives out with Dr. McNeil had been worried sick for months, and all the people who'd been against the expedition from the start were pulling long faces and reminding everyone how nobody'd ever come back from the Far West, and they'd said all along no good would come of such a thing. Then, the day after school let out, a report arrived at the Settlement Office from one of the circulating magicians, saying that the McNeil expedition had passed through a settlement to the southwest a few days before his own arrival, heading home.

If he'd known what a fuss it would cause, I bet that

circulating magician would have put more in his letter than just a couple of lines. The Settlement Office was practically mobbed by people wanting details. Finally, they printed up the whole report on broadsheets and passed them out to everybody, even though most of it was just about crops and planting acreage and weather. People still stood in line outside the office wanting to know more, but they were a lot more patient about it after that.

The Settlement Office sent out a fast rider right away. When he got back a week later with more news, even the people who hadn't been interested got excited. Not only had Dr. McNeil done all the mapping and nature study that he'd planned on, but he had also found the camp where the Lewis and Clark expedition spent the winter just before they vanished! Along with all his own samples, Dr. McNeil was bringing back some things the earlier expedition had left behind.

The news that the expedition had lost two men out of fifteen barely dampened the enthusiasm. A lot of people thought that if Dr. McNeil could go nearly a hundred miles west from the last settlement and spend a winter with only two men lost, everybody else should be able to do it, too, and they were as excited over the idea of the Settlement Office opening up a lot of new territory for settlements as they were over the expedition coming back.

Right away, the city began planning a big welcome-back ceremony and celebration for when the expedition arrived, even bigger than the send-off had been, with fireworks and a picnic and music and a parade and speeches. This time, everybody thought there was a good chance that at least some of the speeches would be interesting, because Dr. McNeil was going to be one of the speechifiers, and of course everyone expected him to talk about the expedition.

"I don't know what Harrison is thinking," Professor Graham grumbled to Papa. "Asking a man to make speeches the day after he comes back from a long, dangerous journey is unreasonable, in my opinion."

"I don't think it'll be a problem," Papa told him. "Dr. McNeil knew what to expect when he left, and even if he didn't, he's surely had enough notice by this time. The Settlement Office has had message riders going out and back every day, it seems."

Papa and Professor Graham were in the middle of the planning right from the start, because the expedition was bringing back live specimens, including two swarming weasels, a baby mammoth, some rocketflowers, and a couple of other things that the Great Barrier Spell had been specifically designed to keep out. That meant that the college magicians had to open a hole in the barrier, long enough for the expedition to get everything across to our side of the Mammoth River. Papa had all of his students down to watch while they did it, and all the boys, too, from Jack right on down to Lan. Mama took some convincing.

"It will do very well for your young men . . ." That was

what Mama called Papa's students from the college. ". . . and perhaps for Jack, but I'm not so sure about Robbie and Lan."

"It's an excellent chance for them to watch the practical application of team spell casting," Papa told her.

"I'm of the opinion they'll be far more interested in watching the baby mammoth," Mama said. "And perhaps more than watching, if you take my meaning."

In the end, she let all the boys go, with Nan along to keep an eye on them. Rennie sulked all afternoon because she thought she should have gone, being older, but Mama said the boys wouldn't mind her as well as they would Nan. Then Mama kept all of us busy for the rest of the day. There was plenty to do — besides regular chores, we'd been asked to make up three dozen little cloth figures of mammoths and wagons and dire wolves and other such things, to use for table favors at the celebration.

When Papa and the boys got back, Rennie insisted on hearing about the whole afternoon in detail, even though all the boys wanted to talk about was the baby mammoth and the magic. "It's as tall as a man, even though it's just a baby," Robbie said. "They had to give it a whole barge just to itself, because it didn't much like crossing the water. Or maybe it was the barrier spell; we couldn't tell from away off where we were."

"I don't see why Father wanted us there at all, if he wasn't going to let us close enough to see anything," Lan complained.

"We were *supposed* to be watching the magic," Jack said, as if he hadn't been just as interested in the mammoth and the swarming weasels as ever Robbie and Lan were, before they left.

"Well, we couldn't see that, either, from way up on the bluffs where we were," Robbie grumbled.

"I could see it," Lan said. "The spells, anyway. Well, not see it, exactly, but I could tell where they were and what they were supposed to do."

"Oh, that," Robbie said. "Anybody could do that. I meant the casting."

"You shouldn't need to see it," Jack told him. "You can look up the words and ingredients and gestures anytime you want. It's the actual magic part that's important, and the way everybody's pieces have to fit together just so."

"Did Dr. McNeil and his men help with the spells?" Rennie asked.

"No, they were too busy with the mammoth," Robbie said. "It didn't want to get on the barge, and then it didn't want to stay on. It almost went over the side twice." He sighed. "I wish I'd gotten to see it up close."

Rennie rolled her eyes, and went on trying to get a proper story out of them. I could see it was no use, but Rennie never could let go of a thing once she'd decided on it. She spent the rest of the evening working at them and getting crosser and crosser, to no purpose.

Three days later, they had the official welcome-home celebration. Dr. McNeil gave a dandy speech, all about the importance of exploration and great discoveries, and following in the footsteps of Lewis and Clark. That last wasn't right, strictly speaking, because Lewis and Clark went up the Grand Bow River in boats from just north of St. Louis, while Dr. McNeil went straight west from Mill City in wagons, so you couldn't really say he *followed* Lewis and Clark. But it sure sounded good.

Dr. McNeil talked a lot about the trouble the expedition had encountered, and the two men who'd died. Then he introduced all eleven of the men who were left. The very last one was Brant Wilson, wearing his squared-off hat with the crow feather so everyone there knew him for a Rationalist straight off. Not too many people had known that there was a Rationalist on the expedition, so there was some puzzled murmuring in the crowd.

Dr. McNeil said in front of everyone that Brant was a hero, and that if it hadn't been for him, they'd have lost more than just the two men. Everyone cheered, even the people who'd been too far back to hear, and that was the end of the speech and the start of the picnic. After the picnic, there was stick ball and other games, and then dancing and fireworks in the evening.

There was a crowd around every member of the expedition the whole time, because everyone wanted to know more about what had happened to them. Most of the folks had no business asking but curiosity and wanting to be first with a good tale, Mama said. They didn't get what they wanted, though. Dr. McNeil and the Settlement Office had agreed in advance to do a series of broadsheets with the whole story laid out neatly in order, and no one on the expedition was to talk about what had happened beforehand, so as to keep wild rumors from starting.

It didn't work very well. Maybe there weren't quite so many rumors as there might have been, but there were plenty of them, and they were plenty wild. They kept circulating even after the broadsheets came out, and some still get told to this day.

We got the real story straight from Dr. McNeil, the day after the celebration. He and Brant came to see Papa, and naturally ended up in the front parlor having biscuits and jam and talking to the whole family. The very first thing the boys wanted to know was what really happened.

"I heard you saved the whole party from a nest of sunbugs!" Jack said.

"I heard you wrestled a spectral bear that caught you bathing in the river!" Robbie put in.

Brant rolled his eyes and groaned. "Don't be daft," he told them. "Do I look like I can wrestle bears?"

"Boys," Mama said in a warning tone. "You know these gentlemen aren't supposed to talk about what happened until the official account is published."

Robbie and Jack and Lan all looked over at her and then sat back in their seats, scowling. Nan and Allie and Rennie had been leaning forward, too, though not as eagerly, and they straightened up quick, hoping Mama hadn't noticed.

Dr. McNeil laughed. "It's not so strict a ruling as all that, Mrs. Rothmer," he said. "In fact, I think there's more harm being done by letting these tall tales run wild."

"You shouldn't have made me out a hero," Brant said to Dr. McNeil. "Anybody could have shot those pests."

"Perhaps, though I don't think many men would have kept their heads under the circumstances," Dr. McNeil said. "But you were the man who did, and it saved the expedition."

"If you don't intend to tell the whole story, you had better stop now," Papa said, smiling.

"If he didn't intend to tell the whole story, he never should have begun," Mama said sternly, but there was a hint of a curl to her lips, so all of us knew she didn't quite mean how she sounded.

"That *is* the whole story," Brant said.

Lan gave Brant a sidelong look. "What kind of pests were they?" he asked. "The ones you shot?"

Dr. McNeil laughed again. "That's the thing in a nutshell," he said. "They were swarming weasels. Our campsite was nearly on top of one of their burrows, and naturally they picked the exit closest to us to come boiling out of. The spells we'd cast weren't intended for such numbers or such close range, and there wasn't time to cast more powerful ones. Fortunately, Wilson here kept his head and had his revolver handy."

"You shot a whole swarm of those weasels with just a revolver?" Jack said, plainly awed.

"No, I shot the two leaders," Brant told him. "As soon as they were dead, the swarm fell apart and the other weasels dove back underground. That was all."

"Leaders?" Papa said.

"Exactly," Dr. McNeil said, nodding. "Nobody has ever gotten such a close look at a weasel swarm and survived — nobody with the training or the sense to observe the way they work. Wilson not only saw that the swarm had a center, but he was able to pick out the critical pair and shoot them before we were overrun. If he hadn't, we'd all have been eaten alive."

Rennie, Allie, and Nan shuddered. "How brave!" Rennie said.

Nan nodded agreement and added, "How did you know?"

"My mother keeps bees," Brant said. "The swarming weasels were moving around the leaders the way a swarm of bees moves around their queen, and I thought it looked familiar, that's all. Then, when I realized what it reminded me of, I looked for the center. The two leaders were larger than the others, and had lighter coats. So I shot them. It was just luck that it didn't send the whole swarm into a frenzy instead of making it fall apart."

"You had the brains to see what was happening, the sense to have worn a loaded revolver, the skill to hit what you aimed at, and the nerve to stand and shoot when the first dozen swarming weasels were within a yard of your feet," Dr. McNeil said firmly. He looked at Papa and shook his head. "I've offered him a permanent position at least a dozen times, but he won't take it."

"I'm much obliged to you, Dr. McNeil," Brant said, "but I'm going with my uncle to found a new settlement as soon as he gets an allotment from the Homestead and Settlement Office. After this, I don't see how they can continue to insist that we have to have a settlement magician."

"Well, if you change your mind, the offer will remain open," Dr. McNeil said, and went back to talking about the expedition. He didn't tell as many stories as the boys wanted; mostly, he talked about the things they'd seen, like striped antelope and a new species of saber cat they'd named a chisel lynx, and something he called a chameleon tortoise that used magic to look like rocks when there was danger near. Nan and Allie left after a while, but the boys stayed until the biscuits and jam ran out, and Rennie and I stayed right up until Dr. McNeil and Brant said their farewells.

I dreamed that night of saber cats and mammoths and insects like tiny flying stars, and when I woke I thought for just an instant that I was in a tent on the endless plains instead of in my bed at home. I couldn't help wishing Dr. McNeil had brought back more of the strange animals he'd found, so I could get a look at them for myself.

Maybe, I thought, he'd go on another expedition some-day, and catch more creatures, and I could see them then.

CHAPTER 12

THAT WHOLE SUMMER, IT SEEMED LIKE ALL ANYBODY COULD TALK about was the McNeil expedition and how it turned out. Every man who'd been along got treated like something special and then some. It got so none of them could poke a nose out of doors without a whole gaggle of "expedition ladies" — upper school girls and young single ladies — following them around, giggling and flirting and fussing over them. Mama said such behavior was a disgrace, so she wasn't pleased to find that Nan and Rennie had been joining in. She gave them both a tongue-lashing and extra chores for a week, which pretty much stopped them going out after the expeditioners. But it didn't keep them from making cow eyes at Brant when he stopped by to visit Papa.

Brant visited a good deal, talking with Papa about the settlement his uncle was going to build and planning how to handle the wildlife without magic. At first it seemed just dreaming, but after dithering for nearly half the summer, the Settlement Office finally offered the Rationalists an allotment after all. The place the Settlement Office picked was a failed site about two days' hard ride from the river, where a settlement group had collapsed three years before.

Some of the Rationalists weren't too happy when they heard what the Settlement Office was proposing, because the previous settlement had used spells to keep the wildlife out. Brant said that was silly. What with all the magical animals and plants and insects on the Great Plains and on west, there wasn't a place that hadn't ever had something magic about it. That first settlement was gone, along with their spells. Even their buildings had mostly collapsed, and their fields had gone back to weeds and wild.

By the time Brant and the ones who thought like him got the others talked around, it was too late in the year for the whole group to set out. Some of the men went ahead to lay out the compound they'd all be living in later. The buildings had to be a lot sturdier than the ones in a normal settlement, and they were going to take a lot longer to put up, all because the Rationalists wouldn't use magic. So Brant said it was just as well they had the extra time.

The expedition ladies made quite a to-do when the Rationalist settler group left. They threw a going-away party for Brant that was near as big as the welcome-home celebration for the whole expedition. Rennie and Nan helped with that, too. They said it was to wish the men well; Mama said it was an excuse for more foolishness, and gave them extra chores again.

"I wish him well, I do indeed," Mama said the day after Brant and the others set out, when Rennie and Nan complained. "But I don't see that making the poor man dance half the night away is any help or encouragement to him, especially when he has a hard day's work ahead of him."

"You don't understand," Rennie said.

"I understand quite well enough for any reasonable person," Mama told her. "Which is plainly more than you'd like me to."

Rennie didn't quite dare to answer back, but she looked a whole book and a couple of extra chapters.

"It's just as well that young man's going to be gone this winter," Mama said. "He's a dangerous fellow."

"Mama! How can you say that?" Nan burst out.

"It's quite true," Papa said. "Brant's an idealist, and he's competent. There are few more dangerous combinations in this world."

Mama glanced at Nan and Rennie, then nodded. I got the distinct impression that she hadn't meant it the way Papa said.

"Brant isn't dangerous!" Rennie cried. "He's a hero — everybody says so!"

"Heroes are even more dangerous than idealists," Papa said.

"Don't tease the child, Daniel," Mama said. "Rennie, while you are working at the mending, think on this: No one has ever yet said just who Brant might be a danger to. A barnyard cat is a powerful danger to mice, but none whatsoever to the farmer."

Rennie gave a sullen nod, and Mama turned away, satisfied. I was still watching Rennie, and it seemed to me that she was paying less attention to what Mama had said than to working out whether it came out a compliment or an insult to Brant.

I wasn't sure whether to be glad or sorry over Nan and Rennie's punishment. Rennie especially. The way she'd been acting all summer, shirking her work to hang about when Brant came to see Papa and then slipping off to gossip with the expedition ladies, it was plain to anyone with sense that she'd get a comeuppance sooner more than later. Also, I was pleased to get help with the mending for a time; not one of the boys seemed able to get through three days that summer without tearing a shirt, and the only pants in the house that still had knees were their Sunday best and Papa's. Even with Allie and me hard at it, we couldn't keep up.

On the other hand, Rennie could sulk and pout and pine worse than anyone, and she knew how to make everyone around her just as miserable as she made out she was herself. Mrs. Callahan told Mrs. Sevenstones once that Rennie acted more like a spoiled child of five than a grown woman of nearly twenty, and it just showed you that even the best families had a black sheep somewhere. Mrs. Sevenstones said she rather thought Robbie was the black sheep, but that was just because her son had bought two of Robbie's fake steam dragons that spring.

Rennie pined a bit after Brant left, though not where Mama could see her. It didn't last long, because less than a week after Brant left, we got a letter from our older sister Diane. Not that we hadn't been getting letters all along from the ones who'd stayed back East, but this one was different. It was four pages long, both sides — but Papa summed it all up in just one sentence.

"It seems Diane has found the position she's dreamed of and the man of her dreams, both at once," he said as he handed Mama the letter.

"What? What?" all the rest of us asked.

"Your sister Diane wishes to be married," Papa told us. "And she has a chair with the New Bristol Traveling Orchestra."

Everyone crowded around Mama, trying to get a look at the letter. Finally, she read it out to us, though usually when a letter came from one of the ones back East, we passed it around so we could all read it for ourselves. Mama might as well have done things the usual way, I thought. Papa had said all the real news; the rest of the letter was a lot of oh-how-wonderful, mostly about John Brearsly, the man Diane had gone and got herself engaged to, but some about the job as well. She'd sent along a short note from Mr. Brearsly, formally asking Papa for her hand, but it was plain as day from her part that they'd settled it between them already.

John Brearsly was third trumpet with the New Bristol Traveling Orchestra. Diane had been one of their substitute violinists for the past two years, and he'd encouraged her to try for the permanent position when it came open. Mama looked less and less happy as she read through the letter, and when she finished, she looked at Papa.

"I can't pretend I like it," she said, and sighed. "She is still so young."

"Diane is twenty-three," Papa pointed out. "You were five years younger than that when you married me."

Mama turned pink. "I didn't mean — Daniel, don't tease! This is serious. We don't know anything about this young man."

"I should hope it was serious," Papa said. "As for the young man, I expect we'll hear more than we want to, one way and another, from Sharl and Julie at least, and probably from my sisters, as soon as Diane tells them the news. Maybe even from the boys. It's not as if she has no family nearby to look out for her interests."

"That's true." Mama looked more cheerful. "Still, I wish she'd chosen someone with a more reliable income. A musician's life is so uncertain."

"But Diane was going to be a musician already, even before she met Mr. Brearsly!" Allie said.

"That's precisely why I wish she'd found a husband with a steadier position," Mama said, sighing again. "I want my children to choose their partners wisely in temperament and moral character, but also in material considerations. Life can be bitterly hard for someone who mistakes her choice."

Allie looked as puzzled as I felt, but she didn't say anything because Rennie poked her and mouthed "later" behind her hand. So I followed them when they went off together after everyone finished marveling over Diane's news, and that was how I found out about my aunt Amelia.

She'd been Mama's sister, Rennie said. She'd fallen in love with a poor young man and had run off and married him over her parents' objections. Afterward, our grandfather had forbidden anyone to even speak of her ever again. According to Rennie, that hadn't mattered to Aunt Amelia. She'd been happy with her poor husband and her hard life, Rennie said, until she took ill and died for lack of money for a doctor. Rennie plainly thought it was a most romantic story, but she said that Aunt Amelia had been Mama's favorite sister, and that accounted for Mama having such strong feelings on the subject of picking a marriage partner.

I thought Rennie was maybe partly right, but not altogether right. I'd heard Rennie and her friends talking sometimes, and the older girls at school, and sometimes even Mama and the ladies from church. It seemed to me that all mothers worried a fair piece about their children getting a good start in life, and the more children they had, the more they worried about every last one of them. Maybe having seen things go all wrong for her sister had made Mama more worried than some, but I thought that having fourteen of us to see launched was just as likely to be what was giving her fits.

Over the next few weeks, we got more letters, and Mama was a bit reassured. Most of the aunts said that Mr. Brearsly was a fine young man, though they liked his profession as little as Mama did. Sharl and Julie wrote, too, and even our oldest brother, Frank. And of course there were lots of letters from Diane herself.

Diane had evidently been thinking about her wedding for some time, and she didn't much like the notion of coming out to Mill City to be married, when she didn't know anyone here but us. She wanted us to come back East, every last one of us, so she could be married in Helvan Shores with all her family and friends. She proposed that most of us come home a month or so early, to visit and help with the wedding preparations. Papa would stay until the end of school, and they'd have the ceremony as soon as he arrived.

The plan seemed to suit everyone. Papa said it was very considerate of Diane to think of his students. Mama was pleased that she'd have a month to give Mr. Brearsly a looking-over for herself. The younger boys were glad to get out of a month of day school, though Mama told them we'd all still have lessons, which damped their enthusiasm some. The girls were excited about the wedding plans, and chattered about dresses and linens and wedding presents like an entire flock of blue jays.

I was the only one who didn't like Diane's plan, and nobody asked me what I thought. But all that fall and winter, while we sewed our dresses for the wedding and hemmed sheets and table linens for Diane's starter trunk, I had a hard knot in my stomach. I tried not to think about going back to all the cousins and their teasing, and the suspicious looks of the aunts and uncles, but it was hard not to think about something when everyone around me would talk of nothing else. I changed the subject when I could, and when I couldn't, I found some excuse to leave after a few minutes. There were always chores, if I couldn't think of anything else.

I didn't think anyone had noticed until Lan caught me in the pump room near the end of winter and gave me what for.

"You're fretting over nothing," he said flatly.

"I am not," I said.

"Are, too. And if Mama or Papa notices, it'll be trouble."

"It's not over nothing," I said. "I thought at least you'd understand. And they won't notice."

Lan snorted. "They'd have noticed already, if they weren't watching Rennie so close."

"Rennie? What about Rennie?"

"If you'd been paying attention, you'd know," Lan said in his most irritatingly superior tone. Lately, he'd taken to acting as if he was really a year older than me, instead of just a year ahead in school.

"If it's that plain, I don't need you to tell me," I shot back. "I'll figure it out myself in a day or so."

"Go ahead and try," Lan said. "Maybe it'll keep you from worrying about going home for Diane's wedding."

"Helvan Shores isn't home," I said without thinking. "Not for me."

"Me, either," Lan said, but he didn't sound like he really meant it. Then he added, "But it is for Mama and Papa, and all the older ones who stayed, and even Rennie and Hugh."

"Huh." I paused for a second. "I never thought of that."

"No, you were too busy worrying when you shouldn't be."

"When I shouldn't be? How can you say that? You remember how they were, all the cousins and the uncles and aunts. Don't you?"

"Sure I remember," Lan said. "But unlike you, I've actually thought about it. This is Diane's wedding; nobody will want to spoil it for her. And she always liked you when we were little, so she won't mind if you stick close. And besides —"

"Besides what?"

Lan gave me an evil grin. "Besides, if it hasn't occurred to them that you're the twin sister of a double-seventh son, they'll remember it pretty sharp if they try anything nasty."

"Lan! You can't magic people just because they're mean."

"Why not?"

"You can't! Uncle Earn will get a policeman to come arrest *you* this time!"

Lan looked at me and shook his head. "You goose! I won't have to put a spell on anybody. All I have to do is remind them what I am and what I can do, and make it plain that I'll have a mind to do something pretty quick if they don't watch how they behave to you."

"You think that'll work?" I said hopefully.

"Of course it will." Lan patted my shoulder. "So stop fretting."

I hesitated. "I'll try."

If I didn't manage to stop worrying completely after that, I could at least reassure myself that Lan was on my side. It even worked, sometimes, as long as I didn't think too much about Uncle Earn.

CHAPTER
13

Brant Wilson came back to Mill City in early spring that year, a month and a half before we were to leave for Helvan Shores. He and the other men had finished building out at the Rationalist settlement, and he'd come to town to take back the first round of womenfolk and supplies. While he was in Mill City, he stopped by to let Papa know how the settlement was getting on and to say thanks for the help. He said he'd be back as soon as the plowing and planting was finished, if not before, and he seemed disappointed when Papa told him we'd be out East for the spring and summer. Most of the expedition ladies had given up by then, but Rennie and three others saw him off when he left.

Then, in mid-May, it came time for most of the family to leave for Helvan Shores. There was a lot of arguing about exactly who was going to go on the first trip. Papa had to stay in Mill City to finish teaching his classes. Rennie wanted to stay in Mill City and take care of the house for Papa while Mama and the rest of us were gone, and I wanted to stay just to keep away from my cousins for as long as possible. Papa insisted that he didn't need any more taking care of than Mrs. Callahan looking in twice a week, and Rennie should go along with the rest of us.

Mama wouldn't hear of leaving me behind, but she was all for Rennie staying in Mill City. She said Mrs. Callahan couldn't finish planting the garden, or keep it weeded and watered, in just two visits a week, and Papa was sure to get caught up in his study and forget. She and Rennie argued hard, but Papa just shook his head.

So Rennie packed her trunk and got ready to go with us. She didn't even pout. Jack said it was because she still expected to change Papa's mind, but Nan said he was being unfair and nobody could pout with something as splendid as a wedding coming up. Nan had been old enough when Julie got married to remember how it was, and she was pleased as anything about being a bridesmaid this time.

In the end, it seemed, Jack turned out to be right. On the very last morning, while we were getting ready to go to the train station, Rennie came flying in through the door, crying, "Mama, Papa's changed his mind! I'm to stay here after all!"

"What?" Mama looked up from her sewing box, where she was hunting for dark blue thread to sew back the button Robbie had just torn off his good suit. "Never say it!"

"He did!" Rennie said, frowning. "Right before he left for class."

"But the trunks have already been sent off!" Mama said.

Rennie's face cleared. "Oh, I'll come to the station with you and get mine, and change my ticket. Papa explained it all to me, and gave me the money to pay for the ride back." She held out the coins for proof.

"Well, if that isn't just like him," Mama said. "Why couldn't he have changed his mind last week, if he was going to do it at all?"

"Maybe he didn't want to come right out and admit to your face that you were right all along, Mama," Allie said slyly.

Mama laughed. "It wouldn't be the first time. Jack, stop that — we'll be late to the train if you tear your trousers and have to change. Rennie, would you finish this?"

So Rennie finished sewing on Robbie's button and helped round everyone up, and we all took the hired wagon to the train station. Rennie went straight to the ticket window to change her ticket, then saw us off. I felt a little hollow as I waved good-bye.

The train trip back went by much faster than I wanted. I tried not to let on how scared I was, and mostly I succeeded. Lan noticed, but he just bopped me on the head and whispered "Goose!" which made me feel better.

When we got to Helvan Shores, Uncle Stephen and our two oldest brothers, Frank and Peter, met us at the station with enough carriages to hold all of us and the luggage. Mama exclaimed about the expense, but Uncle Stephen only smiled. "It's not as if we hired them for the occasion, Sara. Now, where's that list Tilly made up? We'll need it to load the carriages properly." He started rummaging through his pockets, but Frank stopped him.

"I have it right here, Uncle," Frank said. "Mama and Rennie are to stay with Aunt Tilly; that's closest to Diane's rooming house, so it'll be most convenient. Allie's with Sharl, and Nan's with Julie." He looked at them apologetically. "The aunts thought you'd be a help with the little ones, and they neither of them have space for more than one person."

"It's fine with me," Allie said. Nan looked thoughtful for a minute, then smiled and nodded.

"Uncle Thom and Aunt Grace are taking Robbie and Jack," Frank continued. "Hugh is already bunking with me, and Lan's going with Uncle Stephen. Eff —" he hesitated "— is going to stay with Cousin Marna."

My heart sank. I hadn't thought at all about where we'd be staying, but now that I did, it was plain as plain that we wouldn't all fit in any one house. Sharl and Julie both had tiny homes that were full up with childings; Diane and the boys were still rooming out. Some of us would have to stay with aunts and uncles, and it only made sense to spread us out so the work wouldn't all fall to any one family. But with all that, it was even plainer than plain that none of them had wanted to have me.

Mama frowned slightly, but before she could speak, Lan said, "I'm sorry, Uncle Stephen, but that won't do. Eff and I are twins; we stay together."

Everyone looked at Lan. Lan lifted his chin and stared right back. He didn't add any arguments, or whine the way a childing would. He just stood there, quiet and more sure of himself than any thirteen-year-old had any right to be.

Uncle Stephen frowned and stuck his chest out, and I knew he was going to tell Lan that what the aunts had decided was settled, and no amount of fussing would change it. But then his frown deepened and he hesitated.

I looked back at Lan. His brown eyes had narrowed just a little, his shoulders were set, and his lips were pressed together firmly, like a man readying for a challenge. He'd grown in the last year, and though he wasn't full size yet, he didn't have that suddenly-stretched look that a lot of boys get. But he was still a boy, not a man.

And then I thought to wonder what else Lan was, and right away I saw why Uncle Stephen was frowning so hard. He wasn't seeing an uppity boy wanting his own way. He was seeing a double-seventh-son magician — a double-seven old enough to have had three years of who knew what kind of training out West, who looked to be very sure he could get what he wanted, one way or another, and who maybe was fixing to do something about getting it, right there in the train station.

"Lan," Frank said uncertainly. He looked at me, then down at his list, then at me again. Then he started to look at Uncle Stephen and stopped. "I don't think Uncle Stephen has room for you and Eff, too."

"Then we'll have to stay somewhere else," Lan said. "I'm staying with Eff. There's no telling what'll happen if I don't."

Mama's head whipped around, but it wasn't Lan she was looking at. It was Uncle Stephen, and if he hadn't been shamefaced before, he surely was when her eye lit on him. "Do tell, Stephen," she said in that mild tone that always meant trouble for somebody.

I looked back at Lan, and suddenly I saw something else. He looked the way Papa did sometimes, when he was casting a spell. As soon as I thought that, I felt the magic curling out of him, the same way I'd felt the magic of the steam dragon during Miss Ochiba's after-school class. "Lan!" I said, shocked. "What are you doing?"

"I told you before," he said in an aggrieved tone. "You're my twin. I'm going to make sure you're all right."

"That's not necessary," Frank said.

"No, it isn't," Mama agreed. "Eff and Lan can stay at Tilly's with me. Rennie stayed behind; she'll be coming later with your father. So that's no problem."

"Ah . . ." Uncle Stephen gave me a sidelong look that made Mama frown. "There was some talk of having Eff stay with you, but Janna felt it would be safer to keep her away from the center for the wedding preparations. Not that it's your fault, honey," he added, looking at me straight for once. "But everybody knows —" He broke off, because everybody, including Frank, was looking at him with identical expressions of disgust.

"Janna," Mama said, like she'd just found a nest of spiders in a kitchen cupboard. "I might have known she and Earn would come up with something like this. And don't tell me he wasn't in on it, for I won't believe you. Janna does whatever her husband wants, and he's never gotten over having a thirteenth child in the family."

"That's why you wanted Eff off by herself?" Hugh said in tones of outrage. "Because she's thirteenth-born?"

"And why stick her with Cousin Marna?" Jack demanded. "She was one of the ones who used to pick on Eff all the time, even though she was years older than us. I remember."

"You didn't tell Sharl or Julie about this, did you?" Nan said. "They'd never have gone along with it."

"They have childings," Uncle Stephen said. "And Earn thought it'd be safer . . ."

"Uncle Earn can go jump in a lake," Robbie said fiercely. "Why do you listen to him? Just because he's oldest? I wouldn't listen to Frank if he said stupid things like that."

"You won't ever have to," Frank muttered.

"Robbie!" Mama said. "Mind your manners."

"But, Mama, you agree with me, don't you?" Robbie said. "You practically said so!"

"I may agree with your sentiments, but I very much disapprove of your way of expressing them," Mama told him. "Earn Rothmer is still your uncle, and you should be polite when you speak of him."

"Is there a polite way to tell someone to go jump in a lake?"

"We can discuss it later," Mama said.

Allie stepped forward. "If Eff wants to trade with me, she can stay with Sharl," she offered. She looked at Lan. "I know you wanted to stay with her, but Sharl will be just as good, especially now that we know."

Somewhere in the middle of the conversation, the feel of magic pouring out of Lan had stopped, and he didn't look like a powerful magician anymore. He looked more like my plain old brother, trying to keep up with things that had gotten out of his control. "I —"

"Eff and Lan will stay with me," Mama said firmly. "If Tilly has some objection, we'll find other arrangements. It's not required that all of us stay with family, after all, and I still have good friends in town. One of them will surely be willing to put us up, especially after I explain the situation."

Uncle Stephen looked horrified, and all the argument went right out of him. You could see he still didn't care for the notion, though. He might have put up more fight if Lan hadn't been so insistent on staying with me, but he wasn't about to let the precious Rothmer double-seven magician stay with someone who wasn't family. So he went off to the baggage room, muttering, and got our trunks sorted out so they'd be delivered to the right places. Then we all got in the carriages and rode to Uncle Stephen's house for a big welcome dinner.

The aunts and uncles and cousins were all a bit startled when they heard about the new arrangements, but they didn't dare say much straight out, not after Mama told Aunt Janna that she was sure Aunt Janna had the best of intentions, but she preferred to keep me near to hand as I was still delicate from the rheumatic fever three years before. It made a dandy excuse, but I wished she hadn't used it. Aunt Tilly forgot all about being flustered over me staying with her and went straight to fussing over me like a broody hen. She didn't stop for the next three weeks.

Lan stuck close by for the first few days, until he was sure everyone was clear on how I should be treated. It didn't stop people from giving me funny looks and shifting away from me at dinner, but it kept them from doing much besides making an occasional nasty remark, and even that, they didn't often do when they knew I could hear. Lan was very pleased with himself about it all.

I wasn't so sure, myself. Those first few days, I had more chance to watch Lan than I'd had for a while. It seemed to me that he was enjoying making the uncles and cousins a little scared of him, and I was just a handy excuse for doing it. When I tackled him about what he'd done at the train station, he just laughed and shrugged it off.

"It's not like I was casting any spells," he said when I persisted.

"Then what were you doing?" I demanded. "There was magic coming off you like heat from the stove in winter!"

"It wasn't a spell." He laughed. "It was the part before a spell."

"The part before a spell? What does that mean?"

"It's something Dr. McNeil does when he wants people to pay extra-close attention. I saw it when he was talking at the college. He calls up magic, as if he's going to work a spell, but then he just lets it all go again without doing anything. Most people, even magicians, don't notice anything they could put a name to, but it makes them pay attention." He looked at me curiously. "I think it took me three times before I realized that he was doing anything, and two more to figure out what it was."

"You looked just like Papa does when he's spell working," I told him. He nodded, satisfied. I wasn't satisfied, not all the way, but I could see I wasn't going to get any more from him then, so I let it go.

Being back in Helvan Shores wasn't as bad as I'd expected, those first three weeks. I got to meet my nieces and nephews, and Sharl and Julie even let me take care of them a time or two. John Brearsly was nearly as nice as Diane's letters had made him sound. He wasn't fussed at all about me being a thirteenth child, though I was sure he had to know.

The uncles weren't around much, only the aunts and girl cousins, and all of them were so busy with wedding plans that they hardly had time to think of me at all. They didn't like me helping, though. The one time I tried, Aunt Janna sniffed and looked disapproving, and Aunt Mari took away the tablecloth

I'd picked up for hemming and gave me some charity mending instead. Apparently she thought it was fine for my bad luck to rub off on my sewing as long as it got sent out of the house right away, but she didn't want me anywhere near something Diane would be using. I didn't tell her that I'd already spent a month hemming two of the ruffles on the petticoat Diane was going to be wearing under her wedding dress, and put lace on them, too. Aunt Janna would've had an apoplexy right on the spot.

After that, I spent most of my time by myself, doing the regular lessons Mama had brought, or practicing the Aphrikan foundation work Miss Ochiba had taught me. I couldn't practice regular spells without making everyone except Mama and Lan nervous, but nobody could sense me doing foundation work. I even tried Lan's trick once or twice, calling up magic and then letting it go, just to see if I could. It worked just the way he said — it made people notice me without knowing why they were noticing me — but I didn't like it. Being noticed made me nervous, especially in company with my aunts and cousins.

Then, barely a week before Diane's wedding, Frank turned up one afternoon looking serious and insisted on seeing Mama privately, at once. They were holed up in Aunt Tilly's second-best parlor for an hour, and then Mama called Diane in. The aunts were all buzzing, wondering what it could be about. Aunt Freda thought something dreadful must have happened to Papa, but Aunt Tilly said no, there hadn't been a telegram, and that was how such news always came. Cousin Marna said Frank could have gotten the telegram, couldn't he? Aunt Tilly sniffed, and everyone started choosing up sides. They were in such a tizzy they didn't even think to send me out of the way.

When Mama and Diane and Frank finally came out of the parlor, Diane looked like she'd been crying. Mama was pale and stiff-faced, and all I could think was that Aunt Freda had been right. Then Mama took a deep, shuddery breath and said, "I'm afraid I have bad news."

The room went so still you could hear the elms outside the window rustling in the wind. "You know my daughter Rennie —" Mama's voice broke. She closed her eyes and went on after a minute, "My daughter Rennie stayed in Mill City, planning to come East with my husband in a few days." She paused again, and swallowed hard. "It seems she won't be coming."

A little shiver ran through all the aunts and cousins, but nobody quite had the nerve to interrupt to ask why. Mama raised her chin and finished.

"She eloped with Brant Wilson the day we left Mill City."

CHAPTER

14

THE NEXT FEW DAYS WERE MISERABLE FOR EVERYBODY. NONE OF THE aunts or older cousins wanted to take time to explain to us younger ones just what had happened. We had to figure things out on our own, as best we could. And when the aunts caught us hanging over the banister listening, they relieved their feelings by scolding fiercely — or at least they scolded me. Nobody quite dared to scold Lan, no matter how annoyed they were with him.

So Lan did most of the listening, and we eventually pieced the story together. Papa had never changed his mind about Rennie staying. She'd only said that so she could take her trunk and the money for her train ticket and go off with Brant, without anyone being the wiser. She and Brant had planned it all out. Papa thought she'd come to Helvan Shores with us; Mama thought she'd stayed home with Papa. No one would have known better until Papa arrived for the wedding without her, except that Allie had forgotten to pack her new gloves, and Mama wrote home to have Rennie bring them.

When Papa got that letter, he knew something was wrong, but he didn't want to worry Mama until he knew what it was. So he telegraphed Frank to find out if Rennie was in Helvan Shores. When he found out she hadn't arrived, and that everyone thought she'd stayed in Mill City with him, he started looking for her.

It didn't take him long to find out where she was. She'd been so sure that no one would miss her for a solid month that she hadn't tried to hide at all. She'd planned to be out at the settlement by the time anyone found out, with no chance of having to face any of us. She ended up having to face Papa, right enough, but it was too late. Rennie and Brant had already gotten married.

That was all that everyone agreed on. Aunt Mari thought that Rennie should be formally read out of the family and never spoken of again, though she certainly spoke plenty about Rennie every chance she got. Aunt Janna said it was a family disgrace, and just what you'd expect from bringing a girl up out in the Western borderland, especially when there was family history. She only said that once, because Aunt Tilly threw her out of the house for "raking up the dead past." Aunt Ellen pointed out that Rennie was only twenty, so Papa could have the marriage declared void. Several of the other aunts thought he should do just that. I couldn't see the point. Rennie would be twenty-one in September, and as stubborn as she was, she'd run off and marry Brant all over again, and make the talk even worse.

What I couldn't understand was why she'd done it. Even if she thought Mama and Papa would object to having their daughter marry a Rationalist, she could have waited a few months and not spoiled Diane's wedding. And it would have been just plain sense for her to wait until she was legal age. It wasn't until much later, when I thought to count back from when their first boy was born, that I understood why she'd been in such a fearsome hurry, and why Brant had gone along with her.

After a day or two, when the uproar began to settle, everyone started wondering what would be done about John and Diane's wedding. Nobody was quite sure how to ask, and there wasn't much opportunity because Diane spent most of her time in private with Mama. Finally, Aunt Mari took it on herself. She caught me taking a cup of tea up to Mama and followed along. When Diane came out to collect the tea, Aunt Mari asked her point-blank what her plans were.

"Of course, you'll put off the wedding," Aunt Mari told her. "So you really ought to notify the guests officially as soon as possible."

"Put off the wedding?" Diane repeated, staring.

"Oh, dear, hadn't you thought of that?" Aunt Mari said. "But I'm sure you see how it is. You don't have to decide now how long you'll wait; indeed, I think it will be better if you don't, just yet. Give people time to forget this unfortunate event before you announce a new date. Three months might be long enough — it's not as if that girl ran off from Helvan Shores, after all."

"Three months?" said Diane on a rising note. "Aunt Mari, whatever gave you the idea that we were going to put off my wedding?"

Aunt Mari stiffened. "It's the obvious thing to do. With all this talk, and your father stuck in Mill City dealing with the matter —"

"My father is not stuck in Mill City, and he's already done as much dealing with things as can be done," Diane said tightly. "I am not putting off my wedding just because my brat of a younger sister, whom I haven't seen in eight years, has behaved like a selfish little tramp."

"I sympathize with your feelings, I really do. But my dear, you can't have thought —"

Diane glanced back toward the door of Mama's room, and lowered her voice. "I've thought of nothing else for two days, nearly. And I'm not postponing my wedding because of Rennie."

"I suppose a small, quiet ceremony would be all right," Aunt Mari said with visible reluctance. "Though there will be talk."

"There'll be talk whatever I do," Diane said flatly. "Rennie has seen to that. Well, I don't care. I'm not putting off my wedding. I'm not having a small, quiet ceremony. I haven't done anything to be ashamed of, and I'm not changing a single thing that I don't absolutely have to change."

"Have you considered your Mr. Brearsly's feelings about this? I can't believe that he will like such an arrangement."

Diane's expression softened for a moment. "John agrees with me. I've already asked one of my friends to take Rennie's place as bridesmaid, and Frank has telegraphed back to Mill City to tell Papa."

"You actually intend to embarrass the family like this?" said Aunt Mari.

"I'm not the one who has embarrassed the family, and I'll thank you to remember it," Diane snapped. "If you don't like it, don't come."

As Aunt Mari stared at her in stunned disbelief, Diane turned and almost ran into me. She looked down at me and the teacup for a second as if she'd forgotten who I was. Then she opened the door and whisked me into Mama's room ahead of her and closed the door again right in Aunt Mari's face. I spilled half the tea, but I didn't care. I was just glad to get out of that hallway before Aunt Mari got her voice back and went looking for someone to take things out on.

When the rest of the aunts found out what Diane was planning, they were more upset than ever. Aunt Janna even said that Aunt Mari must have misunderstood. She was so sure that she nearly convinced some of the other aunts, until Diane came down and straightened them all out. Aunt Tilly was the only one who seemed to think that it was all right for Diane to go ahead with her wedding just as she'd planned it.

Papa arrived two days later. He looked tired, and he went straight in to Mama and stayed there until the next morning when he and Mama came down to breakfast. It was the first time Mama had been out to see the family since she'd made the announcement.

After that, things sped up considerably. Whether the aunts approved or not, there was still a passel of wedding work left to do, and they weren't about to let Diane's friends take over. So Aunt Tilly's house was busier than ever for the next few days. If I poked my nose out of my room, some aunt would pounce and send me off on an errand, thirteenth child or not. I didn't mind much, because it made me feel that I was finally part of the preparations, but Lan took to running off with the older boys right after breakfast.

Despite everything, Diane's wedding was beautiful. She had it in our old church, that the Rothmer family had been going to since the day Grandfather first moved to Helvan Shores years and years before. It was a tall stone building with a square tower for the bells. Charlie told me the congregation had sent all the way to Albion for those bells, which he thought was a great waste when they could have got them easier from Philadelphia or New Amsterdam. Inside, the church was like an enormous cave, cool and gloomy even on a hot summer day with all the candles lit.

Diane looked lovely in her pale gray wedding dress, with the bridal wreath on her head. The wreath had taken Allie and

Nan and three of my cousins most of the previous day to make. The pincushion flowers kept falling out between the rosemary and love-be-true, or ending up in the wrong order. Bridal wreaths are important to get right, because everything in them means something magical.

After the ceremony, we all went from the church to Uncle Gregory's house, which was the only one that had a lawn big enough for everyone. I don't know what we would've done if it had been raining — what with Papa's brothers and sisters and their children and children's children, we'd have filled up two or three houses, easy, and all Mama's family was there, too. I'd forgotten I had so many relatives. And on top of all of them, there was John's family, and the people from the traveling orchestra, and all sorts of friends from town. Even Uncle Gregory's enormous back lawn barely had room.

At first, it seemed that everyone had forgotten about Rennie eloping and our family being disgraced. Everyone laughed and talked while the hired girls brought out the roast chicken and the jellied clams and the new bread and wine and all the other good things my aunts had been fixing for the past two days. John's best man made a toast to the bride and groom — health and happiness, I think — and everyone clapped and drank. Then Papa made a toast, and John's father made one, and after that I lost track.

Once the speechifying was over, I started to feel uncomfortable. They'd put our family at a special table up front, next to where Diane and John sat, where everyone could look at us. And from where we sat, facing everyone else, it was easy to see the sidelong glances, the people whispering together and the headshaking. Nobody had forgotten about Rennie, not really.

As soon as I finished eating, I left the table. Uncle Gregory had collected lawn games from all my other relatives, to give the childings something to do while the adults finished eating and got ready for the dancing. I didn't try to join any of the games myself. I just wandered from one to the next, looking. I was watching some of my cousins-once-removed play wickets with John's younger brothers and sisters when a hand fell on my shoulder. I looked up and froze. It was Uncle Earn.

"So here you are, after all," he said. His face was red, right up through the thin white fringe of hair and across his bald head, as if he'd been out in the sun too long. "Aren't you satisfied yet, hellspawn?"

"S-satisfied?" I could hardly speak for terror. I'd gotten so used to being in Helvan Shores and not seeing Uncle Earn, and so taken up with Diane's wedding, that it'd slipped my mind that I'd have to avoid him afterward.

Uncle Earn gave me a hard shake. "Humiliating everyone like this. Wasn't it enough that that girl ran off with her lover? But no, you had to make sure that all this —" he waved a hand, taking in all of Uncle Gregory's yard, the older people still sitting at the tables or moving slowly from one to another, the younger folk gathering around the musicians setting up for the dancing, the children running in and out of the crowd

"— that all this went on, instead of being delayed a decent interval until the talk died down."

"I — I never —"

"Liar!" Uncle Earn shook me even harder. "I heard the whole thing from Mari. If you hadn't been there, Diane would have agreed to wait, like a sensible person."

"I didn't say anything to Diane!"

"You don't have to say anything. You're bad luck, wherever you are. It was your influence, you snake-in-the —"

"Earn!" Papa's voice came from near to hand, startling both of us. Uncle Earn let go of my shoulder so fast that I lost my balance and sat down hard on the grass. "What do you think you're doing?"

"Seeing to the well-being of this family," Uncle Earn said. "You certainly won't! I expected you to learn a lesson from having that other girl of yours run off, but no, you still let this demon child run loose. And see the results!" He waved again, so extravagantly that he staggered.

Papa glared at Uncle Earn, and for a minute he was very still. Then he said in a careful, controlled tone, "This is Diane and John's wedding, in case you've forgotten, Earn. It's nothing to do with Eff."

"You're blind," Uncle Earn said flatly. "It's her fault, that misbegotten thirteenth child of yours. Open your eyes!"

"I think you've drunk a few too many healths to the bride," Papa said. "You'd best go in and lie down for a while."

"Oh, you'll find any excuse to ignore my advice," Uncle Earn snarled. "You think you're better than the rest of us because you're a seventh son. Well, I'm not drunk and I'm not letting you off so easily this time. It's time you heard a few home truths, like it or not!"

Right about then, I pulled myself together enough to scoot back out of the way and look around. Papa and Uncle Earn were facing each other like a couple of prizefighters, and a ring of guests had collected around them. The cousins had stopped their game of wickets to listen, and I could see people hurrying over from farther off. Uncle Earn was ranting on about Papa being too proud of being a seventh son, and being so stubborn about having a seventh son himself that he'd gotten a thirteenth child, and then running off West with his double-seventh son, just when he'd finally gotten well enough known to do the family some good. I got a sick feeling in the pit of my stomach just listening to him.

Then I felt magic gathering around us, and I heard Lan's voice say "Uncle Earn," just as cold as the air the day the steam dragon fell on Mr. Stolz's feed store, and I felt even sicker. I didn't think Lan was going to pull the magic in and let it go this time. He was going to let loose, and there was no telling what the result would be. My legs were wobbly, but I struggled to my feet, just as Uncle Earn turned toward Lan and opened his mouth.

"Uncle Earn," I said, loud and clear as I could. "If it's me you have a grudge on, it's me you'd ought to be talking to."

Uncle Earn whipped around and stared at me, and I looked at him, and suddenly, I was madder than I'd ever been in my whole life. Because this time I didn't see the frightening oldest uncle who'd tried to have me arrested when I was five. I saw a selfish, pompous, ignorant old man, who didn't even think about how he was ruining Diane's wedding worse than ever Rennie had. He didn't see that Papa and Lan were just before doing something dreadful because of the things he'd been saying. And he was certain-sure to blame me for everything, when he got around to noticing the consequences of what he'd done.

Well, if he was going to blame me anyway, I decided that I was going to give him something to blame me for. At least I could try to keep Lan from cutting loose — no matter what I did, I figured it couldn't possibly be as bad as a double-seventh son letting go of his temper.

"Uncle Earn," I said again, before anybody could get over being surprised, "if I'm such a dangerous person, why did you let my cousins pick on me all that time? And why do you keep egging everyone on to badger me?"

Uncle Earn just gaped at me, and the anger inside me grew. I saw that he'd never even thought that plaguing me might make things worse, and he wouldn't have cared if he had thought of it. He'd only ever cared about showing everyone he was right.

"If I was going to do evil to someone, it wouldn't be to Papa and Mama or my sisters, who haven't ever done anything bad to me," I said. Then I thought about some of the punishments Mama and Papa had handed out, and about some of the pranks my sisters and brothers had pulled on me, and I added conscientiously, "Well, they haven't done anything bad out of pure meanness, anyway."

I looked Uncle Earn straight in the eye, and my anger nearly boiled right over. And then along with the anger, something else woke inside me, something that was already just as strong as the anger that had been building up for all my life. Magic.

"If I was going to do evil," I said slowly, "I'd do it to those who've troubled and tormented me, over and over." I couldn't help smiling as I spoke, because it felt so good to say what I'd been thinking for years. "I'd do it to you, Uncle Earn," I told him. And then the magic and the anger swirled together and exploded out of me, right at him.

MAKING MAGIC IS NOT AN EASY THING. IT TAKES FOCUS AND CON-
centration, on top of years of study to know the exact right
combination of words and objects that will do just what the
magician wants it to. If you get one tiny thing wrong, the spell
can fizzle like a wet firecracker, or worse yet, turn back on the
magician in some unexpected way. Or tear into the people
standing around nearby.

That's what they taught us in school, anyway, and I
believed it. I'd seen enough times what happened when Miss
Ochiba's older students got careless — looking like they'd been
dipped in green paint was the least of it. Papa's students were
more careful, but they were also doing harder spells, so when
things did go wrong it could be pretty spectacular. Once
when a spell went wrong, it punched a hole the shape of a duck
in every pane of glass in every west-facing window in every
building for three blocks around the magic lab, in spite of all
the shields and mufflers they had up.

But when all that muddle of magic and fury burst out of
me at Uncle Earn, I knew that even though I hadn't been

focused or concentrated or even practiced it as a spell, it was going to do exactly what I wanted. Not what I'd told it to do or meant for it to do, because I hadn't thought about either of those things. It was going to do what I wanted. And what I wanted right that minute was for Uncle Earn to pay for all his meanness, and pay handsomely.

For one tiny snip of a second, just as that magic left me, I knew all that and I was happy to know it. Then, in the next instant, I was terrified. I grabbed for that mess of magic, trying to pull it back before anything dreadful happened, the way sometimes you can catch a sentence right at the edge of your teeth before you actually say it and get yourself in trouble.

I didn't quite catch this, but I did something. The angry tangle of magic fell apart right before it got to Uncle Earn. The air filled with a cloud of sparkles, bright enough to see clearly even in the daylight. Uncle Earn flinched and batted at them with his hands, like he was trying to shoo off a cloud of gnats. The crowd of people who'd gathered around us all gasped. Papa and Lan stared at me with identical expressions of surprise and alarm.

The sparkles floated higher, hovering over the crowd like fireflies, except they twinkled like the sun on lake water instead of blinking slowly. They hung there for near a full minute before they winked out, while I stood there panting and hoping they wouldn't do anything but sparkle. Uncle Earn kept batting at them until they rose too high for him to reach. Then he started sputtering at me instead. I didn't understand most of it, until he turned to the people behind him and said, "You saw her attack me! You all saw!"

People stirred at one end of the crowd and started moving off. Uncle Gregory came through them toward us and gave the rest of the onlookers a glare that got them moving, too. He put one big hand on Uncle Earn's shoulder — Uncle Gregory was the biggest of my uncles by a fair margin — and said cheerfully, "Earn, you're drunk as a skunk. You'd better come along before Janna finds you, or you'll hear about it for the next month."

Uncle Earn sputtered some more, but he didn't have much choice. When Uncle Gregory decided to move someone along, he moved. I found out later that as soon as Aunt Tilly heard there was a ruckus going on, she'd hunted up Uncle Gregory and told him that poor Diane had been through enough already, and it was his house and his responsibility to see that nothing more happened to spoil the party. So he had come straight over to put a stop to whatever was going on.

Papa watched for a minute, then said, "Eff, you're overwrought. Lan, take your sister into the house and find somewhere quiet. I'll be along in a minute." He sounded very stern. He didn't wait to see that we did as we were told, but started purposefully after Uncle Gregory and Uncle Earn.

Lan nodded even though Papa didn't see, and grabbed my arm. As he hustled me away, he asked, "How did you do that?"

"I don't know!" I said. I pulled my arm free. "I didn't do it apurpose. It just happened."

"Well, you're in for it now," he said. "Uncle Earn isn't a good enough magician to spot anything but those sparks you did, but Uncle Stephen is, and so is Aunt Irma, and they were both watching. It'll be all over the family in no time."

I just nodded miserably. Uncle Earn would have me arrested for real this time, and I didn't even care. All the things everyone had been saying about me for all those years were true. I'd almost hurt Uncle Earn badly, and I'd been happy about it. That wasn't right, no matter if he deserved it. And Papa and Lan knew it, too, or they wouldn't have looked at me the way they had.

By the time Papa came to find us, I'd sunk into a black despair. Papa took one look at me and sent Lan away, then held me for a while, as if I was a childing of three instead of near grown. Then he asked me to tell him what happened, from the beginning. When I finished, he told me he was going to put a dampening spell on me until we got back to Mill City. It'd work on my magic like a soggy blanket smothering a fire, so there wouldn't be any more accidents. Once we got home, he said, I'd have to take a whole long list of tests to see how and why I'd been able to let loose a spell like that and then stop it cold.

I nodded, though I didn't see that it mattered whether I agreed or not. Papa told me I was overexcited and overtired, and made me lie down until it was time to leave, so I missed the rest of Diane's party. If I thought about it at all, I was glad. It wasn't even a punishment; it'd have been worse to go back out and see everyone looking at me sideways and whispering and backing away as I was sure they would. I didn't want to spoil Diane's party the way Rennie had spoiled her wedding, not any more than I'd already done.

On the way back to Aunt Tilly's after the party, Lan told me that everything had gone fine for the rest of the evening. John Brearsly even laughed when Diane fussed about Uncle Earn and me, and told her that there was no harm done that he could see, and that it'd make a good story to tell at their fiftieth anniversary. That made me feel a little better. At least there was someone who didn't mind what had happened.

The next morning, Papa took me into Aunt Tilly's music room and did the magic-dampening spell. I didn't understand most of it. All I had to do was stand in the middle of a clean sheet while he ground some herbs and sprinkled them in a circle around me, then burned some other plants and sprinkled me with water and I forget what else. He didn't explain it, and I was still too miserable to ask questions, before or after.

The dampening spell made me sleepy, and even when I was awake, I felt as if I was walking around in a thick fog. I didn't like it at all, but at least I didn't have the energy to fret over the dark looks and the scared whispers that swirled around me for the rest of our stay in Helvan Shores. Truth to tell, the memory of it is still foggy, even after all this time.

As soon as we got back to Mill City, Papa cleared the spell off me. Right away I was almost as miserable as I'd been back in Helvan Shores. When I said as much to Papa, he told me not to worry, that as long as I was away from Uncle Earn's "irritating influence" it wasn't likely that anything else would happen for a long time. By then, I'd have the training to control my magic.

I nodded and smiled, but for the first time in my life, I didn't really believe what Papa said. I didn't think I could control the kind of anger I'd felt toward Uncle Earn. More than that, I was sure that I'd never be able to control the magic. I knew that the power I'd felt was just a beginning. What would I do when it grew stronger? I wouldn't have a hope of controlling it then. But I could see that Papa wouldn't understand.

Papa left me to myself for three days, to let any lingering effects of the magic-dampening spell wear off all the way. It was like I was sick all over again, only this time I was in quarantine. Finally, he started the tests he'd promised. First he cast a magic-detecting spell and made me work all the minor spells I'd learned at the day school, over and over. Then he did it again, with a spell for detecting a different sort of magic. That went on for about a week, and then he went over to the engineering department and borrowed a bunch of their instruments for measuring the level of magic in a spell and did it all again, and again.

I spent nearly the whole summer in Papa's study, I think. Every time I cast a spell, I felt that lump of magic power inside me grow a little. It worried me more every time, until I found a way to sort of move sideways in my head so that practicing spells didn't make the power grow.

In the end, the tests didn't show anything unusual about me at all. Papa sat down and explained it all to me very clearly. The magic that had gone off at Uncle Earn had been a fluke; such accidents happened to young people sometimes, he said, especially when they were turning from childing to full-grown. People didn't grow evenly; sometimes their legs got long and clumsy before the rest of them caught up, and sometimes they went wide, or skinny, from growing one direction faster than another. In me, the magic part had grown too fast and burst out without any control, but the rest of me was already catching up. Once everything was back in balance again, there was no chance of anything similar happening again.

The only trouble was that what Papa described didn't sound anything like what I'd felt. Or like what I was still feeling. I tried to tell Papa that, but he only smiled and said I was worrying over nothing. How someone felt didn't have anything to do with spell casting, he said.

Maybe it didn't have anything to do with normal spell casting, but the way I felt about Uncle Earn had plenty to do with that spell burst I'd sent at him. And it was me switching from angry to scared that made it fall apart just in time; I'd worked out that much. But Papa just shook his head and reassured me, a little sharply, that according to all his tests, everything was completely normal.

School started up again, and if anything could have made things worse, that was it. The Settlement Office had been busy that summer, and a lot of families had gotten their allotments and moved West. They still couldn't keep up with the people who wanted land, though, so Mill City was growing fast. There were a lot of new faces at the day school, even though a couple more parent associations had formed and started new schools in our part of town. I was the tallest girl in my class, and at thirteen I was also the oldest, and I felt awkward and clumsy and conspicuous. All of the new students knew about Lan being a double-seventh son, and they heard pretty quick that I was his twin. They all gave me curious looks when they thought my back was turned, which made me feel even more conspicuous.

For the first time ever, I had trouble with my schoolwork. I couldn't remember the Columbian Presidents past the first five — George Washington, John Adams, Thomas Jefferson, Eduard Baier, and Herman Augustus Morton. All my sentence diagrams went crooked, with the phrases coming off in the wrong places. I got the signs backward in my algebra. Worst of all, I started having trouble with my magic lessons. The spells I'd worked without any problems all summer began fizzling out, and I couldn't get the new ones to work at all.

Two months after classes started, Miss Ochiba asked me to come back and see her after school. I thought I knew what was coming — a lecture and extra homework, and maybe even the threat of moving back another year, to study with the sixth-grade magic classes.

So I wasn't prepared when Miss Ochiba closed the classroom door, waved me to a seat at the practice table, and said gently, "I am sure you know as well as anyone that your classwork has not been satisfactory this year. It is plain that the cause is neither lack of interest nor lack of effort. You are an intelligent girl, Miss Rothmer, and I should like to know what you think the reason is for your sudden difficulty."

I burst into tears. Miss Ochiba handed me her handkerchief and waited. I gulped and wiped my eyes and the whole summer tumbled out of my mouth in a jumble: Diane's wedding and the new students watching me all the time and Rennie running off with Brant and Papa's tests and the spell I'd thrown at Uncle Earn.

Miss Ochiba listened without saying anything, and I couldn't read the expression on her dark face. When I finished, she nodded and said, "I am not surprised that you are finding your studies difficult."

"Papa says that how a magician feels doesn't have anything

to do with spell casting." I felt torn. I wanted to believe what Papa had told me, but . . .

"Your father is an excellent magician," Miss Ochiba said, "but his background is entirely in the Avrupan school of magic. Furthermore, he is accustomed to students who are older and less . . . volatile than persons of your age. I am a little surprised that he did not recall the incident with your brother."

"The incident with — you mean when Lan got mad and floated William treetop-high?" I said. "How do you know about that?"

"Miss Rothmer." Miss Ochiba gave me a look that was half amused, half reproving. "I teach magic to all of the students at this school, including your brother, all of your other siblings, and their friends as well. It would be more than surprising if I had *not* known about it."

"But what does that have to do with me?"

"Three years ago, Lan lost his temper and cast a spell on William that should not have been possible for a child with little training and no practical experience. You are his twin sister. You lost your temper and cast a spell with more power behind it than you should have been capable of handling at your level of training and experience. I think the parallel is obvious."

"I'm — like Lan?" I stared at her. "But he's a double-seventh son."

Miss Ochiba closed her eyes briefly. "And what else is he?" she asked in her teacher voice.

"He's my brother," I said, reacting automatically to the question she'd asked so often in class. "He's my twin. He's a boy. He's thirteen, and the youngest of us. He's —" I stopped. Saying that Lan was Papa's favorite, and the one everyone always looked to and talked about and expected great things of, would sound petty and jealous. Only it was the plain truth. I'd just never seen it that way before, because I felt that way about him my own self.

"Exactly so," Miss Ochiba said when I didn't continue. "And he's a few other things besides, and no doubt he'll pick up more as he goes along in this life. In some ways, you are alike; in others, you are not. I leave it to you to sort them out. For the moment, that is not my main concern."

I nodded uncertainly. Miss Ochiba tapped her fingers on the tabletop, one-two-three, one-two-three. Then she said, "Thank you for explaining. Now that I am aware of the situation, you need have no fear of any similar accidents occurring in my classroom, Miss Rothmer. Do you understand?"

I nodded again. Then I swallowed hard and said, "But what about everywhere else?"

"There is a Hijero–Cathayan technique that I believe you will find helpful," Miss Ochiba replied. "It will take some time for you to master it, but I do not think that will be a problem. You do not lose your temper often."

I hadn't believed in Papa's tests, and I hadn't believed him when he told me everything was fine, but when she said that, I believed Miss Ochiba. I almost cried in relief.

Miss Ochiba gave a brisk nod, as if I'd said something, and stood up. "We will begin tomorrow, then. That is all, Miss Rothmer." The next thing I knew, I was walking home in a daze, feeling hope for the first time since the start of summer.

CHAPTER 16

Miss Ochiba's confidence in me, and the Hijero–Cathayan concentration technique she taught me, were about all that made that year bearable for me. I did a lot better in most of my classes once I stopped fretting over maybe blowing someone up if I got mad. I still had trouble with magic, though. I was afraid of it — or, rather, I was afraid of what I might do with it. The book-work was fine, but at least half the time, when I started to cast a spell, the fear got in the way and it fizzled. The looks my classmates gave me went from curious to doubtful to sneering.

Oddly enough, I didn't have any difficulty in Miss Ochiba's Aphrikan magic class. Most of the Aphrikan magic we were doing didn't feel like spells, and that helped. We still practiced foundation work at least twice a week, but those of us who'd been in the class for two years already were up to what Miss Ochiba called "advanced world-sensing." It started with being aware of the world, the way we'd learned in foundation work, and then went on to feeling the links between what we were sensing and ourselves. The first time, she had us each give her the slates we used in our regular classes. She mixed them up, then made each of us tell her which slate belonged to which person, without looking at them. She said that when we got really good at it, we'd know if a floorboard was rotten before we stepped on it, or whether an apple had a worm in the middle before we bit into it.

Round about Christmas, or a little after, Papa and Professor Graham got in another row with the North Plains Territory Homestead Claim and Settlement Office over their allotment policy. I didn't know the long and short of it, and neither did anyone else in my class, but that didn't stop some of those whose parents favored the Settlement Office from deciding to choose up sides, with William and me on the wrong one.

At first it was mostly just name-calling. William got into a couple of fights during recess over that. I ignored it as best I could. I had to. I was afraid of what might happen if I got mad. Then someone put damp sand in our lunch pails during the morning, so that our sandwiches were soggy and full of grit. William went straight home and talked his father into teaching him a locking spell, and after that nobody could get into his lunch pail. He tried to teach me the spell, too, but it fizzled, so I just kept a sharp eye out from then on.

Then, on a bitter cold day in late January when we all had to wear our coats in class because the stove in the corner couldn't keep up, someone iced the path behind the general store that William and I always took to get home. If we hadn't just come from Miss Ochiba's Aphrikan magic class and been working on sensing the world, we might not have noticed it before one of us had a nasty tumble. As it was, we spent ten frozen minutes kicking snow and little stones onto the icy part to rough it up so that nobody else would fall.

Things came to a head two weeks later. Four of the boys and two girls who'd been the worst of the name-callers laid for us after school. They'd done it before, and we'd given them the slip, but this time they were ready for us. They caught us on the path behind the store, out of sight of anyone on the street. Before you could shake a stick, they had a ring around us.

"Well, well, lookee here," said Tad Holiger. He was one of the new boys, the oldest and biggest of the group. By his age, he ought to have been starting in the upper school, but he'd started schooling late and never paid much heed to it except in Miss Ochiba's class. "It's the snobs from over on College Way. What do you suppose they're doing here? Come to tell the Settlement Office how to run?"

"Heading home," William muttered.

"What'd you say?" Tad shoved William's shoulder, and the other boys laughed. I got a sick feeling in my stomach.

"I said we're heading home," William repeated loudly. "So if you'll just move out of the way, you can be rid of us."

"Oh, that's cold," Tad said, with an exaggerated look of hurt. He looked around the circle. "Isn't that cold?"

"Cold as the snow," one of the other boys said.

"Let's see," said a third, and scooped up a handful of snow. The other two boys followed his example, while Tad and the girls watched William and me.

"Just leave us alone," I said, and the sick feeling in my stomach got sicker. I'd said the same thing to Uncle Earn. I took a deep breath, trying to start the concentration exercise, but I was too scared — scared as much over what I might do as over what Tad and his friends were planning.

"Oh, the little mouse has a squeak after all," Tad said. "Let's find out which of these two is colder." He nodded and all three of the boys let fly.

The snowballs didn't get within two feet of William. All three of them whizzed sideways in mid-course and plowed into the snowbank. William gave Tad a nasty grin. "There are advantages to having a father who teaches magic at the college," he said. "He likes it when I take an interest in more advanced magic than what they teach at the day school. Or didn't you figure that out when your lunch pail trick didn't work?"

"You can't block it if you're not looking at it," said a girl on William's left. He turned to give her a disdainful look, and the boy behind him pitched another snowball hard at the back of his head.

I yelled, too late, but the snowball veered sideways a foot before it got to William. The girl who'd set him up had to dodge in a hurry, and the snowball hit the side of the store with a solid thunk. William frowned. "There was a rock in that snowball," he said.

"Maybe there was, and maybe there wasn't," Tad said. "But we still haven't found out which of you is colder, and everybody knows your girlfriend is no good at magic. We'll just start with her."

"His fancy spell may stop snowballs, but I bet we can still stuff it down the back of his coat," one of the girls said. She kicked a chunk of ice loose from the bank alongside the path and picked it up.

"That's a really bad idea," Lan's voice said, and a second later he walked around the corner of the store. He was seriously angry, I could tell, though he might not have looked it to anyone who didn't know him well.

Tad looked him over and sniffed. "Says who?"

"Me," Lan replied evenly. "Lan Rothmer."

"The double-seventh son!" the second girl gasped.

"That's right," Lan said. "And Eff is my twin sister, in case you didn't know. That's why picking on her is such a bad idea."

A couple of the boys looked uneasy, but Tad just sneered. He made a show of scooping up another handful of snow, and this time he didn't hide the rock he stuffed in the middle. "So you're the hot-shot magician everybody talks about. How hot are you?"

"Oh, about this much," Lan said, and gestured.

A tongue of flame three feet high shot up from the middle of Tad's snowball. Tad yelled and dropped it.

"Now," Lan said. "All of you. Leave my sister alone." He got a faraway look for a second, and Tad and all five of his friends, boys and girls both, started yelling and hopping up and down. One of the girls plopped down right in the snowbank and yanked off her boots, then buried both feet in the snow.

"Don't just stand there, you dummies," Lan said to William and me. "Let's get out of here."

So the three of us ran. When we finally stopped for breath, I said, "How did you come to be so handy?"

"I had a feeling something was wrong," Lan said. He looked at me, and I could see he was still pretty mad. "How long has that been going on?"

"This was the first time," I said quickly. "Lan, what did you do to them?"

Lan grinned and held up a half-burned matchstick. "Hotfoot spell. Don't look like that — it won't really burn them. It just feels like it. For about five minutes, I think, until it wears off." He sounded very pleased with himself.

"Five minutes, you think?" William asked in a wary tone.

Lan shrugged. "You're supposed to use it on one person at a time. I had to do six at once, so I put a little extra power in it. I'm not sure what that'll do to how long it lasts."

"You're not sure?" I said. I'd burned my hand on the smoothing iron once when Mama was teaching me to iron shirts, and I remembered how much it hurt. Feeling like that for five minutes would be awful, even if you didn't get blisters and soreness after. "If you don't even know how long it'll last, how can you be sure that the extra power won't really burn them after all?"

"You goose," Lan said. "It's an illusion spell; it can't burn anything. More power just makes it last longer." He looked thoughtful. "I wonder how long I could make an illusion last, if I really tried. Days, I bet."

"Lan! You could have hurt someone," I said. "And what about that fire you shot out of Tad's snowball?"

"That?" Lan laughed. "That was just an illusion, to scare him."

"You'll still be in trouble if he reports it," William said.

"He deserved it," Lan said, unconcerned. "Anyway, he won't say anything. If he told, he'd be the one in trouble, for putting rocks in snowballs. Besides, all I did was scare him off."

"You brought up being a double-seven, and then you used magic on them. Even if it was just illusions, that'll bother a lot of people."

"I didn't bring up being a double-seven," Lan objected. "That girl did. I can't help it if people know who I am, can I?"

"I suppose," William said doubtfully. He looked like he wanted to say more, but thought better of it. "Where did you learn that spell, anyway?"

"From Jack. He got it from one of Papa's students, I think." Lan gave William a sidelong look. "I'll teach you, if you want," he offered. "It's easy."

William hesitated, then nodded. I wanted to object, but I didn't. After all, Lan hadn't said anything to Tad about leaving William alone, just about me.

It wasn't until later that night, thinking things over in bed before I fell asleep, that a niggling little worry started in the back of my head. Lan had said that the flame that shot out of Tad's snowball was illusion, but I distinctly remembered hearing the hiss and spit of water hitting a hot surface. I tried telling myself that it was part of the illusion, that Lan had remembered to include sound as well as sight in his spell. I convinced myself well enough to get to sleep, but not enough to make the worry go away for good.

That was just about the end of the nasty tricks from Tad and his friends. The very end came a couple of days later. I was walking back to my seat in class, and I saw Tad shift his feet under his desk. I knew that he was going to try to trip me as I went past him. Only then he looked down and turned white as a bleached shirtfront, and went completely still. His head twitched as I came up next to him, like he'd started to look at me and stopped himself, but that was all.

I looked down at his desk as I passed, and saw his slate with all the math problems we'd been doing. Right in the middle was a blank spot, like somebody had swiped a sponge across it, and in the middle of the blank were three words and two numbers: *Don't even try. 77*

After that, Tad didn't just leave me alone; he avoided me every chance he got. That was fine by me. At the end of that week, Lan asked casually whether I'd had any more trouble. I told him no, and I didn't think I would. I didn't tell him I'd seen his message to Tad, and I didn't ask how he'd done it, though I thought on it more than a little.

Then, just when I figured the worst of the year might be over, Mama slipped on the back steps while she was carrying the wash water and twisted her knee and broke her leg in two places. The doctor strapped her in a heavy cast and she was weeks mending.

Nan had just found a job in the shipping office at the railroad, so Allie and I had to take over running the house. You'd have thought that with Hugh at university in the East and Rennie off in the settlement, there'd be enough less work to notice, but it didn't seem like it. It was harder on Allie than it was on me, because I'd been having as much trouble learning normal housekeeping spells as I did with my other magic lessons, so Allie had to do most of the chores that needed magic. Neither of us complained much, though, except to each other. We didn't want Mama to take the notion she should get up and manage things herself, not until the doctors said she could, anyway.

In the middle of everything, a letter finally came from Rennie. Papa didn't pass it around to us all, the way he usually did with family letters, but he said she was sorry she'd caused a fuss. She was happy at the Rationalist settlement, she said. And she'd had a baby boy, named Albert Daniel Wilson after his two grandfathers, who she hoped to bring to Mill City to meet us all when he was older and better able to stand the journey. She didn't mention a birth date, which annoyed Nan, but Papa added Albert Daniel Wilson and the year to the family Bible and said we'd put the rest in later.

The news from Rennie cheered Mama up some. By the time school let out, she was up and around again, but she tired easily, so Allie and I kept on with the householding. It didn't leave me time to worry over Lan, or Tad, or Rennie, or anything else, all that summer.

CHAPTER
17

THAT FALL, LAN WENT BACK EAST TO A BOARDING SCHOOL IN
Pennsylvania. I'd known, out on the edge of my mind, that he
and Papa had been talking about it all spring while Mama was
in her cast, but I'd been too busy to pay it much mind. Papa
said that it was time Lan had different magic teachers, who
could show him a wider range of techniques.

Lan didn't seem too pleased with the notion. He said
he wanted to stay in Mill City and go to the upper school that
Allie and Robbie were in and study magic with Papa and
the other college professors, the way he'd been doing. But
Papa said the Mill City upper school wouldn't give him the
theoretical grounding he needed, and picking up bits
and pieces from the other professors wasn't anything like
the kind of education he'd get from a top-drawer Eastern
school.

I heard them arguing about it more than once before Lan
agreed to go. After a while, I noticed that Papa never once said
straight out that Lan was a double-seventh son, but he talked
a lot about how Lan needed to stretch and challenge himself and

about reaching his full potential. He'd never talked like that to any of the other boys.

He didn't fool Lan one bit, either. A week after school let out, Lan came looking for me. I was out behind the house with Allie and Nan, beating the winter's dirt and dust out of the big parlor rug. It should have been done weeks before with the other carpets, but we'd left it for last because it was so large, and then had gotten busy with other things. Whaling away with the carpet beaters was usually fun, but that day was warm, with no wind to carry the dust off, so it was just hot, sweaty, dirty work. It is truly amazing how much dust and dirt you can pound out of a carpet in the spring, even one that's been sitting in a room that's hardly ever used.

We'd almost finished going over the carpet when Lan showed up with two buckets and asked if I could go frogging with him. I wasn't slow about putting my carpet beater aside, though I wondered what Lan really wanted. He usually went fishing or frogging with one of the boys from down the hill, or by himself, if they couldn't come.

Lan handed me a bucket, and we started for the creek. As soon as we were well out of earshot, he said abruptly, "You know Papa's been at me to go to this boarding school out East, don't you?"

I nodded.

"What do you think of it?"

"What do I think of it?" I stared at him. "That's for you and Papa to decide, surely."

"Yes, but you're my twin," Lan said impatiently. "And . . . well, what if you need me again?"

"Need you . . . Oh, you mean if Tad Holiger starts in on me again?" I considered. "He hasn't bothered me or William since that time last winter. I don't think he'll start up again. And if he does, I'll just remind him that I'm a double-seven's twin."

"That should work." Lan looked relieved. Then he frowned. "But what if —"

"Lan." I cut him off before I got to feeling cross with him. It was bad enough that he'd be going, even if we had drawn apart some, but it was worse that he was dragging me into helping him dither over a decision that was none of mine. "You'll be at the upper school next year, even if you stay in Mill City. And I'm not totally helpless, just because I'm no good with magic."

Lan snorted. "That's not the point." But he didn't say what the point was. He just stood there, digging the toe of his shoe into the dust and swinging his frogging bucket.

"What do you want to do?" I asked suddenly.

He flushed and looked away and didn't say anything for a long time. Then finally he said, so soft I almost missed hearing it, "It's not fair."

"Fair?" I thought at first that he meant it wasn't fair that he was made to go off East to school, when he wanted to stay. Then I saw his face clear, and all at once I knew that he wanted to go as badly as he'd ever wanted anything in both our lives. What wasn't fair was that he got sent East to school, just for being a double-seventh son, when there'd never even been talk of sending anyone else.

If it hadn't been for Miss Ochiba's teaching, I don't think I'd have seen even that much. I know for sure that I wouldn't have seen, right then, that being a double-seventh son was near as bad for Lan, some ways, as being a thirteenth child was for me. Only nobody'd ever expected me to like being a thirteenth, or to be happy about it.

"No, it's not fair," I said, thinking hard. "But it's not like Robbie or Jack ever wanted to go to school out East."

Lan had to grin at that. Robbie had discovered girls, and there were lots more girls at the Mill City upper school than there were boys, because some of the settlement families let their girls stay in town for schooling when they went off to their allotments, but they took the boys along to help out. The last month of school, Robbie had walked a different girl home every afternoon, sometimes more than one. As for Jack, he hated school, and was happy to be finished with it for a while. When Papa told him he should start studying to get into a college, the way Hugh and Charlie and the older boys had, Jack said he'd only just gotten out of upper school and he wanted a break.

I took a deep breath. "And it's not fair that you were born last and a double-seven, and the rest of us are just regular people." I didn't have to add that it wasn't fair that I was thirteenth-born. I knew that right then Lan was as mindful of it as I was. "It's not fair, but it's how things are."

"I can't change when I was born," Lan said, and stopped.

"But you could change this?" I said for him. "Don't be a . . . a goose! What good would it do any of us for you to give up the chance for the kind of schooling you want? Besides, if you stay, in less than a month you'll be moping around making everyone else miserable. You know you will! How is that fair?"

Lan had to admit I was right, though he was plainly still troubled. He cheered up when we got to the creek, though most of the frogs seemed to have gone into hiding. We barely got half a bucketful between us. That night he told Papa that he'd try the boarding school. So Papa made the arrangements, and in the fall Lan left on the eastbound train.

I missed him more than I'd ever suspected I would. I'd thought that because we'd been in different grades for so long, and because he was off studying with Papa so much when we weren't in school, I'd hardly notice he was gone. Instead, I noticed it all the time, even when I was in school or doing chores like the wash, that the boys didn't ever do. Lan had always been somewhere nearby — nearer than Pennsylvania, anyway — and I'd known it. I felt like I was missing part of myself.

School wasn't much changed from the year before. I still had difficulty with my spells — the fire-lighting spell went off like a Fourth of July sparkler without actually starting a fire, the spell for lightening loads sort of stuttered, so that the weight went from light to heavy and back, over and over, and the far-seeing spell didn't work at all. Even William got impatient with me over that sometimes. He was studying hard for the final examination, along with about a third of the eighth-grade class, the ones who meant to go on to the upper school. The rest were looking forward to finishing with school and going off to work or to their families' settlements.

I felt like I was drifting. I didn't know whether to go on to upper school or not. If I didn't, I could stay home and do more of the housework — the parts that didn't take magic, anyway. Mama was still feeling poorly and not up to heavy cleaning, and with Lan's school expenses, we'd had to cut back on having Mrs. Callahan in to help. Also, there was a part of me that cringed away from learning any more magic, which I'd have to do if I went on to upper school.

But I knew that Papa and Mama would be upset if I told them I didn't want any more education. I was pretty sure William would be upset, too, and I knew for a fact that Lan would give me a tongue-lashing the next time I saw him. I didn't want to face any of them. So I put off making up my mind, and put it off, and put it off.

And then it was March. The weather was cold and we had two blizzards in one week, but in between them the wind was warm and damp, and made everyone restless for the spring that hadn't come yet. The settlement boys started cutting classes, even though there wasn't much of anything to do yet outside of school. Every day there'd be two or three empty seats, except in Miss Ochiba's class. Nobody quite dared to skip out on her.

One morning we came into Miss Ochiba's classroom to find that she was not alone. A tall, strong-featured man was half leaning, half sitting on her desk, swinging a booted foot. His skin was a rich, dark chocolate color, and his hair was clipped close to his head, shorter than his neat beard and mustache. A broad-brimmed hat dangled from one hand, and his jacket and pants were well-worn brown leather with long fringes dangling from all the seams. He grinned a wide, white grin at our startled faces, and said something to Miss Ochiba that nobody else heard.

Nobody ever dawdled getting ready for Miss Ochiba's class, but that morning we were even quicker about taking our seats than usual. Miss Ochiba smiled slightly as she rapped for order and wished us good morning. Then she said, "As most of you have probably guessed, today's class will be somewhat unusual."

A little stirring rippled through the class; Miss Ochiba frowned slightly and it ceased instantly. Behind her, the black man's eyes crinkled at the corners, and he pursed his lips like he had to do something with them or he'd burst out laughing.

"Many of you will be going out to the settlements in a few weeks," Miss Ochiba continued. "You will find that it is one thing to learn in class about wildlife and the spells that hold them back, and quite another to live with their presence day to day. Even for those of you who will remain in Mill City, it will be wise to remember that the Great Barrier Spell runs less than two miles away.

"I have therefore taken this opportunity to have Mr. Washington Morris speak with you today." Miss Ochiba turned to indicate the man behind her, who gave a short nod in acknowledgment. "Mr. Morris has spent most of the past ten years on the far side of the Great Barrier, as an explorer, guide, and independent circuit-rider among the border settlements. He knows a great deal about the country and the wildlife of the settlement frontier, and I recommend that you give him your full attention."

Washington Morris straightened up and came forward. "Thank you kindly, Miss Maryann," he said in a deep, rumbly voice with more than a hint of a Southern drawl. "I think I'd best begin by speaking of what I do, and give you all a chance to collect your thoughts. Once you've got your questions ready, I'll be pleased to answer them."

We all listened in utter fascination. Mr. Morris was a traveling magician, one of those who went from town to town, bringing news and sometimes supplies, escorting folk who needed to travel, and helping the settlement magicians reinforce or expand their protective spells. Traveling alone on the far side of the Great Barrier was difficult and dangerous. The Settlement Office had a regular schedule of circuit-riders for the larger towns close by the river, but the farther out the settlements went, the fewer magicians were willing to take the risks.

So the Settlement Office decided to hire men who'd gone into the Far West exploring on their own and had lived to tell of it. They found six, and authorized them as independent circuit-riders, with no fixed schedule to keep, just a wide section of territory to keep track of. Mr. Morris had been one of their first recruits, and for the past five years he'd been riding the northernmost section of the territory from the tip of the Red River down to the Long Chain Lakes, stopping back to Mill City every so often to report in.

In that time, he'd been hunted by greatwolves and nearly trampled in a bison stampede. He'd been stung by sunbugs and had once awakened to find rattlesnakes sharing his bed-roll. He'd run from wildfires and dodged prides of saber cats and Columbian sphinxes. Once he'd lost all his supplies in a flash flood, and had to hike eighty miles to the nearest settlement. He told us all this in a calm, matter-of-fact way that made his list of adventures seem as commonplace as watching the milk-delivery wagon rattle up the street every morning.

But for all that, it was plain to see that he loved the wide, wild country to the west, and all the people and creatures that lived there. "They were just acting according to their natures," he said when one of the girls asked why he didn't shoot the bear cubs who'd gotten into his food cache. Then he grinned his wide grin and added, "Also, I knew the mama bear was around somewhere, and I can't rightly say I wanted her riled at me. A mama bear who's protecting her cubs is a fearsome thing."

He looked around the class and said more seriously, "There's a thing to remember that's worth as much as a round half-dozen spells: Steer clear of the young ones, no matter what kind. For certain-sure, their mama is nearby, whether or not you see her, and even a prairie dog will fight for her pups.

"There are two kinds of people who get themselves in true trouble on the far frontier," he went on. "The ones who are terrified of the wildlife, who cower in the settlements wanting the magicians to keep every last critter as far away as if they still lived east of the barrier, and the ones who aren't afraid of the critters at all, who act as if they carry a personal barrier spell around with them all the time."

"Mr. Morris, what do folks do who don't ever get themselves in trouble?" one of the boys asked. His family was moving to a settlement in a few weeks, so he had a serious interest in the answer.

Mr. Morris studied him for a minute, then gave him a slow smile. "There's nobody who doesn't ever get in trouble," he said. "But the ones who see the least of it start like you, with questioning those who've been before them. They take care, but they don't let fear cripple them. They watch the wildlife, and learn from them."

"Learn from them, Mr. Morris?" the boy said.

"There's no creature out there that's not wary of something. If you watch them close, you can figure out what they do to stay alive, and apply it to your own self." He paused, then said with another slow grin, "And being as how you're Miss Maryann's students, you can call me Wash, all of you. I'm more accustomed to it, you see."

"What are mammoths afraid of?" another boy demanded.

Wash's eyes narrowed. "Even a mammoth will flinch when a steam dragon flies overhead."

"What about steam dragons, then?"

"I don't rightly know." Wash shook his head. "But I'll tell you this: About twelve years back I took a notion to see for myself those big Rocky Mountains you hear tell of sometimes. It was a hair-raising journey, and I don't propose to carry on about it now, but I got to a place where I could see the mountains rising up off the horizon every time I topped a hill. They had a sort of pull on me. Every evening I'd tell myself I'd come far enough, and every morning I'd tell myself that it wouldn't hurt to go on just one more day.

"One morning I was packing up my saddlebags and having that same conversation with myself, when something made me look west. Suddenly I saw a full-grown steam dragon burst up off the side of the mountain. It tore through the sky like it was running from Judgment Day, and passed overhead without even pausing to consider what a tasty meal my horse and I would make."

"What did you do?" one of the girls asked.

"I finished packing my saddlebags in a right hurry, and headed back east at as good a clip as seemed wise. I don't know what put the fear into that steam dragon, but I knew for certain-sure that whatever it was, I didn't want to meet up with it."

He paused for a minute, and sighed. "We don't know enough about the critters on the far side of the Great Barrier," he said, half to himself. "We don't even know what all of them are yet. I've seen things on the far frontier that no one here can tell me names of. You can't ward things off if you don't know what they are or when they're coming."

Those words hit me and sank in deep. I thought of some of the tales I'd heard of failed settlements, and the reasons they'd failed. I remembered Dr. McNeil's expedition, and how they'd almost been killed because they didn't know to look for a swarming weasel burrow near their camp, and how Brant Wilson had saved them with his pistols and knowing about bees and a lucky guess. At that moment, I knew what I wanted to do: I wanted to go into the frontier, not as a settler, but as a naturalist, to study the wildlife the way Dr. McNeil had, the way Wash said was needed. I sat there thinking so hard about it that I hardly heard the rest of what Wash said, and the more I thought on it, the more I knew I wanted to do it.

It wasn't until the recess bell rang that it occurred to me that if I wanted to do all that, I was going to have to go to upper school after all.

CHAPTER 18

ONCE I MADE UP MY MIND TO GO TO UPPER SCHOOL, I WORRIED CON-stantly about the day school's final exam. William had been studying hard for it for weeks, and I hadn't done a thing. I spent the next three weeks with my nose in my books, trying to make up for lost time. It worked, mostly. I didn't do as well as I could have — I missed two of the arithmetic questions, and I got some of the presidents mixed up — but I passed.

William got the best score in the class. He'd worked so hard for it that I thought he'd be happier, but he just looked tense and worried when they announced it. It wasn't until the next day that I found out why. William wanted to go to the Mill City upper school, but his father had been talking about sending him off East, like Lan. He'd been hoping that if he did well on the final exam, his father would see that it was all right for him to stay in Mill City.

Professor Graham wasn't best pleased by the notion, but William was just as stubborn as he was. He argued that he was getting plenty of learning right where he was and the exam proved it. Professor Graham said that doing so well on the exam proved he needed more challenging than he could get in a frontier-border city. I guess there was some yelling involved, but finally they struck a deal. William could have a year at the upper school, but if Professor Graham wasn't satisfied with his progress, he'd go off to boarding school the year after.

I didn't see why William was so set on biding in Mill City, and I said so.

"I just want to stay here for a while," William said crossly. "Is that so hard to understand?"

"I can see that you're dead set on it," I said. I was near as cross as he was, for him snapping back at me when I'd asked a civil question. "What I don't see is why. The best magic teachers don't come out to the far edge of the country — they're all back East. If you're going to be a magician like your father —"

"I'm not going to be *like* anybody," William burst out.

I stared at him in surprise. "But you're good at magic. I thought you wanted to be a magician?"

"Of course I want to be a magician. That's not the problem!"

"Well, what is, then? You're not making any sense."

William was silent for almost a minute. Then he sighed. "Sorry, Eff. It's just that my father . . . he used to be worse, I think. It's all right."

"William Graham, you explain what you're talking about right this minute, or I'll put ants in your lunch pail every day from now 'til the end of school!"

"There's only a week left. I can stand it that long," William said, but he grinned. We walked in silence for a bit, then he sighed again. "My father wants me to be like him, only better. Or if I can't be like him, he wants me to be like Lan. That's the real reason for this boarding-school idea. He never talked about it even once, before he found out Lan was going."

I couldn't think of anything to say that wouldn't sound nasty, even if I didn't mean it that way. Lan was a double-seventh son; there was no way William's magic would ever be a match for his, no matter where they went to school. Both William and Professor Graham had to know that already.

"My father wants me to be a teaching magician, the way he is," William went on. "Only I'm supposed to be better and teach at a famous Eastern school. The New Bristol Institute of Magic, maybe. He has my whole life planned out, to make sure I'll have all the knowledge and skills and experience I'll need. It's not what I want, but he won't listen when I tell him that."

"What do you want, then?" I asked.

"I don't know all of it yet." William tilted his head back and looked up at the sky, and spread his arms wide. "But I want — first, I want to be *me*. And then I want to do something large. Something as large as all that country out there that people are settling. Even if I'm not a double-seventh son." He dropped his arms and ducked his head. "And I'm never going to find out what the something is, if I keep going along with my father's plans."

I nodded, though it seemed to me that William might be a sight better off at a boarding school out East, where his father wouldn't be looking over his shoulder every minute. I could see that right then wasn't the time to tell William that, but I figured I'd have other chances.

Lan only came home for three weeks that summer and had to miss our fifteenth birthday, because the boarding school had year-round classes. He wouldn't have been able to come at all for such a little time if Nan hadn't been working in the railroad shipping office so he could ride the train for free. He'd shot up another couple of inches, passing me by for height, and he wore his hair long and slicked back. All his talk was about the school and his new friends and teachers — for the first few days, anyway. Then we had a glorious two weeks, and then he was gone again.

I didn't miss Lan quite so much this time. I had too many new things of my own to pay attention to, what with starting at the upper school and leaving the day school — and Miss Ochiba — behind. William was just as unhappy about leaving the Aphrikan magic class as I was, and he wasn't much inclined to resignation. He went and talked to Miss Ochiba, and then to the principal at the upper school, and in the end he arranged for the two of us to keep on with our Aphrikan study as a special tutorial. I was happy because we'd finally learned enough to start doing actual spells — or at least things that were more like the sort of spells we learned in our regular classes.

Aphrikan magic isn't much like Avrupan magic, or even Hijero–Cathayan magic. Avrupan magic is individual. Even when teams of magicians work together on something, they do it by each casting one particular spell that fits together with all the other spells, like the teeth on a set of gears fit each other. If one magician gets it wrong and his piece fizzles or blows up, the big spell doesn't work, but it doesn't hurt any of the other magicians or affect their magic. Still, you have to be very precise to work as part of a team of Avrupan magicians, because nobody wants to waste all that effort just because someone else got it wrong.

Hijero–Cathayan magic is group magic. They hardly have any small, everyday magics that one magician can do alone, like fire-lighting spells. They're good at big things, like moving rivers and clearing out dragon rookeries — at least, they say it was the ancient Hijero–Cathayan magicians who cleaned out the last few nests of dragons in Ashia and Avrupa and made all the land safe for people to live in.

Hijero–Cathayan magicians almost always work in groups, with all the magicians linked together by a spell so they can pool their power. The trouble is that if even one of the magicians makes a mistake, the whole spell can come apart, and when it does, it can hurt or kill every magician who is part of it. The leader of the group, who channels all that power, usually burns out after a couple of years, if his group works steady. I could never make out why anybody would take up magic at all, if they knew that was in store for them, but I guess the Hijero–Cathayans don't see it that way.

But different as they are, both Avrupan and Hijero–Cathayan magic have one thing in common: The main idea is to raise up and control enough magic to do things. That's why learning either of them starts the same way, with doing small spells, and then bigger spells, using more and stronger magic to do larger and larger things each time.

Aphrikan magic starts with looking, not doing. Instead of calling up magic and controlling it, Aphrikan conjurefolk find the places where magic is already moving and then guide it somewhere else. It means that Aphrikan magicians can work together a lot more safely and easily than Avrupan or Hijero–Cathayan magicians, because they don't have to match up their spells precisely, or worry about burning each other out. It also means that Aphrikan spells hardly ever work the same way twice. Sometimes what the magician wants to make happen is too different from the way the natural magic is moving, and he can't get it to do what he wanted at all. Because of that, most Avrupan magicians think Aphrikan magic is unpredictable and unreliable.

Looking at things the way Avrupan magicians do, I suppose they're right. But there's other ways to look, and one thing Aphrikan magic is well and truly good at is dealing with other kinds of magic, especially natural magic, like steam dragons and sunbugs.

That was what Miss Ochiba started teaching William and me, our first year in upper school. Since Mill City is east of the Great Barrier, we didn't have much in the way of magical creatures to practice on. Once a week, we went over to the little menagerie where the North Plains Riverbank College kept its wildlife specimens, and tried to persuade the animals to move where we wanted them to go or eat one part of their feed first, rather than another.

Most of the specimens were ordinary creatures, like the mammoth and the prairie dogs Dr. McNeil had brought back. There were only three samples of magical wildlife, and one of those was a plant. The other two were a scorch lizard and a daybat, and Professor Jeffries, who ran the menagerie, wouldn't let us anywhere near them, even though they weren't particularly dangerous.

In truth, Professor Jeffries didn't much like having us there at first. He sniffed and muttered and peered over the top of his spectacles at us when we arrived, and sniffed and muttered some more when we left. I never could make out what it was he disliked most — that William and I were only in upper school, that we'd gotten permission because our fathers were professors, or that we were doing Aphrikanstyle magic. William and I could see that he was just looking for an excuse to stop us coming, so we were extra polite and very careful about following his rules. That just seemed to make him fuss even more, right up until the end of October.

It was one of those warm, clear days in fall when all the leaves have turned shades of red and gold and half of them have fallen and gone crunchy underfoot. The sky was pale blue around the edges, and the slanting sunlight made everything shimmer in the breeze.

Miss Ochiba, William, and I had been working with the prairie dogs, which were getting slow and fat, storing up food in their tunnels against winter. The prairie dogs were especially good for us to practice on, Miss Ochiba said, because we had to concentrate a little harder to tell them from the squirrels and mice and chipmunks that lived around the college buildings. Once we'd finished persuading the prairie dogs to take particular bits of food and store them in spots we'd chosen instead of where the prairie dogs wanted, we went out to the field where Professor Jeffries kept the mammoth.

The mammoth was four or five years old, Professor Jeffries thought. That made it about half grown, though it was hard to think of something the size of a stagecoach as half grown. Its tusks were already three feet long, but they hadn't started curling yet, and its coat was getting thick and shaggy for winter. Normally it was a peaceable animal, but it got restless every fall, when its cousins in the west started walking south to their winter feeding grounds, so Miss Ochiba made sure that we stayed outside the split-rail fence.

That day, Professor Jeffries had brought his fall class out to observe the mammoth, so there were eight men in the field when we arrived. The seven students were listening respectfully to Professor Jeffries' lecture, paying heed to the mammoth while Professor Jeffries waved in its direction.

When he saw us, Professor Jeffries frowned. It was clear he'd forgotten it was our day to visit the menagerie, and equally plain that he didn't want us anywhere near the class he was teaching. Miss Ochiba just nodded and took us across to the other field, where they kept regular farm animals. We worked with them sometimes, too, because she said that we needed to know the feel of useful, tame animals as well as the wild ones. There was a yearling colt that the horsebreaker thought was still too young to work on a line, though he'd been halter-broke. William thought we could use Aphrikan magic to teach it not to spook at flapping sheets, and after consulting with Miss Ochiba, the breaker had said we could try.

We'd just started work when we heard a shout and a great trumpeting noise behind us. We all turned, just in time to see the young mammoth charge up the field, swinging its head side to side as it came. It knocked two of Professor Jeffries's students out of its way — the others had sense enough to scatter on their own — and slammed into the rail fence. The fence posts leaned over and the rails bent outward and cracked. The mammoth trumpeted and rammed the fence again. The rails flew apart.

William and I stood frozen as the mammoth charged toward us. Then Miss Ochiba stepped forward and raised one gloved hand. Just before the mammoth reached her, she clenched her fist and said a word. The surge of magic that followed was so strong that I fell right off the fence I'd been sitting on. It stopped that mammoth right in its tracks, just as if it had run into a solid wall.

The mammoth couldn't move forward, but it was still plenty mad. It stomped its feet and swung its head, then lashed out with its trunk. Miss Ochiba stood there cool as anything, holding the mammoth in place with an invisible cage of magic.

Nobody could hold an angry mammoth for very long, though, even if it was only half grown. I groped around for the trickle of magic we'd been using to gentle the colt, and urged it toward the mammoth. I felt it take hold, but what was plenty enough, for a yearling was nowhere near strong enough to calm an angry mammoth. It snorted and stamped some more, and its big beady eyes glared at Miss Ochiba.

William shouted a warding spell we'd learned in our regular classes. The air shimmered as it went up around us. I climbed to my feet, slow and careful so as not to startle the mammoth any more than it already was. I wasn't sure what to do next. William's spell wasn't strong enough to hold the mammoth off if it broke free of Miss Ochiba, but I didn't much like the thought of walking out of it.

And then Professor Jeffries and his students ran up at last. Between them, they got a good solid restraining spell up, so Miss Ochiba could relax, and then Professor Jeffries sent one of them off to the main building, to get the ingredients for the charm Dr. McNeil had used when he'd brought the mammoth through the Great Barrier Spell. They all had a nice, busy time of it, but in the end, they got the mammoth calmed down and back in its field, and a temporary fence up with lots of reinforcing spells to keep it there.

As soon as they finished, Professor Jeffries called one of the students over, a big man in a long brown muffler, and started giving him what for. Seems he'd been the one to set the mammoth off, flapping his scarf at it to find out what it would do. Professor Jeffries told him that would have been a foolish thing to do to an elderly, well-broken cart horse, and it was downright idiotic to do it to a wild mammoth three times as big. It made me see clear and personal what Wash had meant about people who weren't afraid of wildlife at all.

After he was done getting yelled at, the man who'd started it came over and apologized to Miss Ochiba and William and me. By then, I wasn't paying too much attention, because I was starting to worry that when Mama and Papa heard about the mammoth getting loose, they'd make me stop coming to work with the menagerie animals. But there wasn't anything I could do to keep them from hearing about it, so all I could do was hope.

CHAPTER
19

WORD ABOUT THE MAMMOTH GOT HOME BEFORE I DID THAT DAY. Mama was waiting for me on the front porch, and she swept me up in a big hug as soon as I came within reach. My heart sank. I could tell she'd been scared bad by what she'd heard. When she let loose of the hug enough to take a good look at me, and saw all the mud on my coat from where I'd fallen off the fence, she wouldn't listen to a thing I said, but made me go in and lie down.

Papa wasn't near so put out as Mama was. He'd heard the whole story from Professor Jeffries, and he said that the professor had commended my presence of mind and was quite happy to have William and me and Miss Ochiba continue our visits. Papa also said that if Miss Ochiba could teach me to stop a charging mammoth, he'd be more pleased than not, and in any case the incident showed that I was a sight safer with her than running around the college on my own. He got Mama soothed down enough to see that I wasn't hurt, and asked what I thought of the matter. Of course I said that I wanted to keep on with my lessons.

That wasn't the end of it, though. Seeing all the mud on my coat gave Mama the notion that working with the menagerie animals was a hard and wearying job, like mucking out stables, and she said she didn't want me tiring myself out. It was no good pointing out that hauling the wet laundry every Monday was harder work than doing spells at the menagerie. She'd been used to thinking of me as delicate, ever since the rheumatic fever, and that was that. She didn't put a stop to my lessons, but she fretted over them until it drove me to distraction.

Still, I loved the animals at the menagerie too much to let them go. After the incident with the mammoth, Professor Jeffries kept his classes outside the fence, and I snuck close enough to listen as often as I could. When he saw that I was interested in the animals, and not just in Miss Ochiba's lessons, he let me help with feeding and tending them sometimes. I didn't mention any of it to Mama.

In February, right after his eighteenth birthday, Jack announced that he'd gone down to the North Plains Territory Homestead Claim and Settlement Office and signed up for a homestead claim. Mama was almost as upset by that as she'd been over the mammoth, and Papa wasn't any too pleased, either, but there wasn't a thing they could do about it. The law said that at the age of eighteen any citizen who had a sound body and the will to work a claim could put in for a settlement allotment, and Jack had gone and done it.

Papa wasn't much for yelling, even when he wasn't happy about something the boys had done, but he came awfully near it with Jack that time. He couldn't see why Jack would want to go out to the settlements at all, and if he had to go, Papa thought he should put in a few more years at school and become a settlement magician. It was a bit safer than homesteading, and it was an easier and better living, because the Settlement Office chipped in with the homesteaders to pay settlement magicians. Also, Papa was aggrieved that Jack hadn't said anything before he went down to the Settlement Office, like he thought Papa would forbid him from doing it.

Jack heard Papa out with more patience than I'd ever thought he had. Then he rolled his eyes and said that he'd told Papa time and again that he didn't want more schooling, and that he wanted to go out and do something real. It wasn't his fault if Papa hadn't believed him.

Mama just looked sad and said she didn't want the Far West swallowing another of her children. Jack told her that he wasn't getting swallowed up and he wasn't sneaking off the way Rennie had, either. Also, it wasn't like he was leaving right away. He'd have to wait for a place in a settlement group, because the Settlement Office hadn't let anyone go out alone since the very first year, when over a hundred farms were overrun by wildlife because the magicians were stretched too thin. It might take two or three years for a group to have an opening for a single man. Meantime, Jack meant to hire out to one of the farmers on the far side of the river, to get some practical experience in an established settlement.

Once they saw that Jack was determined, Mama and Papa quit arguing, but it took a couple of weeks. I think Papa was impressed by the way Jack had worked out his plans, though he wouldn't say so straight to Jack's face.

Jack found himself a position and moved across the river in April, just in time for spring planting. He promised he'd come home every Sunday, since it wasn't far, but the first week he was so tired that Mama told him he wasn't to ruin his health for her peace of mind, and once a month after planting finished would be plenty. She and Papa still grumbled when Jack was gone, though.

I was more on Jack's side than not. Jack had always hated school and loved adventure, and he'd had a hankering for the Far West since the day he heard we were moving to Mill City. And with so many of our school friends moving out to the settlements every year, it felt like a natural thing to do. I thought Robbie might mean to go the same way, if he didn't find himself a town girl, but I surely wasn't telling any of that to Mama and Papa.

What with all the grumbling at home, I took to spending more of my free time at the menagerie all through April and May. Which was how I happened to be there when Washington Morris turned up in mid-May, looking for Professor Jeffries.

"I'll fetch him for you, Mr. Morris," I told him.

He looked at me in considerable surprise, for he hadn't given his name. Then he smiled that wide, white smile and said, "You'll be one of Miss Maryann's students. I thought I told you all to call me Wash."

"You'd have been a sight more taken aback if I had," I pointed out. "You jumped when I called you Mr. Morris."

"I never," he said. "I was merely looking behind me for the Mr. Morris person you were addressing. But it strikes me that you have me at a disadvantage, when it comes to names."

"I'm Eff," I said. "Eff Rothmer."

"Pleased to meet you, Miss Rothmer," Wash said gravely, raising his hat.

"Nice to see you again, Mr. Morris," I said, and gave him my best curtsy.

"Wash," he corrected sternly.

"Wash, then," I said, and went off to find Professor Jeffries. He was out by the mammoth field, fiddling with the fencing spells. I told him that a Mr. Morris was waiting for him over at the classroom building. Then I followed him back, because I was curious what business Washington Morris would have with our college wildlife professor.

"You're the circuit-rider Miss Ochiba spoke of?" Professor Jeffries asked when Wash introduced himself. "Has she told you what I'm looking for?"

"Just that you've a job that's suited to a circuit-riding magician," Wash said in his deep drawl. "Miss Maryann is a great one for letting folks see for themselves."

"I see." Professor Jeffries frowned. "I need someone to collect information on wildlife behavior in their natural habitat. It's all very well to study these creatures in captivity, but to expect me to predict something like the Batterson fiasco with nothing to go on but this . . . Well, I'm sure you see the difficulty."

Wash nodded soberly. The Batterson settlement had been half destroyed the previous summer when a flock of cinderdwellers had flown in and burned most of its crops, two barns, and at least one homestead. The settlement's one magician had been keeping off cinderdwellers in ones and twos for a good six years, but a flock of sixty birds had been too much for him. Everybody had heard about it, and everybody wanted to know why a flock that size had suddenly showed up after so long. All the nearby settlements had been jumpy for months, not knowing if another big flock would turn up before they finished harvesting.

"I can see why you'd want better information," Wash told Professor Jeffries. "But you have to understand that when I'm out in the borderlands, a lot of other things have to come first." He smiled. "I can't rightly see myself stopping to make observations when a bear's after my supply cache, for instance."

"Your notes won't do me any good if you're not alive to bring them back," Professor Jeffries said with a small smile of his own. "And, frankly, whatever you provide will be more than what I'm getting now, which is nothing."

"I'll see what I can do for you," Wash said. "Always

provided you don't mind an uncertain schedule. I go where there's trouble and stay as long as I'm needed, which doesn't lend itself to a regular correspondence. I wouldn't be in town now if I hadn't wanted the sawbones to look over a bit of an infection I picked up last winter that was slow clearing up."

"You can mail me your notes whenever it's convenient," Professor Jeffries assured him.

A month later, a tatty-looking packet arrived for Professor Jeffries, containing ten pages that looked like they'd been crumpled up, sat on, and maybe used to strain coffee. Every one was covered, both sides, with tiny, meticulous notes that drove the professor from ecstasy to despair and back. When we came for our next Aphrikan magic class, he told Miss Ochiba that the bits he could make out were exactly what he wanted, but it would take him months to figure out what the rest of it said.

Miss Ochiba glanced at the page he held out and nodded. "I apologize for not warning you."

"No, no, I'm very grateful to you for putting me in touch with Mr. Morris," Professor Jeffries said. "But I wish he were a tad less inclined to abbreviation. What, for instance, can he mean by 'J3,8m/n fr Klein set.'?"

"June third, eight miles north from Klein settlement?" I suggested after a minute, when Miss Ochiba didn't answer.

Miss Ochiba and Professor Jeffries both looked at me. "Yes, that would be it!" the professor said.

"What do you make of the rest of it, Miss Rothmer?" Miss Ochiba asked, plucking the page from Professor Jeffries's hand and giving it to me.

I studied the page for a minute. It didn't seem much worse than the hen-scratch that some of my brothers called writing. The abbreviations were harder, but when I thought of Wash's deep voice saying the parts I could see right away, all the other parts came clear. I started reading it out slowly.

"June third, eight miles north from Klein settlement. Red fox and three kits at watering hole. Deer mice tracks. Iceweed at water's edge; haven't seen this far south before. Looks spindly."

Right about there, Professor Jeffries stopped me. "Remarkable!" he said. "It took me hours to get that far."

"Young eyes, plus experience," Miss Ochiba said drily, and I remembered that she'd taught three of my brothers, including Jack, whose penmanship was the most hen-scratchy of them all. Plus it was pretty clear that she'd known Wash a good while. Her eyes glinted with amusement as if she knew what I was thinking, and she added, "Perhaps you would be willing to make a fair copy for the professor, Miss Rothmer?"

I agreed at once. The professor thanked me several times, but truth to tell I was as grateful to him as he was to me. I'd been dying of curiosity ever since I found out that the first set of notes had arrived, and now I was going to be the first to find out what they said!

For the rest of that summer, whenever one of Wash's letters arrived, I'd spend a day or two copying it out for Professor Jeffries. At first, he used my copy as a sort of crib sheet to help him read Wash's notes for himself. After a while, when he saw that I was careful about copying exactly what was there, he only referred to the notes once in a while.

I found Wash's letters even more fascinating than the actual wildlife in the menagerie. He wrote about things I'd only ever seen in sketches in books — greatwolves and Columbian sphinxes, curly-horned deer and heatherfish, silvergrass and flower moths. Mostly, he wrote where and when he'd seen the creatures. Once in a while, he added a comment on what they'd been doing when he saw them. *Jy31 by LngL e.shr — sfb.etg bkby, n/dsrt fr me* was one of my favorite entries — *July 31 by Long Lake, east shore — short-faced bear eating blackberries, no dessert for me.*

Wash wrote about the weather, too — rain and dry spells and temperature, with a note on whether it seemed normal to him or not. Once he mentioned a strong smell of smoke on the wind, coming from the west, that lasted three days. It drove Professor Jeffries wild. He was sure it meant a big fire somewhere farther out, but it never got close enough for Wash to see even a glow on the horizon, so there was no telling whether it was fifty miles away or two hundred.

Professor Jeffries had a big map in his office, stuck with pins to show where things were. Green pins were settlements, brown ones were large wildlife like bears or mammoths, pink ones were birds, red ones were for really dangerous things like swarming weasels or saber cats, and so on. Each pin had a little paper wrapped around it, with the date and a reference code so you could look up more in the little brown book that went with the map. The professor had tried to persuade some of the settlement magicians to send him word of any wildlife that came around their areas, but only one or two had agreed, so if it hadn't been for Wash, the map would have had almost nothing but green pins.

Mama relaxed a good bit when she heard I was spending most of my time at a table, copying letters. It made me see that all her fretting was partly my own fault, because I hadn't shown her that I was all the way healthy again. Truth to tell, I'd been happy to keep on doing the lighter chores, right up until she'd broken her leg. And then she'd been too distracted to notice that I was working just as hard as Nan and Allie, and since then, she just hadn't had to think on it.

From then on, I made a point of mentioning it when I helped Robbie stack firewood, or dug over a piece of the garden, or helped haul feed for the horses. Mama frowned at me the first few times, but she couldn't rightly complain about me doing chores with the others, and gradually she got used to the idea that I really was strong enough to do them.

Much to my surprise, I liked doing some of the heavier work. It wasn't like the housekeeping spells that still fizzled on me five times out of six; when I hauled a bucket of water to the sink, it stayed hauled. I loved working with Professor Jeffries, too, and deciphering Wash's cramped writing.

For the first time in as long as I could remember, I was happy all summer long.

CHAPTER

20

LAN DIDN'T COME HOME AT ALL THE SUMMER WE TURNED SIXTEEN. One of the teachers had arranged some special tutoring for him in advanced elemental recombination, with a professor from the Broadbent University of Pennsylvania who could only do it during those few weeks. Lan's letter sounded excited, and of course Papa was very pleased. I was sorry that Lan wouldn't be home, but by then I was used to him being gone, and I was busy at the menagerie.

Around August, Wash started sending samples along with his letters. The first was a small red flower, pressed and dried between two of the sheets; the second was an orange-and-black butterfly whose wings had come off in the mail. None of the samples that followed were alive — they couldn't have gotten through the barrier spell if they were — and most of them were things the professor didn't have in his collection. Once there was a big round beetle, the size of a quarter, with mirror-bright wings and a tiny black head. The note Wash sent with it said: *Found five of these along a line from Birch Creek to south end of circuit. First time. Mean anything?*

Professor Jeffries was excited by the beetle, but he didn't have anything to tell Wash because no one had ever seen one before. Right away, he sent a message to the settlements south of Wash's circuit area. One of the magicians there said he'd seen one, but it had flown straight into the protective spell around the settlement and died, so it wasn't anything to worry about. The professor shook his head when he read that, and said that wasn't the point, and didn't those settlement magicians think about anything beyond watching out for the crops? Still grumbling, he put six shiny silver pins in his map and moved on to other things.

That whole year was the happiest I could ever remember being. I was doing well enough in most of my classes to please Papa and Mama. The class in practical spells was the only one I had trouble with, but as long as I could show I'd done the setup and procedure correctly, the teacher would give me enough marks to pass, even if the spell fizzled. I had friends, Rindy and Susan, two boarder girls who would be moving out to settlements when they finished school. Rindy was hoping to pass her teacher examinations the next year, so that her settlement could have a lower-grades school; Susan just wanted all the learning she could get while she had the chance to get some. I had my extra class in Aphrikan magic and my work at the menagerie — even during the winter months, Professor Jeffries found things for me to do.

Best of all, William had talked his father into one more year at the Mill City upper school, before he was to go East to prepare for college. All summer, I hadn't dared ask when he'd be leaving. And then, there he was on the first day of school. My face must have shown what I was thinking, because he snorted the way his father did when he thought someone was being foolish.

"You," he said sternly, "are a blithering idiot. Did you really think I wouldn't tell you if I were leaving?"

"I thought maybe you just didn't want to talk about it," I said. "I wouldn't, if it was me being sent off."

"I'm not you," William said. "And I agreed to go. One more year here will be enough."

"Enough for what?" I asked, but he just shook his head. I was too happy to pester him about it, especially when he'd made it plain that this would be his last year. I didn't want to break my happiness by thinking too much about that.

William had friends, too, and it wasn't long before all of us — me, Rindy, Susan, William, and William's friends Alec and Max — grouped together to do things. We ran the apple bobbing at the school Harvest Festival party, made up a team for the spelling bee, went sleighing and sledding in the woods north of town. We danced together at the early spring square dances, and split the cake Rindy won in the cakewalk at the church sociable in March. By the end of the year, William was sweet on Susan, Alec was courting Rindy like he really meant it, and Max was pretending he liked me, just to keep everything even.

What with friends and school and the menagerie and the

Aphrikan magic class and my chores at home, I was busy nearly every minute. The best of it, for me, was that it all felt so normal and ordinary. Even working at the menagerie — most of my classmates worked at some job after school and Saturdays. Sometimes I thought that my life would be completely perfect if only Lan were around, too.

And then it all came apart.

The first hint came in early May. The westernmost settlements began reporting problems — a plague of fat yellow grubs that destroyed the sprouting crops. They were normal insects, not magical ones, and they didn't seem much bothered by the spells the settlement magicians cast to stop them. They ate everything on or under the ground. Wash's notes said he'd seen tall trees tip over in a breath of wind because their roots had all been eaten away. Some places, he said, you couldn't take a step without grubs boiling up after your shoe leather. He had to hang his saddle and bridle well up in the air every night, and he'd taken to using a hammock himself, though he'd been used to a bedroll. The grubs wouldn't eat him, or any still-alive animal, but they went for the wool in his blankets, and he said once was enough to wake up to a squirming carpet of the things all over him.

The grubs disappeared after a month, as suddenly as they'd come, but by then the damage had been done. The settlers couldn't even replant enough to get themselves through the winter; they'd have to hunt, or borrow, or send folks back to Mill City for paying jobs, if they could find any.

Susan's family was from one of the Far West settlements, and in June they sent her word that they would have no cash crop that year because of the grubs. There would be no money to pay for her board and schooling in town, come fall. When she got the letter, Susan cried a little, where only Rindy and I would see. Then she put on a brave face and found work with a seamstress that would pay her board and leave a little extra to send home to her family.

Next, Miss Ochiba told William and me that our last Aphrikan magic class of the year would be our last class, period. "The school board has found someone else to teach magic at the day school," she said. "The chairman's sister, I believe."

"That's not fair!" William burst out. His face was very red. "They can't — they shouldn't —"

"Mr. Graham." Miss Ochiba's voice was as cool and level as ever. "That is certainly one way to look at the matter. There are others."

I stared at Miss Ochiba. For once, I couldn't think of any other way to see it. William was right. It wasn't fair.

Miss Ochiba looked at us and smiled gently. "I have been teaching magic at the day school for twelve years," she said. "It's high time I did something new."

"But what?" William said.

"I shall go to my oldest brother in Belletriste," Miss Ochiba said. "He is head of the Aphrikan Magic Department at Triskelion University, and has asked me several times to take a position there."

"You're going away?" I blurted. Then the rest of what she'd said sank in, and I just stared. I'd never thought of Miss Ochiba having a brother somewhere.

"Everything changes," Miss Ochiba said. "I may not be gone for good. I believe Triskelion is hoping to expand, and my brother is one of those who favors opening a western branch. However, that is only a possibility, and some years in the future. For now, I am afraid you must accustom yourselves."

We had a very somber class. Neither William nor I paid as much attention as we should have. At the end, Miss Ochiba handed each of us a small blue book instead of the summer assignments she usually gave us. "I am pleased to say that you have both reached a point where you should be able to work on your own — indeed, some would say it is past time you did so. Whether you choose to continue is up to you. If you do, you may find this useful."

"Oh, Miss Ochiba!" I said, and burst into tears.

Miss Ochiba let me cry for a bit, then handed me a handkerchief. "You may keep that as well," she told me when I went to hand it back once I'd wiped my face. I almost started crying again.

On the walk home, William was silent for a long time. As we came around the corner and started toward my house, he said, "Well, at least it will be one in the eye for the chairman."

"What? What are you talking about?" I asked, then added quickly, "From the beginning." Sometimes William got to having whole conversations in his head, and when they finally started coming out his mouth, he'd just carry on from wherever he'd left off inside. You had to make him back up and start over, or you'd never figure out what he meant.

"Miss Ochiba going to Triskelion University," William said. "If she's teaching there, the school board can't say this new person is a better teacher."

I nodded. Triskelion University had been founded shortly before the Secession War, and it made a point of teaching all three types of magic. Even though it was so much newer than the other schools that specialized in magic, it was almost as well known as the New Bristol Institute of Magic or Simon Magus College in Pennsylvania. I'd been surprised to hear that Miss Ochiba had brothers, but if she had them, I didn't find it at all surprising that one of them would be teaching at Triskelion, or that he wanted Miss Ochiba to come teach there, too.

By the end of July, Miss Ochiba was gone, and William was preparing to leave for boarding school. Professor Jeffries, Professor Graham, and Papa were off in the Far West settlements with most of the other college magicians. The grubs, it turned out, hadn't vanished; they'd just changed into pupae for a few weeks. They emerged in mid-July as round, yellow-and-green-striped beetle-like bugs. They didn't have any wings, but they crawled like crazy. Anything above ground that the grubs hadn't eaten, the beetles got, and the settlement spells didn't work on them any better than they had on the grubs. So the Settlement Office called on the college magicians to find or invent a new spell to take care of the beetles, or at least keep them from spreading farther east.

With Professor Jeffries gone, I didn't have much to do at the menagerie. Wash was as busy as all the other magicians, so his packets of notes had stopped arriving, and there was no one to look at them anyway. The two students who were caring for the animals didn't need my help. After a week, I stopped going over. I told myself I'd start again once Professor Jeffries came back.

But Papa, Professor Graham, and Professor Jeffries didn't come back right away. In late August, just before classes were supposed to start at the college, the basic protective spells at several of the settlements failed. It took all of the magicians another three weeks to get them back up again, and everyone said it was just luck that none of them had any serious problems with the wildlife while the spells were down. All the college magic classes were late starting, and when the college magicians weren't teaching, they were meeting with people from the Settlement Office and the Farmers' Society and the governor's office, as well as writing letters to people back East about the problems with the settlement spells.

Things changed faster and faster. William left for boarding school before his father got back from the settlements. Nan took up with a young man from the mills, whom she'd met at the railroad shipping office, and by Christmas she was wearing a ring and planning her wedding. Allie took the teacher's exam and went to work at one of the new day schools. Robbie had graduated from the upper school in spring, and everybody expected him to spend a year or two studying, the way Hugh and our older brothers had, and then go East for his schooling. Instead, he surprised everyone by going straight into the Northern Plains Riverbank College.

I felt lonelier than ever. Lan was gone; William was gone; Miss Ochiba was gone. Except for Rindy, my friends from the year before were gone — back in the settlements or working, like Susan — and Rindy was studying grimly for the teacher's exam and didn't have time for anything else. For the first time in a long while, I caught myself thinking that maybe Uncle Earn had been right after all, and I was bad luck for everyone I knew.

I had more trouble than ever with my magic classes. By mid-year, my spells weren't just fizzling anymore — they were going off in little explosions. The teacher shook his head and said it was only to be expected, since the class was moving on to more difficult spells. He told me to just do the set-up and write out the procedure for him, and for a while that worked. But then the people on either side of me started having trouble getting their spells to work, the same way I'd had trouble at first. I knew it was my fault, but I had no idea how to stop it from happening.

Working with the little blue book Miss Ochiba had given us was the one bright spot for me all year. It wasn't like the lesson books we'd used in the day school or the texts we used in the upper school, and it wasn't a list of exercises like the ones we'd done in her after-school class. Instead, it was full of stories and tales, some of which didn't seem to have anything to do with magic at all. I didn't know what to make of it at first, but I still read them over and over.

My favorite ones were the transformation stories, like the one where a frog turned himself into a bird to help a chief's daughter, or the one where a lion turned into a snake because he'd lied to his wife. I still didn't see what any of them had to do with Aphrikan magic, though. Until one day, when I was specially cross and frustrated. I'd just read three of the stories over again, and I knew I wasn't getting anywhere. I dropped the little blue book on the table with a thud, and said out loud, "This is stupid! It's just a lot of tales."

As I glared at the book, I remembered Miss Ochiba, and all the times she'd said, "That is certainly one way to look at the matter. There are others."

"What others?" I grumbled, but I knew better than to expect an answer. Even if she'd been there, Miss Ochiba wouldn't have said anything. In all the years I'd known her, she'd never once told anyone *how* to look at things. She just insisted that we look.

So I spent the rest of that year looking for different ways to see each of those stories. I saw that if you looked at it a little differently, the frog turned into a bird because he wanted to fly, not just to help the chief's daughter. It was a story about the way natural things change in ways that aren't natural to them, once people get involved. The more I looked, the more I found, and the more I found, the more I could see.

And then it was May, and the grubs were back worse than ever.

STRICTLY SPEAKING, THE GRUBS AND THE SETTLEMENT SPELLS WEREN'T my worries, I suppose. But Papa had been part of the group that invented the new spells that were supposed to keep the grubs from spreading, so when the grubs showed up in three-quarters of the settlements — nearly all the way to the river, in some places — people came to him and the others to complain. Papa was very annoyed about it. He said that he and the other professors didn't have time to waste settling down a bunch of bureaucrats when they ought to be figuring out what had gone wrong and how to fix it.

Professor Jeffries came around to our house on the second or third day after the news about the grubs reached Mill City. "Good afternoon, Miss Rothmer," he said when he saw me on the porch. "Is your father about?"

"Papa isn't home yet," I said. "I can send Robbie over to the college to fetch him, if you like."

"It'd be a mercy, if he's still tied up with those idiots from the governor's office," Professor Jeffries said, so I went and found Robbie. When I got back, the professor was staring west, toward the river, though you couldn't see it from our porch. "This is a bad business," he muttered as I came up.

"You mean the grubs, Professor?" I said.

Professor Jeffries nodded. Then he looked at me as if he'd only just realized I was there, and his eyes narrowed like he was seeing me for the first time. I'd put up my hair and lengthened my skirts since last he'd seen me, and I couldn't deny it made me look like a grown woman, though I was only middling tall. "It has been some time since we've seen you at the menagerie, Miss Rothmer," he said after a moment.

"I . . . didn't want to be in the way when everyone was so busy," I said.

"The stacks of notes that have been piling up are much more in the way than you would be," the professor said. He looked at me over the tops of his spectacles. "I shall expect you on Thursday at the usual time. Do not hesitate to interrupt if I am occupied with persons from outside the college when you arrive."

The next Thursday I went over to the menagerie office. Professor Jeffries hadn't been exaggerating by much when he'd said he had stacks of notes piling up. I started with the most recent notes and worked backward. It wasn't easy, with so many people around. When I was copying out Wash's notes, I could use a table somewhere else and get away from the visitors, but when I was updating the professor's map, I had to be right there in the office, and it was very distracting.

Even so, I was nearly finished by the time Lan and

William came home at last. Lan was taller again; he said he'd gotten nearly to six feet and he didn't want to hear any jokes about beanpoles or the air up there from any of us. He'd grown himself a pair of muttonchop sideburns, and he wore a green paisley waistcoat under his single-breasted frock coat. William was taller, too, but not by much — he was a good four inches shorter than Lan, barely taller than me. He was wearing a pair of eyeglasses and a beaver hat, but he was just as sandy-haired and serious as ever. I was quite startled when he greeted me with a bow and called me "Miss Rothmer."

"What do you expect?" Lan said. "How long has it been since you put your hair up? You ought to be used to it by now."

"Months," I said. "And I am used to it, from other people. It just sounds strange coming from William."

"'Miss Eff' would sound even stranger," William pointed out. "And I don't think you'd like 'Miss Francine.'"

I rolled my eyes at him, and then Lan asked William about the school he was attending. The two of them spent a few minutes comparing the larks they'd had when they weren't in class and the scrapes they'd gotten into. Well, the scrapes Lan had gotten into, anyway. Then William turned to me. "What have you been doing while we've been gone?" he asked. "Are you still helping Professor Jeffries?"

I explained how I'd stopped for a while, but now I was back at work and nearly caught up despite all the visitors. William gave me a sharp look, but Lan just nodded and started asking questions. The next thing I knew, all three of us were heading for the menagerie office.

Professor Jeffries was bent over his desk, muttering. He looked up as I hesitated in the open door and smiled at the three of us. "Ah, Miss Rothmer, Mr. Rothmer, Mr. Graham! Come in."

"I didn't mean to disturb you, Professor," I said. "But William and Lan were curious about your map."

The professor sighed. "I'm curious about it myself. Perhaps one of these days I'll have time to look at it again."

"If you're busy —"

"It's just more Settlement Office foolishness," Professor Jeffries said. "Harrison was in here this morning and saw that." He waved at the wall map with all the colored pins. "Now he wants one that shows where these grubs are."

"That sounds reasonable to me," William said.

"Well, that part of it makes sense," the professor admitted. "But he wants a portable map. With pins. That stay put when he folds it up. The man's a magical imbecile; does he think spells like that are easy?"

"Could you use an illusion for the pins?" Lan asked.

"That's an idea," Professor Jeffries said. He considered a moment, then shook his head. "Illusions don't last long enough. I'd have to renew the spell every few days, and if I have to trot over to the Settlement Office that often, I'll never get anything done."

"I could try it," Lan offered. "I've always wanted to see how long I could make an illusion spell last."

Professor Jeffries frowned, and I thought he was going to turn Lan down. But then he reached into his desk, fumbled around for a minute, and pulled out a piece of paper. "See what you can do with this map, young man," he said. "The settlement layout has been out of date these five years, but the geography hasn't changed. Just duplicate this pattern here." He spread out a newer map beside the old one and ran his finger along a penciled line.

William and I crowded around to watch. Lan studied the two maps for a minute, then asked, "Might I have some string, Professor? And a couple of those pins you use, please?"

While the professor brought the string and pins, Lan took a small leather case from his pocket. It was full of little vials of powder, held in place by loops of leather. Lan slid one of them out, opened it, and carefully dusted the first map with the powder. He replaced it and dusted the other map with something from a different vial.

"That's an unusual design for a magician's case," Professor Jeffries commented as Lan replaced the second vial. "May I?"

Lan handed the case to the professor, who tipped it this way and that, studying the vials without touching them. "Nice workmanship," he said. "You're a bit low on sulfur."

"I haven't refilled it since my exams," Lan replied.

"Do so at your earliest opportunity," the professor advised.

"You don't want to be caught without supplies when you need them."

Lan gave him a startled look, but accepted his case back without comment. William, the professor, and I watched in silence as he cast the illusion spell. I was half afraid it would fizzle, but after a minute, a network of pencil lines appeared on the old map, with pins at the places where the lines crossed.

"Well done!" Professor Jeffries said.

"Did you miss a spot?" William asked. He looked at the original map. "No, it's on this map, too." He pointed at an area almost in the middle of the map that had no pencil lines at all, and squinted. "Why don't they have any grubs?"

"What's that? Oh, that's just a gap in the reports. The Oak River Settlement doesn't have a settlement magician, and they're not on any of the regular circuits for some reason, so I haven't any information about their infestation level."

"Oak River is the Rationalist settlement," I said. "Where Rennie is. My sister," I added in response to the professor's puzzled look. "They aren't on the regular circuits because they don't use magic."

"That's right, one of you girls married that Rationalist fellow Dr. McNeil was so pleased with," Professor Jeffries said. "So she's out in their settlement now, is she? I don't suppose you could get her to send us some data about the grubs in that area? I'm sure they're as bad as they are everywhere else, but it would be nice to have actual figures."

"Professor, I'm not sure they are," I said slowly. "I mean, I'm not sure there are as many grubs there. We just got a letter from Rennie last week, and I remember she said they'd finished planting and it looked like being a good crop this year. She couldn't have said that if they had grubs all over the way everybody else does."

Professor Jeffries stared at me for a minute. Then he went to the coat hooks and took his hat. "Where's your father?" he demanded. "I need to talk to him about this immediately."

Papa was with a summer class, but the professor collared him as soon as it was over. Then we all had to go back to the house to look at Rennie's letter, and after that, things really started jumping. By evening, there was a special courier on his way to Oak River. Two days later he was back with word that the Rationalists had had a few grubs, but nothing like what the other settlements had been seeing.

That set everyone looking for reasons why. People pretty nearly tore the college and the Settlement Office apart, getting hold of records of wind and rain and temperature for every settlement in the North Plains, and marking up maps to see if there was a pattern that fit where the grubs were. Lan was kept busy making more illusion maps, and William volunteered to help me copy some in pencil, so we wouldn't need to have the illusion spell renewed. Right in the middle of it all, Mr. Harrison came storming into Professor Jeffries's office, waving the first map that Lan had done up for him.

"Jeffries!" Mr. Harrison shouted. "What do you mean by this?"

"Blast it!" Lan muttered as all the lines on the map he was trying to enchant disappeared. He straightened and walked around the table where we were all working. "Professor Jeffries isn't here, Mr. Harrison," he said a little too politely. "Is there some problem?"

"There certainly is, young man," Mr. Harrison said. "This map is incorrect."

"It's an exact copy of the professor's," Lan said even more politely than before. "I made it myself last week."

"*You* made it?" Mr. Harrison growled. "You mean Jeffries has been passing off student work on the Settlement Office? What's your name?"

"Lan Rothmer."

There was an awful silence. Then Mr. Harrison said in quite a different tone, "Oh, I see. Then — you're the one who enchanted this map? You're certain."

"Quite certain, Mr. Harrison. What seems to be the problem?"

Mr. Harrison spread the map out over the top of the one I'd been working on and jabbed his finger at it. "This clear area is supposed to be around the Oak River settlement, but instead it's around something called River Forest."

"It's the same thing," William said. "This is an older map that shows the name of the first settlement, that's all."

Mr. Harrison reddened. Then he huffed and glared at the

three of us. "I require a map that is up-to-date," he said stiffly. "I can't be forever explaining this discrepancy."

"I'm sure that's made this past week very difficult for you, sir," William said. Mr. Harrison looked at him suspiciously. William picked up one of the maps he'd finished, and held it out. "I'm sure this one will suit you."

"Very good," Mr. Harrison said after a cursory glance over the map. "I'll tell Jeffries about this myself. Good afternoon." He tucked the map into his pocket and left.

"I see why Professor Jeffries says he's an imbecile," William said in a thoughtful tone.

"He didn't even thank you!" I said. "Or ask your name."

"It's just as well," William replied. "He really hates my father. He'd probably have exploded again if I'd told him my name. That is, if he'd realized I was Professor Graham's son. He might not have; it took him a week to notice the difference in the map, after all."

"I'd forgotten that the Oak River settlement site had been used before," Lan said. "How long ago was that?"

"The River Forest settlement collapsed about eight years ago," William said. We both looked at him. "I was curious, so I looked it up. They didn't make it the full three years from when they started, and their claims reverted to the Settlement Office."

"Eight years," Lan said slowly. "It's a long time, but there've been cases where there were still traces after ten or even fifteen years. I wonder if anyone has checked?"

"Checked what?" I asked.

"Checked for traces of old spells," Lan replied. "I did a special project on the subject last year. The River Forest settlement wasn't run by Rationalists, so they must have had settlement protection spells and a settlement magician like everyone else. There might still be shadows of those spells around. It takes a long time for them to fade out completely, if the magician doesn't erase them on purpose."

William bent over the map Mr. Harrison had left. "Look. When it was founded, the River Forest settlement was right at the far edge of the frontier. Way out there, they'd have needed a really good magician to make it even for two years."

"Wash said once that the magicians in the farthest-out settlements are always trying things to make the protections work better," I said.

We looked at each other, and I could see we were all thinking the same thing. Lan was the one who put it into words.

"I wonder if something that old settlement magician did is what's keeping the grubs away from Oak River?" he said.

CHAPTER
22

LAN AND WILLIAM AND I DIDN'T WASTE ANY TIME TELLING PROFESSOR Jeffries about Lan's guess. I thought for sure somebody else must have noticed the same thing, but nobody had. Right away they started looking for the old River Forest settlement magician. Unfortunately, it turned out that the reason the settlement had collapsed was because their magician had died of a fever, and they'd been wiped out by a herd of woolly rhinoceroses before the Settlement Office sent a replacement.

Papa spent the next week wobbling between being proud enough of Lan to bust his suspenders and being mad enough at the Settlement Office to spit railroad spikes. Mr. Harrison made a terrible fuss over how long it had taken the college to figure out that there might be old spells at the Rationalist settlement, and never mind that his office had more maps and better ones, since they were the ones who handed out the settlement allotments. He sent people from his office over to the college labs and workrooms every day, and even came over himself a few times, until President Grey told him the visits were disrupting the college and wouldn't be allowed any longer.

That only helped a little, though, because right away he switched to peppering us with notes full of demands and suggestions.

We all ignored Mr. Harrison's notes as best we could, and got on with our work. Everybody knew we didn't have much time before the grubs emerged from their pupae as beetles, and if they kept on spreading, they'd be all the way to the Gulf of Amerigo in another two years, leaving nothing at all of the farm settlements west of the Mammoth River. So the college didn't want to waste any time getting a group out to the Rationalist settlement to see why they didn't have grubs, when everyone around them did.

The trouble was the Rationalists. The ones in Mill City flatly refused to let any magicians go out to their settlement. It took nearly the whole first week to get them to agree that if the people in the settlement itself were willing to let some magicians in, maybe it would be all right. Then the college had to negotiate with the settlement, which took even more time.

"I don't understand those people," Professor Graham said to Papa one evening. Professor Graham and William had been coming to dinner fairly often since the whole muddle began, because it was the only time they could be sure of talking without interruptions. "Don't they understand how important this is?"

"They don't like magic," Lan said calmly. "Or magicians. That's more important than anything else, to them."

"It's not that they don't like it, exactly," William said. "They think it's a weakness to depend on it. At least, that's what Brant Wilson said, when we used to argue while he was visiting Miss Rothmer."

"They really wanted to prove people don't need settlement spells to survive in the West," I said. "I bet they're pretty unhappy, hearing that they're maybe doing so well because of some old settlement spells. We haven't heard from Rennie since that came out."

Papa set down his fork and pursed his lips. Then he looked at Professor Graham. "You know, Anthony, we may have been approaching these folks the wrong way."

"Wrong way?" Professor Graham snorted. "We've told them what we need and why. The rational thing to do would be to stop all this pussyfooting around and let us do the investigation."

"Even Rationalists are people first," Papa said. "They don't want to be proven wrong, and having taken a position, it's as hard for them to back down under pressure as it would be for anyone else. But if we can find some way for them to save face . . ."

"Such as?"

"I haven't seen my daughter in a good five years," Papa said. "Nor met my grandsons. If we present this to the Rationalists as a family visit first, and an investigation second, perhaps they'll be more agreeable."

Professor Graham was skeptical, but no more so than usual, and by the end of the evening, he'd agreed it was worth a try. He and Papa put it to the college representative next morning, and within three days, they had the answer they wanted. The Rationalists agreed to let Papa and some other friends and family members come out to visit Rennie, with the understanding that while he was there, he could spend some time looking into the possibility that there were still spells around from the earlier settlement.

Things moved pretty quickly after that. There wasn't even a lot of arguing over who to send; everyone was in a hurry to be off, and there weren't that many possibilities anyway. Papa would go, of course, and Lan, because even if he was only eighteen, he was a double-seventh son and the Rationalists couldn't object to Rennie's brother coming to visit. Professor Graham wanted to go, but Dean Farley told him straight-out that they needed someone with a sight more tact, so he sent William as his representative. Professor Jeffries was going, and to my complete astonishment, he asked if I could come along, too, as his assistant.

Papa and Mama weren't too keen on the notion at first, but they warmed up to it pretty fast. Papa was pleased because Professor Jeffries said I'd been doing such good work at the menagerie. Mama thought a little longer, then said that she'd go herself if she was up to it, but since she wasn't, it'd be good for Rennie to see at least one of her sisters along with all the menfolk.

And then, just when everything looked like being finished, Mr. Harrison announced that because of the critical
situation in the settlements, he would be coming along to
observe firsthand. Professor Graham nearly had a fit, and
nobody else was happy about it, either, but there wasn't much
anyone could do to stop him.

"It might actually be useful to have him," Papa said once
everyone had calmed down. "The Rationalists could change
their minds at the last minute and decide they don't want magicians in their settlement, but they can't keep out the head of
the Settlement Office even if their three years are up and the
land is all theirs."

"You're too inclined to give people the benefit of the
doubt, Rothmer," Professor Graham said. "The day Harrison
does anything useful will be the day ice dragons turn vegetar-
ian and start hunting for coconuts in the Arctic Circle."

Professor Jeffries made a noise like he'd swallowed something down the wrong pipe.

"The question is, what's Mr. Harrison after?" William
said thoughtfully. "He's been in charge of the Settlement Office
for a good ten years, and I've never heard of him going west of
the Mammoth River even once. Why now?"

"He's up to something," Professor Graham said, nodding.
He looked at Papa and Professor Jeffries. "Perhaps I should
come with you after all."

I went back to packing supplies, while everybody else
pointed out to Professor Graham all the reasons why it would

be a bad idea for him to come along. He took it pretty well, considering, but I couldn't help wondering if maybe he was right. For someone as straightforward as he was, Professor Graham was surely good at seeing all the twisty ways other people played politics.

Thanks to Mr. Harrison, we left Mill City a day later than Papa had planned. We met at the north ferry landing, three miles from our house. Robbie and Mama came to see us off, and Professor Graham arrived with William a few minutes later. Mr. Harrison was so late that we nearly started without him, never mind the fuss he'd have made. The wagon and the horses had been loaded on the ferry for nearly an hour when he finally showed up, driving a light two-wheeled buggy with a rack on the back bulging with packages and bandboxes. Right off he made a fuss about starting immediately, as if it wasn't his fault we were so behind schedule.

The head boatman looked at the buggy, spat, and told Mr. Harrison in no uncertain terms that only a fool would take a buggy like that over the Mammoth River.

"Nonsense," Mr. Harrison snapped. "The settlement lands are my business, and I know my business well."

"Suit yourself," the boatman said, shrugging. "It'll just break down five miles out and have to be hauled right back."

It took another half hour to get Mr. Harrison's horse and buggy loaded on the ferry, but finally we got underway. I stood in the back of the ferry and waved to Mama and Robbie. I felt scared and excited both. I'd been so busy getting ready for the trip that I'd hardly thought about seeing Rennie and Brant again. After five years, I wasn't as cross with Rennie for running off and messing up Diane's wedding, but I wasn't sure I'd forgiven her, either. I didn't know what I'd say to her. I had a suspicion that Lan felt the same way, though we'd never really talked about it.

Halfway across the river, the head boatman rang the big bell at the front of the ferry to warn everyone that we were starting to pass through the Great Barrier Spell. Then for good measure he yelled, "Sit down and brace!"

I turned. Up close, the Great Barrier Spell was more than just a hazy shifting in the air. Thousands of tiny rainbows flickered and flowed in all directions, marking the surface of an otherwise invisible curtain. The front end of the ferry was almost up to it, and I grabbed the railing just in time.

The ferry hit the barrier spell with a bump, as if it had struck a rock. It hung there for a moment, then slowly moved into the spell. The horses lurched and tried to spook in spite of the calming spells Professor Jeffries had cast on them before we left the dock. I couldn't blame them. It was unsettling, watching the front end of the ferry ripple and go all shimmery while the rest of the boat stayed solid and normal. Watching the shimmers creep along the deck toward me was even more unsettling.

My skin tingled as the shimmer reached me. Without thinking about it, I relaxed and looked at the rippling air the way Miss Ochiba had taught me. The feelings Miss Ochiba called "sensing the world" flooded in. William and I had gotten plenty of practice sensing the normal spells around the menagerie during that last year, and if I'd thought about it, I'd have expected the Great Barrier Spell to feel just like them, only larger and stronger.

It didn't. Oh, it was large and strong, no question, but it wasn't strong the way Papa's spells were strong. It was strong the way an ancient oak tree is strong, and large like looking for the end of the sky at night. I could feel pieces that fit together the way Avrupan magicians do team spells, but they all flowed together into one thing, the way Hijero–Cathayan magic does. And under and over and around it was the steady, endless coursing of the river and the magic that followed the river, supporting and powering the spell the way steam powers a railroad engine.

All of that magic was looking right back at me, almost like it was checking to see whether I was something dangerous that shouldn't be let through. The glitter in the air got thicker around me. I flinched, but there was no getting away from it. I tried to take a breath, but I couldn't. I felt like I was drowning.

Then we were through. The shimmering, sparkling air retreated toward the back of the ferry, and I could breathe again. I collapsed all in a heap on the deck of the ferry with my hands clamped tight to the railing over my head. I took a great gulp of air, and then another. I felt like I'd run all the way home from school, twice. After a minute, I forced my fingers open and wiped them against my skirts. I shoved myself up so I wasn't so much of a heap, and then I just sat there.

The boatmen all jumped up and went back to work right away as if nothing unusual had happened. Papa and Professor Jeffries weren't quite so quick, but they'd both been through the barrier spell every time they made a trip to the frontier. They stood up a second later and started reinforcing the calming spells on the horses. Mr. Harrison was still sitting on the deck looking stunned. When I saw that, I picked myself up fully, though I still felt a little wobbly. I wasn't going to let Mr. Harrison get ahead of me, even if nobody else noticed.

Lan stood looking back at the barrier spell, with his hands clamped to the ferryboat rail as tight as mine had been and his feet spread like he was bracing himself. William was up against the cabin wall, breathing hard. After a minute or two, he pushed off from the wall and dusted his pants, then came over to me.

"Wow," he said. "That was . . . wow."

I nodded. I didn't have to ask what he meant; he'd been part of Miss Ochiba's Aphrikan magic class as long as I had, and if we hadn't felt quite exactly the same thing, it'd for sure been close enough.

He gave me a sharp look. "You all right?"

I nodded again. "I just wasn't expecting it to be like that, is all."

William looked like he wanted to say more, but if he did, he thought better of it. Right then Lan came up, looking halfway poleaxed and shaking his head like he was trying to get water out of his ears. "How the — how did they do that?" he said.

"Yeah," William said. "The theories don't seem particularly likely, do they? Not the ones in my textbooks, anyway."

"I thought Mr. Franklin and President Jefferson wrote down how they did it," I said.

The boys looked at each other and rolled their eyes. "They did, sort of," Lan said. "But Benjamin Franklin was a self-educated double-seventh son, and a lot of his spells he made up on his own. Some of his descriptions aren't very informative. And it's practically certain that he improvised a lot when it came to actually working the spell."

"And Thomas Jefferson never could remember that most other magicians hadn't read four thousand or so books the way he had," William said. "And even if they had, sorting out all the references he thought were obvious is going to take scholars years and years."

Lan nodded. "We spent a month in magic theory class last year arguing over whether 'the adaptation of MacReady's transformation sequence using the principles described by Hamid al-Rashid' meant the Colin MacReady who wrote a treatise on physical transformation spells or the Leon MacReady who worked out how to apply mathematical transformations to magic, and whether it was the thirteenth-century Hamid al-Rashid from North Aphrika or the one from Byzantium in the early 1700s. We never did decide, and we never got around to figuring out how any of them applied to the spell at all."

"Oh," I said. We'd studied the Great Barrier Spell in my magic theory class, too, but we hadn't read the actual descriptions Mr. Franklin and President Jefferson had left, only talked about them.

Lan shook his head again. "I'm going to help with the horses," he said. "That, I can handle. Coming?"

"Too many cooks," William said. "Besides, you think better when you're doing something; I think better when I'm staring into space. And I want to think for a while."

"Humbug," Lan said. "You just say that because it gets you out of work."

William grinned and shrugged. Lan bopped his shoulder in passing and went forward. Despite what he'd said, I thought William would follow him, but he stayed right next to me, leaning on the rail in companionable silence, for the whole rest of the crossing.

CHAPTER 23

THE FERRY TO THE WEST BANK OF THE MAMMOTH RIVER HAD BEEN operating long enough to grow itself a sizable town around its landing point. Near the landing, the dirt streets were lined with big square shipping buildings, and all up and down the riverbank were docks for the flatboats that carried grain and timber down the Mammoth to New Orleans. The streets were double-wide to suit farm wagons, which made it easy to see farther in, along the roofed boardwalk that led from the docks to the storefronts. The oldest buildings, near the ferry head, were built of mortared fieldstone, but nearly everything else was whitewashed clapboard. West Landing was smaller and dustier than Mill City, but at first look, pretty much the same.

At second look, you saw that most of the folks on the boardwalk wore long tan-colored dusters over home-sewn calico or muslin shirts, and that almost all of the men wore gun belts. There were hardly any carriages, and the buggies were sturdier. All of the vehicles, from carriages to farm wagons, had a rifle rack next to the driver's seat, and most of the racks were filled. And every so often the wagons or the horses or one of the buildings had the slightly hazy look that meant someone had cast a personal shielding spell around it.

We got a lot of curious looks as we unloaded our gear from the ferry, mostly on account of Mr. Harrison's buggy and bandboxes. Some of the westbankers lounging on the board-walk hollered advice as the buggy came off the gangplank, most of it uncomplimentary, which was another thing that didn't happen much in Mill City. Mr. Harrison frowned when they started up, but he didn't answer back, which showed he had some sense after all.

With the late start from Mill City and the difficulties unloading Mr. Harrison's buggy, we didn't leave the ferry head until near noon. Papa drove the wagon and I sat beside him, Mr. Harrison drove his buggy, and everybody else rode. All the way through West Landing, people yelled advice and com-ments at us. The boys were a bit miffed, at first, and Mr. Harrison scowled ferociously, but Papa and Professor Jeffries just waved cheerfully.

A couple of folks yelled something about guides or maps, and once a long-faced fellow on a big gray gelding rode up to the wagon and asked Papa if he wanted to hire him. "No," Papa said. "But thanks for the offer."

"Begging your pardon, but it looks to me like you folks are heading for one of the settlements," the rider said. "And it's plain you don't realize what the trip will be like. You need a guide, sir, even if you don't think you do."

"Appearances can be deceiving," Papa said mildly.

"I'll admit that some of our party are green as grass, but Professor Jeffries and I have both been west of the river more than once."

"Ah," the man said. "Professor, is it? And magicians as well, no doubt."

"No doubt at all," Papa said. "Between us, I think we'll have no trouble making it as far as the Littlewood wagonrest, and we have a guide meeting us there. So we've no need of your services."

"Can't blame a man for trying," the rider said. "Good day to you, Professor. Ma'am." He touched the brim of his hat to me and rode off.

I watched him go, and then said, "Papa, you never said anything about a guide before."

"Didn't I?" Papa glanced at me and smiled. "Probably because I took it for granted. And because Professor Jeffries made the arrangements this time. It's nothing to worry about. Even settlers who've lived here for years hire guides when they're going somewhere outside their usual stomping ground."

I didn't find that as reassuring as Papa meant it to be, but I didn't get overly exercised about it because I was busy wondering whether Professor Jeffries had asked Wash to be our guide. I finally decided he wouldn't have, because Wash already had plenty of work to do out on the far frontier and wouldn't want to come all this way east just to escort us. But maybe he'd asked Wash to recommend somebody. That made me smile. Anybody Wash recommended would be interesting to talk to.

The storefronts lining the street gave way to houses, and then, abruptly, to open land. Papa told me that most folks didn't want to build any farther from the river than they had to, on account of the Great Barrier Spell making most people feel safer, even if they were on the wrong side of it. That didn't make much sense to me, and I said so. It's not like most wildlife would give enough warning for everyone to jump in a boat and cross back. Papa said it wasn't a magically sound position, but people's feelings didn't always have much to do with logic, and building near the river didn't hurt anyone.

Outside of West Landing, the road changed from packed dirt to rutted dirt, and the ride got bumpier and bumpier. Papa kept the wagon to one side, where the ruts mostly weren't·so bad, and when things got rough he kept the team moving steady and I held on hard to the running board. Mr. Harrison crossed back and forth across the road, looking for the smoothest places, and of course every time he crossed the ruts in the middle, his buggy lurched and bounced. He had to stop three or four times to pick up bandboxes that jounced right out of their ropes and fell off. Finally, on one particularly bad section, the buggy lurched down a rut with a great crack, and didn't come back up.

Mr. Harrison whipped his horse, but it did no good. The buggy didn't move. Professor Jeffries turned around and frowned. "Hey, Harrison! Stop belaboring that horse. You've broken an axle; the Great Blue Ox couldn't haul that thing any farther."

Mr. Harrison got off two or three good cusses before he remembered me and stopped. He put up his whip and climbed down from the buggy to look at the damage, while Papa pulled the wagon to a halt. It was pretty clear even from where we stood that the buggy wouldn't be going anywhere for a good long while. The front wheels were splayed out until the floor of the buggy nearly scraped the ground, and one splintery end of the broken axle had jammed solid into the side of the rut.

"How far do you think we've come from West Landing?" William asked as he and Lan pulled up alongside the wagon.

"About three and a half miles," Papa said. "Why?"

The boys looked at each other, and Lan smirked. "I win," he said.

"You wouldn't have if he hadn't kept zigzagging all over the road like that," William replied.

Right about then Mr. Harrison yelled for everyone to come help unload his buggy. Papa and Professor Jeffries exchanged looks, and then Papa handed me the reins of the wagon. "I'll be back in a minute, Eff," he said.

As Papa walked back toward Mr. Harrison, William started to dismount, but Lan put out a hand to stop him. "What?" William said.

"Papa didn't say for anyone else to come with," Lan said.

William stared at Lan for a minute, then looked at me. I nodded. William looked after Papa with a very thoughtful expression.

Papa and Mr. Harrison had quite a talk, though none of us could hear any details from where we were. In the end, Mr. Harrison rearranged his boxes himself, and picked out a few things to pack on his buggy horse, while Papa came back and sat on the wagon, waiting. After a bit, William commented that things might go faster if someone helped, but Papa said we had to wait for someone to come along the road anyway, someone local who could report the broken buggy and arrange for it to be picked up and maybe mended. Lan said we should just leave Mr. Harrison to it, but that made Papa frown.

"This is the west bank, Lan," he said sternly. "No matter how difficult a man is, and no matter how safe it seems, you don't leave him alone out here."

The words sent a little shiver down my spine, and I looked around. Just like West Landing, it didn't seem too different from the countryside east of the river, at first. Fields of soybeans and alfalfa and northern wheat stretched off on either side of the road, broken up by occasional ponds and wood lots. Off to the south was a steep ridge covered in scrubby trees. But the only buildings anywhere near were a couple of toolsheds tucked in the near corners of the fields, hazy with protective spells.

I looked again, and saw a clump of houses and barns in the distance to the south, surrounded by a palisade wall. East of the river, they'd have been strung out along the road, each house in the center of its own fields.

By the time Mr. Harrison got his boxes rearranged and repacked to his liking, Papa had unbent enough to let the boys help him move the buggy to the side of the road. Once that was done, Professor Jeffries pointed out that we'd never get to the Littlewood wagonrest by nightfall if we waited around much longer, and Lan said we could just as well report the broken buggy when we got to the next tinytown, couldn't we? So Mr. Harrison tied his buggy horse to the back of the wagon and crowded onto the seat with Papa and me, and we set off again.

Three on the wagon seat was too many, especially when two of them were Papa and Mr. Harrison being cross at each other. Even without the bouncing, it would have been a very uncomfortable ride.

We reached the first tinytown about an hour later. It stood on a low hill beside the wagon road, with an old log palisade wall circling the houses at the top, and two newer walls making loops around newer houses on either side. Over it all hung the brown haze that was the sign of settlement spells. We turned off the road, and the town sentry opened the gate for us. I tensed as we went through, but the settlement spell didn't react the way the Great Barrier Spell had. It felt like any other protective spell.

Inside, the buildings were crammed together tighter than the row houses on the north side of Helvan Shores. I asked Papa about it later, and he said that keeping everything close together made it easier on the settlement magicians, because they didn't have to stretch their spells so far. Even the streets were narrow. We had to leave the wagon just inside the gate and walk, which made Mr. Harrison complain some more.

Papa had been to the town before, so it didn't take as long as it might have to find the blacksmith and make arrangements about the buggy. Nobody was willing to part with a saddle, so Mr. Harrison had to go on sharing the wagon seat. Still, another hour was gone before we were ready to leave. Professor Jeffries was squinting at the sun and muttering, but he didn't actually object. Papa stopped to speak to him before he swung up on the wagon seat beside me, and the professor's expression lightened some.

"We need to travel fast," Papa called as we all rode out through the gates. "Stick close. Wagon first — it's slowest. Jeffries, you take the back."

Professor Jeffries reined in his horse and waited for Lan and William to get between him and the wagon. "What is this?" Mr. Harrison demanded.

"They're going to work a speed-travel spell," Lan said. "To hurry us up so we'll get where we're going by nightfall." He sounded like he was explaining to a three-year-old, but Mr. Harrison didn't pick up on his tone.

"But travel spells are factored into normal travel times," Mr. Harrison said.

William threw him a disgusted look. Everybody knew that travel spells interfere with the protective spell you need when you're traveling west of the Great Barrier. Nobody in the

West used extra travel spells unless they had a really, really good reason. I swallowed hard.

"Lan," Papa said. "Pick your spot."

Lan nodded and fell back to ride beside Professor Jeffries, where he could see everyone. I frowned. Even I knew that it only took two people to do a standard fast-travel spell, and that would be Papa and Professor Jeffries. Then I saw that Lan was holding a shiny gold disc about the size of the locket Mama usually wore, and I realized that he was going to cast the protective spell for us. I felt a little better, but only a little. I was pretty sure Lan hadn't done anything like this before, and power isn't everything.

Papa handed me the reins and pulled a gyroscope and a pink quartz crystal from his pocket. "Keep us moving straight and steady, Eff," he told me, and I felt scared and proud that he'd trust me to drive the team while he did his spell casting.

His eyes got that faraway look and I felt the surge as he and Lan and Professor Jeffries all drew power toward themselves to start working. Mr. Harrison started to say something else and William shushed him. Papa said the words and set the gyroscope spinning on the wagon seat. Behind us, I heard Professor Jeffries and Lan reciting their parts.

And then I felt the spells . . . waver. It wasn't quite the same as in my magic classes at school, when the people next to me had everything explode, but it was near enough. I gasped and stiffened right up straight. My fingers tightened on the reins and the horses slowed, just for a second. The change made the gyroscope on the wagon seat wobble, and Papa broke off to say, "Easy, Eff."

"Yes, Papa," I replied. I forced my fingers to relax. I put all of my attention on driving that wagon. I shut off every bit of magic-sensing I had, and I shut out every sound except the horses' footfalls and the creak of the wagon wheels. I looked straight ahead, watching the road, though there wasn't much I could do about the ruts and rocks. Slowly, it got harder to see. The landscape around went all dim and shadowy, as if there was a heavy fog. I realized that Papa's speed-travel spell had taken hold. A minute later, Papa's hands took the reins from mine.

I didn't say anything to him. I knew better; a magician has to concentrate all the time to keep up spells like the speed-traveling one. Besides, I was afraid that if I paid attention to anything besides the horses and the road and not sensing magic, I'd upset the spell. I didn't know what that would do, but I was sure it wouldn't be good.

I don't know how long I sat there trying not to do anything or even think anything. Finally I heard Papa say, "That should do it," and the light came back.

Cautiously, I looked around. Then I stared. The sun shone low in the sky ahead of us, clear and midsummer-bright. It sent skeleton shadows of the nearly leafless trees crawling across empty fields and dead-brown hills. No birds sang; no squirrels scrabbled up and down the tree trunks. We'd run out of road some while back; I couldn't even see wheel tracks in the dirt to steer by. The only sounds were the whisper of the wind through bare branches and the creak of our own wagon wheels.

Behind me, I heard a low whistle of surprise. Stiffly, I turned my head. Lan and William and even Mr. Harrison were staring just as hard at the fields as I'd been. Hearing about the damage the grubs did was different from actually seeing it. Papa frowned. "This far already," he muttered.

We rode in silence for nearly another hour through the creepy, dead landscape. We passed another tinytown off to one side, but we didn't stop. The wagonrest was several miles farther on, an empty palisade area built around a well. The Settlement Office set them up so that settlers who were traveling out to their allotments would have a safe stopping place that wouldn't put a strain on the already established settlements. As we drove up to the palisade, the gate swung open. Professor Jeffries rode forward.

"Welcome at last, Professor," said a deep rumbly voice from the darkness inside. "You all are a bit behind time. I was just pondering whether to head out to look for you."

"Wash!" I said.

It was Wash, all right. His hair was considerably longer than I remembered, and his beard wasn't so neat, but that was only to be expected when he'd been out riding circuit for two or three months. Professor Jeffries introduced him to Papa and Mr. Harrison and Lan, but when he got to William and me, Wash smiled broadly and said, "I remember Miss Rothmer fine, and Mr. Graham, too, though it's been a while."

"I wasn't expecting you to come yourself, Mr. Morris," Professor Jeffries said with a glance at Mr. Harrison. "Your work —"

"Well, now, you haven't seen the state the settlements are in out on the edge of the frontier," Wash said. "They need help, and fast. And I figure the fastest way for me to get an answer out to them is to be there when you all work it out." He shook his head, and added, "Besides, I need supplies. I ran out of coffee a couple of weeks back."

"We have coffee," I said. "It was right at the top of Papa's list, and I packed it up myself. I can make up a pot right now, if you like."

"Miss Rothmer, your father is a wise man," Wash said. "And you are an angel straight from heaven."

Papa smiled. "I've never known a guide who didn't appreciate a little extra coffee."

So I made coffee while everyone else buckled down to setting up camp. Wash had already cast the protective spells to keep the wildlife away, and even started a cookfire, so all that was really left to do was pitch the tents and lay out the bedrolls. Wash didn't have a tent. He said he wasn't accustomed to bothering with one in fine weather. When the boys heard that, they decided to sleep out under the wagon. They said they wanted to see what it was like, but I thought they just wanted to get out of putting up another tent.

While we worked, Wash asked about our trip out. He didn't make any comment about Mr. Harrison's buggy, but he said we'd been lucky on the last part. Where the grubs had eaten all the grass and grain and leaves, there was no food for the small animals, like mice and squirrels and birds, so they died or moved on. That left no food for the larger animals, and some of them had gotten hungry enough to attack travelers and even settlements in spite of the protective spells.

"That wasn't luck," Mr. Harrison said. "That was having a double-seventh son working the spell for us." Papa frowned when he said that, and Lan looked uncomfortable, but neither of them said anything.

Over dinner, Papa and Professor Jeffries and Wash talked about the grubs and how things were in the Far Western settlements. Wash said the thing that was the biggest puzzlement was how the grubs spread so fast. Mr. Harrison said that it wasn't the grubs that spread, it was the beetles that they turned into, and Professor Jeffries pointed out rather tartly that while that might be so, the beetles didn't have wings and couldn't crawl very far. And even beetles with wings didn't usually spread over a hundred miles in a single year.

Wash said it was certain-sure that something odd was going on, because the grubs weren't the only odd new critters that had been showing up in the Far Western settlements. That got Professor Jeffries's attention right away, and Papa's, too. Wash gave them a list of new wildlife he'd been seeing, including a new kind of cinderdweller, some antelopes with curly horns, a bear-like scavenger that seemed to avoid areas with magic in them, and some fat round beetles with wings like mirrors.

"I remember those," I said, and everyone looked at me. "You sent a sample one to Professor Jeffries the first year I was helping out at the menagerie."

"There are more of them now," Wash said. "It's a puzzlement what they eat, since the grubs and the striped beetles have cleared out everything in most of the places I've found them. But the mirror bugs don't do any damage, and they aren't around for long, that I've seen, so I haven't paid them much mind. I'd like to take time to study them, but with things as they are . . ." He shrugged.

Professor Jeffries frowned. "We need more observers," he

said. "Permanent ones, not just occasional expeditions like McNeil's. We could have had a year's warning about these grubs, at least, if there'd been someone out beyond the settlements."

That started Papa and Mr. Harrison and Professor Jeffries arguing over whether such a thing was even possible. It wasn't like there were a lot of folks who'd ever gone west of the far frontier and made it back. Wash just sat back with a small smile and sipped at his coffee.

It didn't take me too long to get tired of listening to the argument, and I could see that the menfolk would go on 'til the fire burned out and never mind the washing up. So I slipped away, filled the tin wash bucket from the well, and set it by the fire to heat. Nobody noticed except Wash and William. Wash gave me an approving nod, and William got up and followed me back to the well. He offered to haul the second bucket of water up for me, which I was pleased to accept, but I could see he had more on his mind than being gentlemanly. So I didn't grab the bucket and head back to the fire straight off. I waited, but he just stood there frowning.

Finally I tired of waiting. "What is it?" I asked.

William sighed and shoved his eyeglasses up on his nose. "What was that about, this afternoon?"

"What was what about?" I said.

"That thing you did. First you started leaking magic all over, and then you sucked it all in and sat on it so hard that I wouldn't have been able to tell you were even there if I hadn't actually looked with my eyes instead of my magic sensing. What was going on?"

"I don't —"

"Don't you go telling me you don't know," William interrupted. "For it's plain as day you do know."

"I don't know all of it," I said, wrapping both arms around myself hard. "I just — remember how much trouble I used to have casting spells in our regular classes?"

William's eyebrows drew together, but he nodded.

"Well, it got worse after you left. The spells didn't just fizzle out; they exploded. And then other people started having trouble casting spells when I was around. It's my fault, I know it. So when Papa and Lan had trouble this afternoon —"

"I see."

"I shouldn't have come," I said. "I should have known better."

"Why do you always do this?" William burst out. I stared at him, which only seemed to make him madder. "Why do you always blame yourself for everything that goes wrong?"

"I —" *I'm a thirteenth child.* The words stuck in my throat. I didn't think anymore that William would believe I was evil because of it, not really — but what if I was wrong? And I was sure he'd be disappointed and furious that I hadn't told him before.

William kept right on, like he didn't expect me to come out with an answer. "Have you talked to anyone about this . . . notion that you're somehow affecting other people's magic?"

"N-not exactly," I said. "When I started having trouble at school, Papa said it wasn't surprising. He said that with twins, when one has lots of power, sometimes the other doesn't have much. And since Lan —"

William snorted. "Lan's a double-seventh son. He has plenty of magic without soaking up extra from you, and besides, you're the elder twin. If anyone was going to walk off with an extra share of magic, it should have been you."

"But —"

"But, nothing," William said flatly. "You have plenty of magic. If you didn't, how could you be interfering with anyone else's spells? If that's what you *are* doing, which I doubt." He shoved his glasses up again and sighed. "You're going to fuss about this for the rest of the trip, aren't you? And nothing I say will make any difference."

William frowned into the bucket for at least a minute, while I tried to think of something to say. I didn't rightly see how I could promise not to worry, though I felt a lot better than I had before William started yelling at me.

"I know," he said. "We'll experiment. I'll cast some spells, and you can try to muck with them, and we'll see what happens."

"I have to do the washing up first," I said. "And besides, I haven't ever tried to — to muck with someone else's spells on purpose. It just happens when I'm close by. And what if I do something to the protective spells on the wagonrest?"

"You can sit close by while I work spells, then," William said. "The protective spells . . . that's a good point." His eyes narrowed, and then he smiled. "Mr. Morris cast the spells on the wagonrest; we'll get him to help. He knows Aphrikan magic, so he can watch what you're doing, and he'll be the first to notice if anything starts affecting his spells. I'll ask him while you're washing up, all right?"

"All right," I said reluctantly. "But if you want him to help, you'd better remember to call him Wash."

When William and I got back to the fire, Papa and Professor Jeffries and Mr. Harrison were still arguing. I collected the tin plates we'd eaten from. As I dumped them in the wash pan, three tin cups landed on top. I looked up to find Lan standing over me with a worn-looking dishcloth in one hand. "That's everything, for now," he said, gesturing at the cups. "Papa and the others are still using theirs. Wash or dry?"

"I'll wash," I said.

We worked in silence for a minute or two. Then Lan said a little too casually, "What were you and William talking about for so long?"

I looked at him, startled. It hadn't seemed long to me. "The way the spells worked on the way here," I said. I took a deep breath. "Lan, when you cast the protective spell this afternoon, did you notice anything odd?"

"Odd?" Lan paused in his dish wiping. "Odd how?"

"Like — like the spell starting to fizzle," I said. "Or — or being hard to cast."

"No," he said. "Well, not to begin with. It got harder to keep the spell going after a while, but that's just because I haven't had much practice keeping spells going for so long. It's more work than I thought."

"You're west of the Great Barrier Spell now," Wash's voice said from behind us, and we both jumped. "Even in the settled places, things are different here, and they get more so the farther on you go."

"Why?" Lan asked.

Wash shrugged easily. "It's how things are. You spend much time out here, you'll see for yourself."

"It doesn't make sense," Lan said crossly. "The Great Barrier Spell is just a big magic wall. It doesn't change anything on either side."

"Magic itself doesn't make sense, if you think on it," Wash said. "Why should burning two sprigs of rosemary and chanting some words make a silver mirror reflect what someone looked like ten or twenty years earlier? Why should spinning a gold disk on a chain keep the wildlife off for hours or days? What works, works, but there's not much rhyme or reason back of it that I've ever seen."

"There most certainly is!" Lan said. "They've known all about it since the Renaissance. Cantel's Theory of Reciprocity —"

"Ah, yes, the foundation of Avrupan magic," Wash said. "One of the foundations, anyway. But there are other points of view."

I gave Wash a startled look. He sounded just like Miss Ochiba. Except he also sounded like he was needling Lan on purpose, and Miss Ochiba never would have done that.

Lan seemed startled, too. Then his eyes narrowed and he said, "You mean Aphrikan and Hijero–Cathayan magic? You could be right. I'm afraid I haven't studied either in any depth yet, so I couldn't say." He sounded rather stiff.

Wash chuckled. "There's a good start," he said. "Now, as long as you keep an eye on what's really in front of you, instead of what you expect to be in front of you or wish was in front of you, you'll do." He glanced across the fire, to where Mr. Harrison, Papa, and Professor Jeffries were still talking. Then he turned to me. "Speaking of keeping an eye out, Mr. Graham tells me you'd like to do some experimenting, Miss Rothmer."

That got Lan's attention right enough, and next thing I knew, the four of us were over on the far side of the wagonrest, with William and Lan taking turns at spell exercises while Wash and I looked on. Or rather, while I watched them and Wash studied me. It didn't take long for William and Lan to make a contest out of what they were doing, picking more and more elaborate spells to show off with.

I was tense to begin with, but neither of them seemed to be having any trouble with their spell casting, so after a while I started to relax. After the first couple of spells, most of the things they did were new to me — things they'd learned off at school in the East. Every so often, one of them would come up with a spell the other hadn't learned, and they'd have to stop and talk about it.

Somewhere in the middle, Papa, Professor Jeffries, and Mr. Harrison came over and joined us. By then it was full dark, and Lan and William had started in on fireworks spells. I half expected Papa to correct Lan point by point when his starbursts came out lopsided, but he just smiled and said it was a good thing for Lan to get some practice. Then William talked Papa and the professor into doing some spells, and in the end all four of them did Washington crossing the Delaware, just as if it was the Fourth of July. William did the flag, and even remembered that it should only have thirteen stars. Professor Jeffries did the boat and the river, with chunks of ice floating everywhere. Papa did George Washington and his men rowing, and Lan did Robert Carradine casting the light spell ahead of the boat for everyone to follow and floating the cannon alongside. Then Papa said that was enough for one night, especially after the day we'd had, and everyone went off to bed.

I glanced over at Wash, who was nearly invisible in the dark. He didn't move or say anything, so I went off to my tent. I thought nothing had happened, but early the next morning Wash came around while I was making coffee and handed me a whorl of wood about the size of a robin's egg. A hole had been drilled into one side for a long leather cord. The wood itself had been smoothed on the surface, and polished to a silky shine between the twists and turns where it curled around itself. I could feel magic in it, but I couldn't tell what the magic was supposed to do. I looked up at Wash.

"You asked for my help last night, Miss Rothmer," he said. "That's about the best help I can give you, time being."

"Thank you kindly," I said. "But I could do with an explanation along with it."

"Near as I can see, you've been storing up magic like a squirrel storing nuts for winter," Wash told me. "But you've also been most carefully not using any of it, so it's been building up awhile. The more you store up, the harder it is to keep from overflowing, and when it starts overflowing without any control, well, it can get in the way of most other types of magic nearby. That —" he nodded at the polished wood piece "— will help drain off some of that extra power you've been hoarding, the way a lightning rod earths lightning to make no harm."

I closed my fingers tight around the wood. "Thank you," I said with a lot more warmth than I had put into the first one.

Wash's eyes narrowed. "It's a temporary measure," he warned. "You'll be needing to do some work on your own if you want to straighten things out permanent-like."

I nodded, only half hearing him. As long as it kept me

from causing problems with the spells Papa and Lan cast, temporary help was good enough for me. I made a loop with the cord and slipped it over my head, so that the wooden charm hung lightly against my chest.

And for the first time in a long time, I had a faint, shaky feeling of hope.

OUR SECOND DAY OF TRAVEL WASN'T MUCH DIFFERENT FROM THE first, for me. I sat with Papa and Mr. Harrison mostly in silence while we drove the wagon across the bare dirt that ought to have been meadows and hay fields and woods. Every so often, Papa or Mr. Harrison would remark on something, but they never got much of a talk going even when I did my best to keep up my part. Everyone else was on horseback, and from what little I overheard, they were having plenty of interesting conversation. I decided right then that no matter what Mama said about being a lady, I wasn't ever getting stuck sitting in a wagon again if all the interesting people were going to be riding.

What with the lack of talking, I spent most of the ride fingering the wooden charm Wash had given me. I was glad that someone else had seen my problem, and gladder still to have something to fix it, but on the whole, if I'd had my druthers, I'd rather that William had been right about it being all in my head.

The little wooden pendant was warm and comforting

under my fingers. Wash had said something about it draining off the excess magic. I decided that if I could figure out how the spell worked, maybe I could drain off more than just extra magic. Maybe I could get rid of all of it. I thought about asking Wash to show me the spell he'd used, but I had a pretty good idea that he'd ask questions, and he wouldn't like my answers.

That gave me pause. If I was that sure that Wash would think my idea was a bad one, I figured I should think about it a lot more before I actually did anything. Maybe I should just join the Rationalists, since they didn't use magic at all. I put the pendant away, but all the rest of the ride I kept touching it, just to make sure it was still there.

We stopped that night at another wagonrest, a few hours short of the Oak River settlement. Lan and William were full of all the interesting stories Wash had been telling, which only made me crosser than ever. After dinner, Mr. Harrison started talking about what steps we should take when we got to the settlement the next day. He wanted to dive right in poking around for the old settlement spells, and he didn't take it kindly when Professor Jeffries told him that the Rationalists would likely throw us straight out again if we did any such thing.

Finally even Papa got exasperated, and said that if Mr. Harrison went on like that, we might just as well have brought Professor Graham along after all, begging William's pardon, for Mr. Harrison was like as not going to upset the Rationalists every bit as much as Professor Graham would have done, just for different reasons. William sort of choked, trying not to laugh. Lan did laugh, though he apologized very nicely. Mr. Harrison scowled, but before he could start up again, Wash spoke up.

"There's times when too much hurrying makes for more delay," he said. "I'm thinking this is one of them. It's true we need to know how the Oak River settlement is keeping clear of those beetles, and we need to know soon — they'll be coming out any day now, if they follow the same timing as last year. But I've stopped by Oak River a time or two on my way back to Mill City, just for curiosity's sake, and Professor Jeffries isn't far off in his guesses."

"Surely the importance of this expedition has been made clear to them," Mr. Harrison said, looking at Papa as if he was sure it was Papa's fault if it hadn't.

Wash shook his head. "Those folks aren't just standoffish when it comes to magicians. They purely dislike them. I'm frankly surprised they agreed to this study at all, let alone as fast as they did. I doubt it'd take much for them to change their minds."

"And we can't afford to take that chance," Papa said firmly. "If you won't recognize that, Mr. Harrison, we'll leave you here tomorrow morning and pick you up on our way back in a few days."

"You can't do that!" Mr. Harrison spluttered.

"I can and I will," Papa said. "You don't seem to realize that this trip was not organized with the backing of the

Settlement Office, nor is it sponsored by the Northern Plains Riverbank College. Officially, this is simply a family visit. You can complain to whomever you like when we get back to Mill City, and much good may it do you, but there's nothing anywhere that says I'm obligated to let you ride along on my wagon when I'm going to visit my daughter."

"There's always walking," Wash added in a thoughtful tone. "The Rationalists do it all the time, though usually not alone. It's easier to hold off an angry bear or a pack of Columbian sphinxes if you've got more than one rifle in use."

Mr. Harrison paled. He sputtered some more, but in the end he had no choice but to agree with what Papa said. Lan frowned, and later on I heard him tell William that if Mr. Harrison tried to change his mind after we got to Oak River, Lan was going to put a laryngitis spell on him. I wasn't so sure that was a good idea, but I was glad that somebody else had thought to wonder whether Mr. Harrison would keep his promises.

Next morning, we started off again. We passed several more tinytowns surrounded by bare land. One of them sent a man out to find out who we were; when he heard that Papa and Professor Jeffries were magicians, he pretty near got down on his knees and begged them for help. Professor Jeffries told him they weren't miracle workers, and Papa said that as soon as they had an answer, they'd let everyone know, but until then, there wasn't anything they could do. Mr. Harrison didn't say anything, but he kept looking at Lan. Nobody said much for a good while after that.

Around mid-morning, I started seeing little clumps of dead grass and weeds every so often, instead of just bare dirt. Shortly after, the clumps came closer together, and then some of them started being green. The wagon ride got bumpy, and then transformed again as the plants got bigger and smoothed out into a meadow. "We must be getting close," Mr. Harrison said.

Papa nodded. A minute later, Lan shouted from up ahead that he could see the Rationalist settlement, and Papa pulled the wagon to a halt.

"What is it?" Mr. Harrison asked.

"Mr. Morris!" Papa called to Wash. "Would you say this is a reasonable distance?"

"It'll make them happier than it makes me," Wash said. "But you're right to say we shouldn't go much farther."

"What are you talking about?" Mr. Harrison demanded.

Papa ignored him. "Jeffries! The settlement's in sight. Time to shut down."

Professor Jeffries nodded and took out the gold disc that he'd used to do the protective spells for us that morning. He breathed on it, muttering, and I felt the spells around us collapse and fade away. I shivered, knowing that if there was any wildlife nearby, it could come straight for us now, and we wouldn't even know until it was close enough to see.

"What are you *doing*?" Mr. Harrison said.

"Canceling the protective spells," Papa said. "It's part of their settlement contract — anyone visiting has to forgo magic while they're on settlement land." Which Mr. Harrison ought to have known, him being head of the Settlement Office, but from the look on his face, he hadn't bothered to check before he came on the trip. I frowned. What else didn't he know about?

Mr. Harrison opened his mouth, looked at Papa, and closed it again. Papa nodded to Professor Jeffries and set the horses moving. Half an hour later, we reached the settlement.

The Oak River settlement was on top of a hill with a palisade of logs around it, like most of the other settlements we'd seen, but the resemblance ended there. At the other settlements, the palisade was more of a tall fence made of branches woven together. It wasn't meant for serious protection; it was just an anchor for the settlement magician's spells.

This palisade was a double wall of logs sharpened to a point on top and then sunk half their length into the ground. The inner wall rose a good fifteen feet higher than the outer one, and there was a gap between them large enough that nothing could climb to the top of the first wall and jump from there to the second. Two log watchtowers stood at opposite ends of the compound, with the national and territory flags flying over each one. Around the outside of the outer wall, about thirty feet from the base of the logs, the hill had been carved away to make the slope steeper.

Professor Jeffries nodded in approval. "Good work. I think those walls would even stop a mammoth stampede."

"They wouldn't stop a steam dragon," Lan pointed out.

"Very few steam dragons come this far east," Professor Jeffries replied.

"It'd only take one."

William was studying the settlement with a thoughtful expression. "They probably have some other way to handle steam dragons," he said. "They'd have plenty of warning, with those towers."

They had plenty of warning of other things, too. By the time we got to the settlement, the gate was open and two men were waiting for us. One of them was Brant Wilson. The other man was older, but he still looked familiar. It took me a minute before I remembered — Toller Lewis, the president of the Long Lake City Rationalists, who'd come with Brant to see Papa the first time, all those years ago. I was more than a little surprised that such an important person had chosen to be a settler.

Papa pulled the wagon to a halt next to them. Mr. Lewis stepped forward. "Welcome to Oak River, Professor Rothmer," he said.

"That's very kind of you, Mr. Lewis," Papa replied just as formally.

Brant looked at Papa and hesitated a second before he said, "Yes, welcome."

Papa nodded at him, and the awkward moment passed over. First I was a little surprised that that was all there was to it, and then I was surprised that I'd expected anything else. After all, it'd been five years, and Papa wasn't one to carry a grudge, especially when he'd recorded Rennie's marriage and childings in the family Bible. Brant would probably never be his favorite son-in-law, but done was done. Papa went right on and introduced the rest of us. When the introductions got to Wash, he and Mr. Lewis gave each other a little nod, and I remembered Wash saying he'd stopped at the settlement a time or two on his way back to Mill City.

When everyone had finished their rather stiff greetings, Mr. Lewis offered to show us around before we went along to Brant and Rennie's house. We started off as soon as we'd stabled the horses. Unlike most settlements, Oak River didn't have an open paddock for visitors' livestock. Everything was covered, and after a minute I figured out why — it was because in a normal settlement, the protective spells kept the flying wildlife off, but here, folks would be taking a big chance if they left everything open. I remembered Lan's comment about steam dragons and shivered. It was all I could do not to keep looking up at the sky every other minute.

Inside, the Oak River settlement was as different from the other settlements as it had been from the outside. For one thing, it looked scruffier, almost makeshift. The buildings were smaller, shorter, and farther apart, and all of them had dirt heaped up around the walls nearly to the roofline. William asked if they'd started as dugouts, but Brant shook his head.

"No — they're deeper and more purposeful than that. Uncle Lewis studied the reports on the western wildlife, then decided we should store most of our critical goods underground. The burrowing beasts are fewer and easier to keep out, for the most part."

"Rather like the storm cellars they build down in the Middle Plains Territories," Professor Jeffries said.

"Like them, but larger," Brant said, nodding. "Every home and store has at least one full room underneath it; most have more." He grinned. "Digging them out was no picnic, let me tell you!"

"They're well worth it," Mr. Lewis added. "We've been glad of them a time or two already. And if we had a major disaster — if a woolly rhinoceros came through the palisade or a tornado smashed the part of the settlement that's above ground — we'd have a lean year or two, but we wouldn't lose all our tools and supplies, and we'd have safe places to live while we rebuilt."

It kept on like that the whole time they were showing us around, with Brant answering most of the questions and his uncle chiming in every now and then. Everyone except me and Wash and Mr. Harrison asked lots of questions, and Brant seemed to get more and more cheerful the more of them he answered. You could see that he was proud enough of the settlement to bust his buttons off, and didn't get near as much chance to brag on it as he'd have liked.

I thought it was all very interesting, but I didn't need to ask questions because Papa and Professor Jeffries and the boys were asking plenty enough without me. Wash didn't say much, but he was studying everything in a way that made me wonder if he was *looking* at things. It bothered me at first, that he'd use Aphrikan magic, even just world-sensing, when the Rationalists made such a point of no one doing any magic on their allotment. Then I remembered the little nod he and Mr. Lewis had given each other, and I wondered if maybe Wash didn't have some arrangement of his own. After all, he'd been here before.

Just about the time I thought that, a woman in a plain stuff dress and deep bonnet came out of one of the buildings and stopped short, staring at us. First she looked surprised. Then her eye lit on Wash and her expression turned dark. She gave him a good glare, then glared at everyone else for good measure, ending with Mr. Lewis. "So you did it after all," she said to him. "For shame!"

"Morning, Mrs. Stewart," Mr. Lewis said, though I noticed he didn't wish her a *good* morning.

Mrs. Stewart ignored the greeting. "Magicians!" She said it the way some of Mama's church lady friends said "saloons" or "actors," like she was cross that the word even existed for her to have to say. "Magicians, in Oak River! It's a scandal, that's what it is, and it's all your fault. I told you how it would be when you first gave in to that nephew of yours." She looked at Brant and sniffed.

Brant's lips tightened. Mr. Lewis gave him a sharp look, then turned his attention back to the woman. "The settlement council agreed to this visit, Mrs. Stewart," he said.

"You've always been lax, Toller, and I make no bones about saying so," the woman went on. "I've half a mind to report you to the national headquarters. We'll see what *they* have to say about all this."

"I'm sure they'd be pleased to tell you, Mrs. Stewart," Mr. Lewis said. His tone was mild enough, but Mrs. Stewart flinched like he'd slapped her.

"Magicians," she said again, scowling at us all. "I never thought I'd see the day." She sniffed once more before she finally brushed past us, holding her skirts aside so they wouldn't come near touching anyone.

"What was that about?" Lan asked after a minute, looking at Mr. Lewis.

"I thought it was fairly obvious," William muttered, but he spoke softly enough that only Wash and I, who were standing right next to him, heard.

"Some of our people don't approve of having magicians here for any reason," Mr. Lewis said with a sigh. "And they'll hold to that no matter what the settlement council has agreed on."

"There are always people in any group who will go along with authority only so long as authority agrees with their opinions," Papa said.

"And sometimes that's not such a bad thing," Wash commented. Mr. Lewis and Papa both gave him startled looks, but he just smiled. "It all depends on the authority and the opinions, doesn't it?"

That put paid to the discussion, and nearly to the tour of the settlement. Mr. Lewis showed us a few more things, but you could see his heart wasn't in it any longer. We saw a few more folks out of doors, and now that I was paying attention, I could see that at least half of them were giving us dark looks of one shade or another. The rest mostly had on polite faces, though one or two of the younger ones looked curious.

Mr. Lewis pointed out one of the little dug-in houses that was maybe a tad bigger than the others, and said that was his, and he'd be pleased if Papa and Professor Jeffries could join him for dinner. And Mr. Harrison, too, he added, just late enough that it was obvious he'd all but forgotten about him. Professor Jeffries accepted right off, but Papa said he'd see once he'd talked to his daughter, which reminded everyone why we were supposed to have come. Mr. Lewis nodded and handed us all over to Brant and wished us a fine visit. Then Brant took us down the street to a tiny house that looked just like all the others. He pushed the door open without knocking and called, "Rennie? We're here!"

RENNIE CAME TO MEET US WHEN SHE HEARD BRANT. MY STOMACH turned over when she stepped out into the sunlight. I'd thought some about meeting her again, but actually seeing her was better and worse than I'd expected. Rennie had always been my bossy older sister. I hadn't always liked her, but I'd always figured she *meant* well, right up until she ran off with Brant. Then I didn't know what to think. Part of me wanted to hug her, and part of me wanted to yell at her, but I wasn't thirteen anymore, and I couldn't do either one, especially not in front of Wash and Professor Jeffries and Mr. Harrison.

Luckily, I didn't have to do much except stand there and nod. Rennie started babbling nervously the minute she saw us, and the next few minutes were mostly exclamations over how tall Lan had gotten, how grown up I looked, how good it was to see everybody, and what a shame it was that Mama and Nan and Allie couldn't have come, too. Then Papa introduced Professor Jeffries and Wash and Mr. Harrison, and Rennie brought her children out to meet us.

Albert Daniel Wilson was a midsize four-and-a-half-year-old; Seren Louise was a tiny two-year-old. Both of them kept trying to hide behind Rennie's skirts. I couldn't quite tell whether they were just shy or really afraid. The baby was two months old, and looked to be ready for a nap and cranky about not getting it. Rennie had all of them dressed up in their Sunday best, and when she wasn't shoving them forward to say hello, she was nagging at the older ones to keep their clothes nice, which didn't make any of them any happier. It seemed a lot of fuss to make over meeting only one grandfather and two out of fourteen-plus aunts and uncles, but that was Rennie for you.

After the first flurry, I stepped back and let Lan and Papa and William do most of the talking while I looked around. The house was tiny, just two rooms, and neither one as big as our second-best parlor in Mill City. The outside walls were peeled logs, but the wall between the two rooms was made of planks.

The dirt piled around the outside walls shaded the windows and made the glass dusty, so looking out was like peering through a tunnel. It also kept the inside of the house cool and damp, which was pleasant enough for a hot day in mid-July, but I wondered how it would feel on a cold, rainy April or September day.

Rennie herself looked older, but not the way Sharl and Julie and Diane had looked older when we went back to Helvan Shores. Rennie didn't look grown-up older; she looked worn-out older. There were hard lines around her mouth that I didn't remember seeing before, and she moved just a little bit slow and stiff, like she'd spent the day doing laundry without any housekeeping spells. Then I realized that she'd likely had to do just that, and not just for laundry — the Rationalists wouldn't want her using housekeeping spells for anything.

That thought startled me, and I took a second, longer look around. This time, I noticed the jars and tins on the shelves by the stove — all things that mice and bugs couldn't get into, even if you didn't have a spell to keep them away. A thin rope ran back behind the stove, where you could hang damp dish-towels and cleaning rags to dry faster if you couldn't use a hurry-up spell. The curtain that served as a door between the front room and the back was a double layer of fly-block net-ting, each piece tacked down around three sides so you could pull them apart to walk through, but they'd fall back together and overlap completely to make it harder for the flies to get around.

Then I blinked. The fly-block netting was shimmering slightly, and I realized that I'd slipped into Aphrikan magic sensing without noticing. And the netting had a spell on it.

It was just a whisper of magic, not a strong spell like the ones on the windows and doors at home, but it was definitely there. I looked around for a third time. Nothing else in the room had the shimmer of active magic, but some things — the wash-tub in the corner, little Albert's trousers, and some of the kitchen pots — had a sharper edge to them that meant they'd had magic used on them not so long ago. And there was only one person in this house who could or would have done such a thing: Rennie.

I wasn't sure why that bothered me so much. It wasn't like she'd run off to join the Rationalists because she believed in their ideas . . . at least, I didn't think that was why she'd run off with Brant. But after all the fuss the Rationalists had made about making a go of the settlement without using magic, and all the trouble everyone else was taking to make sure nobody cast spells in the settlement, what Rennie was doing just seemed *wrong*.

I stewed about it all afternoon, while the boys unloaded some of the supplies from the wagon and Papa and Rennie settled the dinner plans. Everyone but me would go to Mr. Lewis's for dinner, to talk out the best way of investigating the old settlement spells without irking people like that Mrs. Stewart. Rennie couldn't help looking relieved to know that most everybody would be going to Mr. Lewis's and she wouldn't have to cook for so many people. I felt relieved right along with her; I knew good and well who'd have ended up helping with all the work.

Of course, I ended up helping Rennie with dinner anyway, but with only the three little ones and the two of us, it wasn't so difficult. The hardest part was keeping the childings from getting underfoot. Rennie chattered on the whole time, asking about Mama and the family and her particular friends from back in Mill City, and then interrupting me in the middle of my answers. It took me a while to catch on that she always interrupted when it looked like I was going to say something about magic.

After that, I paid more mind to my conversation, and Rennie relaxed some. As soon as we finished clearing up after dinner, we put the childings to bed and went out to sit on the step, waiting for Papa and the boys and Brant to come back.

The sun was down behind the settlement palisade, but the sky hadn't begun to darken yet. Rennie looked up and sighed. Then she turned to me and said, "That Graham boy is growing up well and then some. Is he sparking you?"

"What? Of course not."

Rennie raised her eyebrows at me. "Why 'of course'?"

I sighed. "Rennie, I'm barely eighteen. I haven't even gotten through school yet. And he spent the last year out East getting educated, like Lan. He's only been back a week or two."

"A week or two is plenty of time, if you're of a mind to it," Rennie said, and looked away.

There was a short silence while I groped for the right words to ask what I wanted to know. I didn't find any, and in the end I just blurted out, "Why?"

Rennie knew what I meant. "What does it matter now?" she said angrily. "It's nothing to do with you."

"Nothing to do with me?" I started getting a sick feeling in my stomach, and I clutched at the wooden charm Wash had given me. "Do you have any idea of all the things that happened because you ran off with Brant like that?"

She stared at me, plainly taken aback. "I didn't —"

"You didn't think," I said flatly. "Not then, and not since. Well, if you don't know, it's past time somebody told you." And it all came pouring out of me — the way Mama had looked when she came in to tell everyone that Rennie and Brant had eloped, the way she'd grieved, the cruel things the aunts had said, the row Diane had with Aunt Mari, the whispers at the wedding dinner after, and the whole awful fight with Uncle Earn.

"So don't tell me it's nothing to do with me," I finished. "Or with Diane or Robbie or Lan or any of us. Because —" I choked up at last, half from remembering and half from an anger that I hadn't even known I'd built up over all those years.

The anger and pain were so strong that I felt a flash of fear, thinking I might do to Rennie what I'd almost done to Uncle Earn at Diane's wedding. I felt it building up and didn't know how to stop it. I clutched at Wash's charm and held my breath. And then I heard Rennie's voice say softly, "I'm sorry."

All the anger drained out of me. Rennie was gazing out into the shadows between the houses. "I was young and scared, and I did the best I could at the time." She hesitated, then sighed and went on. "I don't expect you to understand."

I stared in surprise. The Rennie I'd known five years before would have fired right up with some excuse. This Rennie wasn't giving out excuses, or at least . . .

"Scared?" I said finally. "Scared of what?"

"Lots of things." Rennie shivered. "Losing Brant. Losing . . . other things. Being stuck in Mill City forever. Becoming an old maid." She glanced at me for the first time since I'd started in on her, then looked away again. "If it's any comfort, I've paid for it."

Paid? I didn't say anything, just sat there for a long time while the shadows deepened. Then Rennie sighed. "Eff, do you have any idea what it's like to live a life without magic?"

I shook my head.

"I've been trying for five years." Her voice sank to barely more than a whisper, though there was no one near enough to overhear. "It's hard. Harder than I'd ever have believed. These people — most of them grew up this way. They don't understand; they've never known anything else."

"They've only been out here for five years," I said. "They must have seen plenty of magic before that."

"Seeing isn't the same as doing." Rennie's voice stayed low, and I leaned forward to be sure to hear. "Brant's a dear, and more understanding than most, but even he — everything takes twice as long and three times as much effort to do. Even dusting! And everything has to be planned out ahead of time — so long for the dough to rise, so long for the wash water to heat, or the bread won't be done 'til an hour past dinner and the clothes will still be on the line at midnight, because you can't use magic to hurry anything along or make up for lost time.

"But it's the little things that are the worst. Do you know

how horrible it is to climb into a stone-cold bed every night in winter? Or to hear a mosquito whining around your head in the dark when you're trying to sleep? Or worse, to find your baby crying and covered in bug bites every morning, when all that's needed to prevent it is a five-second spell that any twelve-year-old can do without thinking?"

"That's why you put the spell on the fly-block netting," I said softly.

Rennie gave me a startled look. "I couldn't stand it anymore. Brant doesn't know; he thinks the bugs have stopped because of some nasty herbal mixture I soak the netting in every week."

"It's not just the netting, though, is it?"

"How did you —" Rennie stopped, took a deep breath, and shook her head. "Never mind. I forget sometimes just how much magic can do, if you put your mind to it. The people here . . . well, a few of them know enough to sense a strong, active spell if they go looking for it, but most of them haven't had enough training even for that. That's why I stick to small spells."

"I can see why you'd want to magic the fly-block netting," I said. "But the other things — is it really worth breaking the rules, just to make things a little easier?"

"Yes." The word had the intensity of a shout, though Rennie's voice couldn't have carried past the edge of the stoop we sat on. "And it's not just to make things a little easier."

"It's not?"

Rennie raised her chin, and I saw a flash of the old, bossy sister I remembered. "No, it's not," she said firmly. "I don't expect you to understand, because you've never had to go without spell casting. But going without magic is like . . . like going without your eyes, or your hands, or your legs. Sometimes it builds up inside me until I could just *scream*. The first three years, I used to sneak away from everyone when we were outside the palisade, just so I could cast a couple of measly little fifth-grade learning spells where no one would notice. But then Albert got too big and Seren came and I couldn't get away anymore."

"That's awful," I said. But Rennie had always been one for seeing a mule and saying it was a mammoth, so I asked, "If it's that bad, how can anybody stand to be a Rationalist at all?"

"It's different for the ones who believe what the Rationalists say," Rennie said. "If you really do think magic is a crutch, then wanting to use it just proves how much you've been leaning on it and how important it is to give it up. And the ones who've been Rationalists all their lives, like Brant, don't know what they've missed."

"I suppose," I said. I fingered Wash's pendant again, and wondered if what Rennie was talking about was anything like what had been happening to me. If it was, it wouldn't do me any good at all to join the Rationalists. All the magic I'd been so worried about wouldn't stop building up just because I wasn't using it; in fact, if Rennie was right, not using it at all would only make things worse.

We sat in silence for a while, until Papa and Wash and the boys came back from dinner. Professor Jeffries and Mr. Harrison had been invited to stay with Mr. Lewis, since Brant and Rennie really didn't have room for all of us. As it was, we had to shove the table over and lay out bedrolls in the main room for Wash and the boys. Papa got the big bed, Rennie and Brant used a hay mattress they'd made up ahead of time with the baby in its basket beside them, and I shared with the two little ones. There was hardly a bare spot wide enough to step on by the time we finished laying everything out, but at least everyone had somewhere to sleep.

I lay awake for a long time that night. First I thought about all the things Rennie had said. I didn't feel mad at her anymore, though I was still of the opinion that she might have thought a little less about her own self and a little more about all the rest of us. But she'd always been like that. I couldn't get her voice out of my head when she'd said she'd been young and scared. She'd only been two years older than I was now.

Whatever had been in her head when she ran off with Brant, it was five years too late for anything except saying "sorry," and she'd done that. I could hang on to what was left of the hurt, or I could decide to let it go and move on. I remembered Aunt Mari saying that Papa should write Rennie out of the family, and the way Aunt Janna and some of the others had talked, and I decided that whatever else I was going to do, I wasn't going to turn out like them. Rennie claimed she'd done the best she could at the time, and that would have to be good enough for me now.

Once I had that settled in my mind, I rolled over. I could tell from the sounds of their breathing that everyone else was asleep, but I still couldn't get to sleep myself. So I started the concentration exercise Miss Ochiba had taught me back in the day school, when I'd been so worried about losing my temper with Uncle Earn. It was a good way to relax even when I wasn't fussed or upset about something.

It only took me ten or twelve deep, slow breaths to get the first floaty feeling that meant the exercise was working. I kept breathing, counting six in, pause for a three-count, six out, pause, and let my mind float in the darkness.

Then I realized that even though my eyes were closed, I could see a glow in the dark. The wooden charm Wash gave me was glowing.

My eyes flew open. The room was pitch-black. I couldn't see a thing. I fished the pendant out from under my chemise. It still felt like it was glowing, but there wasn't any light at all.

I was so startled that I lost my grip on the concentration exercise. The feeling faded, and I was just lying there in the dark, holding Wash's charm. I thought about that for a minute, then closed my eyes and started counting my breathing again.

It took me a lot longer to get the floaty feeling this time, but when I finally did, I got the glow feeling back right along with it. I didn't bother opening my eyes. I just kept breathing, and tried to do the Aphrikan world-sensing at the same time.

I expected it to be difficult to keep doing both things — the concentration exercise and the Aphrikan sensing — especially since Miss Ochiba had said the concentration exercise was a Hijero–Cathayan technique. But the two went together like molasses went with pancakes. All of a sudden, everything was much clearer. I could sense Rennie's fly-block spell, and what was left of the spells she'd used to patch Albert's trousers and lighten the washtub and keep the pots from boiling over.

But the spell on the pendant was different. I could tell what all the other spells were or had been, but Wash's charm was . . . slippery. Every time I tried to look at it, it slid away. So I stopped trying to look at anything in particular, or even think about looking. I just breathed and floated and let whatever I could sense just *be*.

All of a sudden, the spell on the charm came clear, just for an instant. It wasn't one spell; it was a gathering of spells all layered together. Some of them felt like Aphrikan magic, some like Avrupan magic, and some like nothing I'd ever seen or felt before. All of them worked together, hiding and absorbing and using and feeding and changing the magic that fed through it.

That moment of insight didn't last long, but it didn't need to. I'd gotten a good, hard look at how that pendant worked, and I remembered. I opened my eyes and stared into the darkness. It wasn't any small working that Wash had gifted me with, and it wasn't anything he'd thrown together over an evening. Some of those spells were very, very old.

At least now I understood why no one else had said anything about the spell — a good chunk of the magic on the pendant was going to making sure nobody noticed it. I shook my head. It was one thing for me to take a minor charm from him, but this was something else again.

As I finally drifted off to sleep, I resolved to have a long talk with Wash in the morning.

CHAPTER 27

Talking to Wash didn't turn out to be as easy as I thought. First there was breakfast to make, which meant rousting out Wash and the boys so Rennie and I would have room to move around the stove. Then Professor Jeffries arrived right after breakfast to start setting things up to look for the old settlement spells.

"What on earth are you doing?" Rennie demanded when Lan and William showed up with the first of the supply boxes from the wagon.

Papa glanced at Brant, then explained about the old settlement spells and finding out what was keeping the grubs away from the Oak River settlement.

Rennie scowled. "That's nonsense," she said. "We've had grubs and beetles here, just like everywhere else. You should have asked about it first, before you came on a wild-goose chase."

"What's that?" Professor Jeffries said. He frowned at Wash. "I thought Oak River was clear of those grubs!"

Wash shrugged. "I haven't found any, passing through, and you saw the difference in damage for yourself on the trip here. But if Mrs. Wilson has seen some, I expect they were here. Some of them, anyway."

That got Professor Jeffries so interested that he almost forgot about setting up the detection spells. He wanted to go out looking for grubs right away, and it took Papa reminding him that all the grubs were pupating into beetles right at the moment to settle him down some. Then Wash suggested that he and Brant and Lan and William go out and try to find some of the pupae for the professor to study. Wash said he knew just the sorts of places to look, even if there weren't as many grubs around Oak River as there were in other places.

Professor Jeffries agreed that looking at the actual pupae might be very useful, especially since they should be just about ready for the beetles to come out. Papa was dubious about the whole thing, at first. He didn't like the idea of letting the boys outside the settlement when there weren't any spells to keep the wildlife off. But Brant told him the settlers hadn't found it as dangerous as everyone said, and Wash promised to keep an extra eye on them (which made Lan and William very cross, as they felt quite old enough to keep an eye on themselves). Finally Papa let them go. So the boys and Wash all left, and Papa and Professor Jeffries went back to setting up their spell.

Rennie wasn't too happy about what Papa and Professor Jeffries were doing. She said she had enough trouble with the neighbors on account of being a magician's daughter, without Papa and everybody doing actual spells. I thought that was awfully two-faced of her, when she was doing all sorts of spells on the sly herself. I almost told her so, but she caught me frowning at the fly-block netting and closed her mouth with a snap, so I didn't have to say anything after all.

Setting up the detection spells was a long and fiddly business. In order to keep the spell casting to a minimum and not upset the Rationalists too much, Papa and the other magicians from the college had decided not to do things in stages, the way they usually did. Instead, they'd wrapped everything up into one big spell that was supposed to do everything at once — detect the residue of the old settlement spells, find the places where it was strongest, collect as much information as possible about it, and analyze the information to find out how they were different from normal settlement spells.

That meant every element of all those spells had to be balanced and combined into a new spell. Papa said that what they'd done was a big step forward that would help magicians all over with combining spells, once they'd tested it a few more times and gotten some of the bugs out, but for now it was a cranky, fussy, delicate bit of magic.

Mr. Harrison was another big problem. He arrived around mid-morning, and right away wanted to know where Lan was. He got really angry when he found out that Lan was off hunting for pupae and beetles instead of working on the detection spell.

"It is foolish for you to waste such valuable talent on something anyone could do," he said. "Digging for beetles? Bah! And the risk — the wildlife —"

"I'm quite confident that Brant and Mr. Morris will take good care of *my son*," Papa said.

"*Your son* is a double-seventh son!" Mr. Harrison retorted. "Surely the power he has would be of enormous use here."

"This spell requires skill and finesse, not power," Professor Jeffries put in. "As you'd know if you'd read any of the reports the college sent you. Or understood them."

Mr. Harrison scowled. "A double-seventh son has luck as well as power," he pointed out.

"I think my luck will be quite sufficient," Papa said in a dry tone.

"Your . . . oh." You could just see the moment when Mr. Harrison realized that if Lan was a double-seventh son, Papa had to be a seventh son. I don't think that it had occurred to him before.

Mr. Harrison subsided at last, still muttering. Papa and Professor Jeffries finished setting up the spell while Rennie and I finished the household chores. Rennie did most of the housework herself, with baby Lewis in tow, while I watched out for Albert and Seren. The little ones were a handful and then some, but at least it was a change from the chores I had at home. Still, I couldn't help wishing that I was out with the boys, hunting pupae.

Right around mid-afternoon, Papa and the professor

finished laying out the materials for the spell. I didn't get to see them cast it, because I was outside with the childings. When we came back in, Papa and Professor Jeffries and Mr. Harrison were in the middle of another argument, and Rennie was glowering at all three of them.

"What is it?" I asked Rennie in a low voice.

"Their precious spell didn't work," Rennie said bitterly. "Or maybe it worked but didn't find anything. They can't decide. So they're going to try it again tomorrow."

I just looked at her. Thinking about it, I could see why the spell casting bothered her. Even if she'd been doing everything exactly the way all the Rationalists wanted, Papa's magic was bound to make some of them suspicious. And it was Rennie who'd have to deal with them; we would be gone in a few days, but she had to live here.

On the other hand, I'd seen the bare hills and fields where the grubs had been. Rennie hadn't. So she didn't realize how bad things were, other places, or how important it was to find some way to stop the grubs.

The argument went on and on. Just when it seemed that Mr. Harrison was going to start yelling, there were noises outside. A minute later, Wash and Brant and the boys came in.

"Is that the detection-spell setup?" Lan asked, making a beeline for the table with the measuring sticks and detection meters all over it. "Did you cast it while we were away?"

"Did you find any pupae?" Professor Jeffries asked.

"Everyone except Lan," Wash said. He held up a small covered bucket.

Lan gave him a dirty look. "I found plenty of cases, but they were all empty. And the only bugs where I was looking were those mirror-winged things. Not the beetles we were hunting for."

"That's very odd," the professor said, frowning. "Were you looking in a different area from everyone else?"

"No," Lan said. He sounded cross.

"Nobody found very many," William said. "We only got about twenty among us, all day, and maybe five or six beetles. You just didn't have any luck today, that's all."

Mr. Harrison gave William a strange look. "There, you see?" he said to the professor. "I told you it was a waste of talent to send this young man out on a pointless bug-hunt."

Professor Jeffries didn't even hear him. He had his little black notebook out, and was flipping through the pages, muttering. He looked up at Wash. "How many pupae, exactly? From how large an area?"

"We didn't stop to take a count," Wash said. "And we did spot checks on a three-foot square; among us, we probably covered about a quarter acre."

"Well, let's count them, then." The professor took the bucket from Wash, opened the cover, and spilled the contents out onto the table. Rennie made a noise of protest. Professor Jeffries looked up with a puzzled expression that changed to sheepish when he saw Rennie frowning at her dinner table. "Beg pardon, Mrs. Wilson. We'll clean up in a jiffy as soon as we've counted these."

Rennie sniffed, and for once I didn't blame her one bit. Bugs all over the dining table, and nearly time for dinner! If Professor Jeffries had been family, I'd have given him a good scolding right then, and never mind the company.

Professor Jeffries didn't notice Rennie's sniff or my expression. He was frowning down at the little pile of pupa cases. Something bright was moving slowly among them. "Mr. Morris, why did you bring two mirror bugs along with these others?" the professor asked.

"I didn't." Wash gave Lan and William a stern look. Lan looked indignant; William just shook his head.

"Then how did they get in here?" The professor stirred the pupae with his forefinger. Even from several feet away, I could see several dull green beetles crawling among them, along with the two — no, three — mirror bugs. "Look, there's another one."

"What are those things?" Brant asked, leaning forward with interest. "I've never seen one before."

Lan scowled. "I did *not* put any mirror bugs in that pail!" he said, marching over to the table. "I didn't put anything in that pail!" He pointed angrily at one of the crawling beetles, the tip of his finger barely an inch away from it. "Wash and William found all the pupae, and Brant caught all of those —"

There was a small popping noise, and the long green

beetle Lan was pointing at turned into a mirror bug. Lan stopped talking and gaped at it. So did everyone else. Then there were more popping noises. Four of the pupae that were closest to Lan's finger broke wide open, and a mirror bug crawled out of each one. The change kept spreading, the way popcorn goes when it starts popping — first one kernel, then two, then four or five, then everything all at once. In another minute, there was nothing left on the table except mirror bugs and empty pupa cases.

"Well, that explains why you couldn't find anything but empty cases," Professor Jeffries said after a long silence.

"But why did they change?" William said.

"Obviously, it's the magic of a double-seventh son," Mr. Harrison said, sounding as if he was talking to a room full of idiots.

Lan looked disgusted. "Don't be ridic — I mean, I don't think that's possible, Mr. Harrison. I wasn't casting any spells."

"No," Wash said slowly, "but still, there may be something to the idea."

"May be?" Mr. Harrison said indignantly. "Of course there is! You all saw it yourselves."

"But what did we see, exactly?" Papa murmured. He was looking at the mirror bugs with an intense expression. "Jeffries, have you seen anything like this before?"

"Not in a natural insect," Professor Jeffries said immediately. "But these have clearly been misclassified. This creature appears to have a five-stage life cycle, rather than the four stages that are usual with insects. The interesting thing is that the mirror-bug stage is the only obviously magical one, and that it could develop from the wingless-beetle stage as well as directly from the pupae. That is not —"

All at once, half the mirror bugs stopped crawling around the table and took off. Most of them flew straight at Lan, who yelled and batted at them. The others zoomed around the room, sparkling whenever the light hit them and banging into things.

"Get those bugs out of my house!" Rennie yelled. She reached for the fly swatter, but Papa stopped her.

"We'll take care of it, Rennie," he said. He looked up and muttered a shoo-fly spell, the one he used at home to clear the flies out of a room after someone left the door open.

But instead of flying out the door, all of the mirror bugs — including the ones on the table and the ones that had been buzzing around Lan — zeroed straight in on Papa. He looked quite startled, but he didn't bat them away the way Lan had. He let them light on his coat and then walked slowly toward the door, just as if he'd planned it that way. The mirror bugs clung to his shoulders and arms without trying to fly off, and a minute later, he had them all outside.

Rennie gave a sigh of relief and picked up a cleaning rag to wipe down the table. Wash got there first; he scooped all the empty pupae back into the bucket, picked up the bucket lid, and headed out the door after Papa. After a second, everyone but Rennie followed.

Outside, Wash was picking mirror bugs off of Papa's shoulders and slipping them into the covered pail. "Hold on a minute," Professor Jeffries said. "I want to test something."

He held out his hand, and Wash passed over the bucket. Professor Jeffries frowned for a minute, then took a nickel from his pocket. He flipped the nickel into the air and called out the spell for keeping something moving. The nickel hung in the air, spinning faster and faster. All the rest of the mirror bugs launched themselves from Papa's shoulders at the nickel and latched onto it, forming a glittering ball the size of a baby's fist. There was a rattle from the bucket as the bugs inside hit the lid, trying to get out. Professor Jeffries slid the lid back without ever taking his eyes off the spinning ball of mirror bugs, and the bugs from the bucket whizzed up to join the others.

The ball spun slower and slower, sending silvery flashes of light in all directions. After a few seconds, it started to sink toward the ground. Professor Jeffries held up the bucket and gasped the closing word of the spell. The ball of mirror bugs dropped into the bucket with a soft rustle. The professor slid the lid into place and sat down on the steps with a plop, like all the energy had gone out of him.

"What sort of nonsense was that?" Mr. Harrison demanded.

"So they're attracted to magic, even after they've changed," Papa said to Professor Jeffries, completely ignoring Mr. Harrison.

"And they absorb it," Professor Jeffries said. He pulled out a handkerchief and wiped his forehead. "They were sucking up power faster than I could feed it into that spell, though fortunately not by much. Which no doubt explains their attraction to you, young man," he added, nodding at Lan.

"But I wasn't casting any spells," Lan objected.

"Neither was anyone else," William pointed out. "As soon as someone did, all the mirror bugs went for the spell. But before that —"

"Lan was the strongest source of magic in the area," Papa said. He frowned slightly. "The question is, does the change from beetle to mirror bug occur based on the strength of the magic available, or on the amount?"

"We'll have to find some more pupae to test," Professor Jeffries said. "But I'll wager it's the amount of magic available that's the critical factor, and strength just speeds up the transformation."

"It's too late to find any more tonight, I'm afraid," Brant said.

Mr. Harrison broke in to huff about wasting time on mirror bugs when it was the grubs that were the problem, which irritated everyone and led to another argument that kept on right through to dinner.

I went back to helping Rennie with the housework, but even having three childings to look after didn't stop me turning over everything in my mind. And the more it turned, the more worried I got.

The pupae and beetles absorbed magic and popped into mirror bugs. The mirror bugs absorbed even more magic, enough to make Professor Jeffries tired after just a few minutes. There hadn't been very many mirror bugs to begin with, but the longer there were lots of beetles around the normal settlements, absorbing magic from their spells, the more mirror bugs there would be. And all of them would be soaking up magic from the settlement spells.

What would happen when there were so many mirror bugs that the settlement magicians couldn't keep their protective spells up anymore?

CHAPTER
28

THE NEXT DAY, PROFESSOR JEFFRIES TOOK BRANT, WASH, AND William out to look for more pupae and beetles. Lan stayed with Papa to help redo the detection spell, instead of Professor Jeffries. It didn't take as long to set up the second time, and it didn't have any more results than it had the first time. There just weren't any old settlement spells left for it to detect, Papa said.

Of course, Mr. Harrison didn't believe it. He said the college must have made a mistake when they designed the spell. Papa told him that in that case, he was welcome to redesign it himself, and arrange for his own people to do the testing. They were going at it hammer and tongs when the professor's group came back with their bucket of pupae. They'd ridden out to the edges of the Oak River settlement's allotment this time, and they'd found a lot more pupae and beetles than they had the day before.

Professor Jeffries was extremely pleased with their results. He was even more pleased when Papa told him they couldn't find any traces of old settlement spells at all, which irritated

Mr. Harrison even more. "If there aren't any spells, what's keeping those damned grubs away from this settlement?" Mr. Harrison shouted at last.

Rennie looked up, frowning. "Mr. Harrison," she said coldly. "I don't care what position you hold; this is my home, and I'll thank you not to use language like that where my children can hear!"

Mr. Harrison choked, but he must have known he was in the wrong because he apologized right off. When he turned back to Professor Jeffries, he didn't look so angry and he wasn't shouting. "Well?" he asked. "What's keeping the grubs away?"

"Nothing." Professor Jeffries gave Mr. Harrison one of the smuggest smiles I'd ever seen.

Mr. Harrison scowled uncertainly. Wash grinned. Papa's eyes narrowed, and then he smiled, too.

"Of course," he said, nodding at Professor Jeffries. "The beetles are attracted by magic. Oak River uses no magic, and is surrounded by settlements that use a normal number of active spells. As soon as the beetles emerge, they head toward the other settlements, and that's where most of them lay their eggs for next year's crop of grubs."

"Exactly," Professor Jeffries said. "I'm still not clear where the mirror bugs fit, but that's what we're here to look into." He rubbed his hands.

When Mr. Harrison realized no one was listening to him, he went off in a huff. Papa, Professor Jeffries, Wash, and the boys spent the rest of the day experimenting with the pupae.

By evening, they'd established that the pupae and beetles would transform into mirror bugs for any magician, just as Professor Jeffries had thought, and they were working on finding out how strongly the bugs were attracted to magic, from how far away. Papa, William, Lan, and Professor Jeffries were standing in a circle casting spells of different strengths, and Wash and Brant were in the middle with the mirror bugs and the few beetles that were left, counting how many moved in which direction.

All of a sudden, all the bugs and beetles stopped moving. Then the mirror bugs all leaned back on their rear legs and pivoted around, like they were looking for something. One after another, they took off, heading southwest. The beetles headed southwest, too, but they could only crawl. None of them got very far, though; even the flying mirror bugs had barely cleared the edge of the circle before they all dropped back to the ground and walked in little circles for a few seconds. After a minute, they all resumed crawling back toward Papa and the boys.

"Now what's this about?" Professor Jeffries muttered.

They collected the bugs and beetles and put them back in the buckets for the night, then talked it over all through dinner. Nobody had any real idea what had made the bugs behave that way, though Lan suggested it might have something to do with sunset coming on.

The next morning over breakfast, Papa decided to go bug-hunting with Professor Jeffries and the boys, since there was no point in doing any more spell detecting at the settlement. I was getting more than a mite tired of helping Rennie all the time, though she wasn't as bossy as I remembered. I wasn't sure whether the difference was in her or me. Pinning my hair up and letting my hems down hadn't made so much difference at home, but everyone there had had plenty of time to watch me growing, so it wasn't so startling a change. Still, however much Rennie had mellowed, I couldn't muster much enthusiasm for another day of housework and childings with no breaks.

So I told Rennie I was going to see everyone off and started down to the settlement gate with them, half hoping to persuade Papa to let me come along. We were hardly halfway there when we heard the ruckus at the gate. We could see four or five men yelling at each other, but we couldn't make out the reason for the argument until we were right on top of them. Seems there was a new arrival who hadn't stopped to dismiss his traveling spells, and the Rationalists were well and truly peeved about it. Some of the things the new man was yelling made it pretty clear that he didn't think much of the Rationalists and their ways, settlement rules or no.

As soon as he saw Papa and Professor Jeffries, the newcomer quit yelling at the gatekeeper and started yelling at us. It took a few minutes to get him settled down enough to make sense. It seemed that the settlement magician two allotments over had been trying something new, and now all the settlement spells had failed. They'd heard that Papa and Professor

Jeffries were visiting at Oak River, so they'd sent this fellow to ask if they'd come help put the spells back up.

Of course, Papa and the professor agreed. Papa decided to take Lan along, so he could observe the spell casting. He offered to take William, too, but William said his studies weren't advanced enough yet for him to get much out of watching, and he'd rather stay behind with Wash and me. Papa consulted with the messenger and told us not to worry if they weren't back for lunch, and they set off.

We had to explain it all to Mr. Harrison and Mr. Lewis, who came along too late to get in on the planning. Neither of them was too happy. Mr. Harrison just seemed to have a grump on about everything Papa and Professor Jeffries did, and Mr. Lewis was cross about having to put up with Mr. Harrison some more. I was a sight more sympathetic toward Mr. Lewis; after all, he hadn't really known what he was getting into when he offered to put Mr. Harrison up while we were in Oak River.

Wash, William, and I walked slowly back to Brant and Rennie's, and on the way I asked Wash about the charm he'd given me. Before he could answer, William jumped in, wanting to know all sorts of things about it, just as if he was one of my older brothers.

"Wash gave it to me," I said. "After that night at the wagonrest when you and Lan had that illusion-casting contest."

"It wasn't a contest," William objected. Then he frowned and looked at Wash. "You mean there really was something to all Eff's fussing about making other people's spells go wrong?"

"You might say that," Wash replied. "I confess to having a certain curiosity over the whys and wherefores of it, but Miss Rothmer seemed disinclined to account for it."

They both looked at me. I sighed. I still didn't want to explain, but I felt like I owed them an answer, even if neither of them had actually asked a question yet. "It's . . . it's because I'm thirteenth-born," I said, looking down at the toes of my walking boots so I wouldn't have to see their faces.

There was a long silence. Then, in tones of complete outrage, William said, "*That's* what you've been worried about all this time?"

"Mostly," I said without looking up.

"That's — that's —" He sounded exasperated, and I was pretty sure that only politeness was keeping him from saying "That's the stupidest thing I've ever heard." And I didn't think politeness would hold him back much longer.

"It's not stupid," I said before he actually got the words out. "It's — there was — I almost —" I stopped and took a deep breath, and before William could start in again or I could lose my courage, I told both of them the whole thing, all about Uncle Earn and the policeman and moving West and Diane's wedding and Papa's tests and the concentration technique Miss Ochiba taught me and the troubles I'd had with magic in the upper school. "I'm sorry I didn't tell you before," I said, mainly meaning William. "I just . . . I just couldn't."

"If you say so." This time, William sounded hurt.

"Fear's a powerful thing," Wash said in his slow, deep drawl. "Habit is even worse, for most folks. I must say, Miss Rothmer, I'm pleased and proud to be your acquaintance."

That got my eyes up from my boot tips, right enough. I stared at Wash. William was staring, too, but not like he was surprised. Wash tipped his hat at me and went on, "There's just one thing more I'd like to know, if you don't mind. Have you ever considered your situation from any other point of view?"

I didn't see right off what he meant, but William did. "Besides Avrupan?" he said.

Wash nodded. I looked down again. "Miss Ochiba told me once that being thirteenth-born doesn't mean the same thing in Aphrikan or Hijero–Cathayan magic. But she didn't say the Avrupans were wrong about it, either. And anyway, I'm not Aphrikan or Hijero–Cathayan."

"Honestly, Eff, if that isn't just like you!" William said. "Where you were born doesn't make any difference to whether the theory works or not!"

"That's not as true as you seem to think," Wash said. "But Miss Rothmer isn't any more Avrupan than she is Aphrikan or Hijero–Cathayan." He grinned at my startlement. "You're Columbian, Miss Rothmer, bred and borne. As is Mr. Graham here, and your talented brother, and even myself, though some might prefer it otherwise."

"I —" My mouth felt dry, and I had to swallow

twice before I could get any words out. "I never thought of that before. But what difference does it make, really?"

"Nobody really knows yet," Wash said. He tilted his hat back and looked down the street, to where the protective palisade blocked the westward view, and his eyes had a faraway look to them. "We're still inventing ourselves. But we're not starting from just one kind of magic, no matter what the folks back East may think. Columbian magic is a mixture and always has been — Avrupan and Aphrikan and Hijero–Cathayan and some traditions that haven't ever grown large enough to make a theory or a style of magic, plus a few bits folks have just made up for themselves at need, all thrown together."

"That sounds messy," I said without thinking.

Wash laughed. "So it is, oftentimes." He looked down at me, and his expression turned serious. "You're still inventing yourself, too, Miss Rothmer. You've been working your hardest to invent yourself right out of being a magician, and it's plain to me that if you keep on, you'll succeed in the end. You'd likely have succeeded already, if your heart had really been in it."

"But my heart *is* in it!" I objected.

"No, it isn't," William said. "Wash is right. You don't want to stop being a magician. You just want to make sure that you don't ever use your magic to blow up that uncle of yours, or anybody else, even if they deserve it."

"It's the same thing!"

"Oh?" William shoved his glasses up on his nose and glared at me. "So if you stop your magic completely, and then one day you grab a shotgun and use *that* to blow up your uncle or somebody, that'd be just fine with you?"

"No!" I could see where William was going, and I could see he was right, and it upset me almost as much as nearly blowing up Uncle Earn had. I'd known in my heart since my first day in Oak River that I didn't want to live without magic; I just hadn't admitted it straight out to myself. Because if I was going to go ahead and be a magician, even just an ordinary everyday magician, how was I going to keep my magic from doing something horrible one day?

William made an angry noise, and I realized I'd said more of that out loud than I'd meant to. Wash just nodded and said, "It's a puzzlement, Miss Rothmer, and not one you're alone in having."

"I — what? What do you mean?"

"You seem to think your magic is a separate thing from you yourself," Wash said. "Something you can pick up or leave alone, like that shotgun Mr. Graham mentioned a minute ago. But magic is as much a part of you as your voice. What you do with it is your own decision. And you're not the only magician with a terrible temper, you know."

"You're not even the only magician in your own family with a temper," William muttered, and I knew he was thinking of the time when he was nine and Lan hoisted him in the air.

318

We'd gotten back to Rennie's house by then, despite walking slower and slower, and Rennie came out wanting to know why Wash and William had come back instead of going off with Papa and the professor to hunt bugs. So I never got to say anything back to Wash and William about tempers and magic, but I worried at the notion all morning long while I helped Rennie with the weekly washing.

Lan had a temper, sure enough. I'd never gotten round to asking him how he'd felt about magicking William that time, but I could see that it hadn't slowed him down even a little when it came to being a magician. Thinking on it, the whole reason I'd started yelling back at Uncle Earn was because I could see that Lan was about ready to lose his temper. I'd forgotten that. And Lan hadn't ever seemed too concerned about misusing his magic by accident, even though he was a double-seventh son and crammed to the rafters with power.

But Lan had been getting special training since before he was old enough to cast spells. And Wash had said something about habit being more powerful than fear. I frowned down at the wash water. Maybe I'd been going about this all the wrong way. I decided to talk to Lan when he got back, and maybe to Papa when we got home to Mill City. I'd have liked to start trying things out right then, but the middle of a Rationalist settlement didn't seem like the best place to suddenly start experimenting with my magic.

Papa and Lan didn't make it back for lunch, and they still weren't back by mid-afternoon when Mr. Harrison came to see what they were doing. Mr. Harrison grumped and fussed at Wash about it, until Wash offered to take him over to the other settlement to check on things. That didn't sit too well with Mr. Harrison; he wasn't much inclined to do things himself, if he could get other folks to take care of them, and he was especially unwilling to do any more dangerous traveling, even though we hadn't had any trouble with the wildlife the whole trip.

Mr. Harrison was just winding up one of his rants when there was a loud rattling noise from the corner. "What's that?" he demanded.

"It's the pail with Papa's mirror bugs," I said slowly. I frowned uneasily at it, waiting for the rattling to stop. It didn't.

Mr. Harrison sniffed and turned back to continue his one-sided argument with Wash. The pail kept rattling, and I kept staring at it. After a minute, I started to feel floaty as well as uneasy. Finally, I couldn't stand it anymore. I walked to the corner and picked up the pail. "William, Wash, could you come outside for a minute, please?" I said.

I didn't wait for them to answer. I walked out the door and around back, to the cleared-off circle where Papa and Professor Jeffries had been doing their magic tests. I felt lightheaded and cut off from everything, as if there was a wall of glass between me and the whole rest of the world. Right in the middle of the circle, I stopped. I glanced back to make sure

Wash and William had caught up, and then I held the bucket out and took the lid off.

All the mirror bugs in the bucket took off in a glittering streak of silver, heading in the same direction. "Wash," I said in a voice that sounded very far away, "what direction was that settlement Papa and Lan were going to?"

"Southwest," Wash said.

We all stared after the twinkling line of mirror bugs, flying as hard and fast as they could toward the southwest.

"Something has happened to Papa and Lan," I said with certainty. "I have to go find them." I set the bucket down and started for the settlement gate.

GOING AFTER PAPA AND LAN WASN'T QUITE THAT SIMPLE, OF COURSE, but it turned out to be a lot easier than it could have been. Mostly, this was because Wash and William both believed me right off. Rennie and Mr. Harrison argued, though as soon as she realized that Mr. Harrison didn't want me to go, Rennie stopped arguing and just glared at everybody. It would have been funny if I'd had an inclination to be amused right then. Mr. Harrison just couldn't get on anybody's right side.

I just kept walking toward the gate, while Mr. Harrison said there was no point in jumping to conclusions because of a few bugs. It was getting late, he told us, and there'd be time to send a messenger in the morning. We collected quite an audience as we went up the street, on account of Mr. Harrison not bothering to keep his voice down. Finally, just as we got to the corral, Mr. Harrison yelled, "You aren't going anywhere, any of you! I forbid it."

I stopped and looked at him.

"In the absence of Professor Rothmer, I am in charge of this expedition," Mr. Harrison said in a slightly more normal tone. "And I will not allow —"

"Mr. Harrison." I kept my tone as polite as I could manage, which I fear wasn't too much because Mr. Harrison's eyes went wide and he stopped in mid-sentence. "Papa told you before that this was a family trip. You aren't my family by a good long ways."

"That was a ruse to get into this place, and you know it!" Mr. Harrison said. A lot of the Rationalists who'd gathered murmured angrily and glowered at him, but he didn't seem to notice. "This expedition is vital to the protection of the settlements, and I won't allow your whims to jeopardize it."

"Whims?" William said. "Eff's the least whimsical girl I know. And she's Lan's twin sister, in case you've forgotten. Of course she'd know if anything happened to him."

There wasn't any "of course" about it; I'd never before gotten a sliver of a notion when anything was wrong with Lan. But Mr. Harrison wasn't to know that, and he'd surely heard the stories about twins who could do such things. Besides, *something* was pulling at me, sure enough, and it wasn't any whim of mine. I kept my mouth shut and let Mr. Harrison sputter.

After a minute, Mr. Harrison glared at William and me and said, "Even if something is wrong, you can't do anything to help. It's better to take these things slowly — to find out what the problem is, if there is one. Then I can go back and send out the right people to handle it."

I looked at him, getting madder by the minute. Ever since he first found out Lan was a double-seventh son, he'd been trying to get at him, or at Papa, but now that they were both in danger, he wasn't in any hurry to help. Ever since . . . I remembered Mama threatening to haul Lan and me back East. All the anger settled down, and I smiled, knowing just what to say.

"That's as may be, Mr. Harrison," I told him. "But I'm not an employee of the college, nor of the Settlement Office, nor of anyone else in Mill City, and you've no authority over me. Papa hired the cart horses that brought us here. One of them will do for me to ride, and if I can't borrow a saddle from Brant, I can manage bareback. There's nothing you can say that will keep me in Oak River, and I can't see you laying hands on me to stop me."

"Just let him try," William muttered.

"So I'm going," I finished. "And that's my last word, and I'm wasting no more time on you."

As I started turning toward the corral, Mr. Harrison said, "You can't go off to this other settlement without a magician to do the protection spells for you!"

"Why not?" I said. "The Rationalists do it all the time."

There was a murmur of approval from the people standing around, and Mr. Harrison seemed to notice them for the first time. "You're hardly more than a girl!"

"I turned eighteen last month," I said.

"And I believe there's a good deal more to Miss Rothmer than you're allowing for," Wash's voice said behind me. I turned to find him leading three horses. "I took the liberty of saddling up our horses," he said to me and William. "Seeing that there may be reason for hurry."

"You can't go with them!" Mr. Harrison shouted. "You work for the North Plains Territory Homestead Claim and Settlement Office, and I'll fire you if you do!"

"Well, now, I don't believe you can rightly do that," Wash drawled. "My contract is with the Frontier Management Department in Washington, not with the North Plains Territory branch office. Still, if you want to write them a note of complaint, I'm sure they'll take as much notice as ever they do."

William choked on a laugh. "You want help mounting, Eff?"

I nodded. I hiked my skirts up, thanking my lucky stars that I'd worn full ones, and stepped into his cupped hands. An instant later, I was in the saddle. Wash held the horse while I tucked my petticoats in around my legs to keep from chaffing too much against the saddle. As he and William went to mount, Mr. Harrison yelled, "You can't just leave me here!"

"Now that's a true thing." Out of the crowd of Rationalists came Mr. Lewis and Brant, leading another riding horse. Mr. Harrison stared at them. Brant walked over and handed him the reins. "You're not welcome in Oak River any longer, Mr.

Harrison," Mr. Lewis went on sternly. "We'll see you on your way."

"You can't do this!" Mr. Harrison said. "I'm the head of the North Plains Territory —"

"— Homestead Claim and Settlement Office," Mr. Lewis finished for him. "So you've been saying these last few days. But we've been here five years and earned out our settlement claim."

"The only thing you have to offer us is the service of your magicians," Brant said. "And we've no interest in them."

"Which is a thing you seem to have a mite of trouble comprehending," Mr. Lewis said, and I couldn't help wondering what Mr. Harrison had been doing in Oak River while everyone else had been working on finding out about the beetles. "So be on your way, before we're moved to be less polite."

Mr. Harrison just stood there staring like he couldn't believe what he was hearing.

"Looks as if you'd best come with us, Mr. Harrison," Wash said.

"He can come if he likes," I said, "but I'm not waiting for him." I nudged my horse with my heels to get him walking toward the gate. I had a tense feeling in my chest and a growing urge for hurry, and I could see that if we let him, Mr. Harrison would talk nonstop for the next two days to keep from having to leave. "Thank you for your hospitality," I called over my shoulder to Brant and Mr. Lewis. Then we were out of the gate.

Mr. Harrison didn't take long catching up, and of course he had plenty more to say. First he wanted Wash to cast the protective spells for traveling right then, even though we were still on the Rationalists' land. Then he wanted us to stick to the areas that had been cleared and planted, so as to be able to see any wildlife at a good long distance, even though that would have meant going far out of our way. He kept on complaining about this and that until William told him that if he didn't shut up his mouth, he, William, was going to test out some of the silencing spells Lan had been telling him about.

Wash already knew where Papa and Lan had gone from the discussion in the morning, and he was familiar enough with that part of the territory to know the quickest route there. He thought that since we were in long-settled territory and moving fast, it'd be safe enough to travel without protection spells, even though Mr. Harrison objected bitterly. We alternated galloping and walking the horses — Mr. Harrison complained about that, too — so it only took us a couple of hours to cover the distance. By late afternoon, we came over the last hill to within sight of the settlement.

We pulled our horses to a halt and stared. A huge, sparkling cloud of mirror bugs hid the hilltop where the settlement was supposed to be. Some of the bugs were flying, but most of them were heaped up over the walls and the top of the settlement in a huge pile. They looked as if someone had taken an enormous ball and stuck mirrors all over it. The sun glittered and flashed on their wings as they flew and crawled, making it seem like the air was on fire and the ground around the settlement was moving.

Then I realized that the ground really *was* moving. Or rather, thousands of dark green beetles were crawling across it toward the settlement and the shiny pile of mirror bugs. If you looked in the right place, you could see little flashes of light as the crawling beetles popped into mirror bugs and joined the swarm around the settlement. It would have been real pretty, if I hadn't known there were a lot of people inside somewhere, and Papa and Lan among them.

Mr. Harrison turned white as a sun-bleached sheet. Wash's face went all stony and grim. William's eyes widened. "Where'd they all come from?"

"Anywhere near," Wash said. He nodded toward the ground, and we all looked down. There were beetles crawling past our horses' hooves toward the settlement. We were far enough away that they didn't make a solid layer over the ground, but there were still plenty of them. Mr. Harrison jerked, pulling his reins, and his horse danced sideways.

"There's no point in going farther," he said when he got his horse under control. "There's nothing we can do here."

He'd been saying things like that since before we left Oak River, but looking at the moving carpet of beetles I wondered for a minute if he was right. But William shook his head. "We have to try something. If we don't, what'll happen to the people inside the settlement?"

"It's just a lot of bugs!" Mr. Harrison shouted. "It's not as if they'll eat everyone!"

"No," Wash said. "They'll absorb all the magic from the settlement spells — which I'm near certain are currently being held by a double-seventh son — and then they'll spread farther east. Toward the Great Barrier."

William's head whipped around to stare at Wash, and I'm sure I looked just as bug-eyed as he did. I hadn't ever thought of that, but now that Wash had said it, it was obvious. If the beetles could absorb enough magic to make the settlement spells collapse, enough of them might do the same to the Great Barrier Spell. And looking at the mass of beetles around this one settlement, I had to think there'd be enough, sooner or later.

"Nonsense," Mr. Harrison said, but he sounded more scared than certain. "They're just bugs!"

A line of beetles a foot wide suddenly popped into mirror bugs, starting at the edge of the pile and heading straight as an arrow for us. It petered out halfway across the dead fields, but I still felt a tug, much stronger than I had at Oak River. This close, I could tell it for one of Lan's spells, only the beetles were soaking up most of it before it could get to me. "Lan's trying to do something," I said. "I have to get closer."

I kicked my horse into motion and headed down the hill toward the settlement. I kept trying to think of something I could do. My horse squashed beetles with every step, but with so many around and more on the way, the few he killed were nothing like enough to make a difference. Burning them might work, but I couldn't see how to get them away from the settlement first. And anything magic, they'd just soak up.

I was getting too worried to think straight, and I knew it. So I took a deep breath, then another, and started counting out the Hijero–Cathayan concentration technique. Mr. Harrison's whining faded into the drone of insect wings, and my mind settled some. I still didn't have any idea what to do, but I just knew there had to be something, if I could only figure out the right way to look at the problem. The beetles and the mirror bugs absorbed magic. The magic turned the beetles into mirror bugs, but what happened to the power the mirror bugs absorbed?

My horse slowed and shook his mane uneasily. We had almost reached the cloud of mirror bugs. Sunlight flashed on their wings as they darted in and out of the center, making my horse even more nervous. He pranced sideways, trying to run. As I brought him under control, I felt a surge of magic from the direction of the settlement.

It was Lan, trying again to reach me. Mirror bugs exploded into the air from around my horse's hooves as the crawling beetles absorbed the magic and changed. My horse reared, and I slid sideways. I had just enough presence of mind to kick my feet free of the stirrups before I fell completely off.

I landed in a pile of beetles and my horse ripped the reins from my hands and bolted. The fall and the beetles had broken that brief contact with Lan's spell. I didn't think he could get through the beetles, and I knew I couldn't reach him myself. I didn't have his power, and anyway my spells always went wrong.

A dark green beetle crawled over my boot. I didn't even have the energy to squash it. Behind me, I heard Mr. Harrison shouting for someone to come back at once. A second later, William pulled his horse up next to me and flung himself out of the saddle. "Eff! Are you all right?"

"It almost worked," I told him. "Whatever Lan was trying to do, it almost worked. But not quite."

"Come on," he said, dragging me to my feet. "We have to get away."

"Away?" I said, puzzled, and then I looked at him properly. His face was pale and he was sweating. Around his feet, several beetles popped into mirror bugs, and he swayed slightly. "The beetles!" I said. "They're absorbing your magic!"

"Yes, I know; now come *on*," he repeated.

"But they're not bothering me," I said. "And Lan —"

"We can't get in," he said doggedly. "And I can't think this close. Come on, Eff."

"Leave the da— dratted girl and get out of there!" Mr. Harrison yelled, and suddenly I was furious.

This time, though, the anger didn't go pouring out the way it had with Uncle Earn, and it didn't settle back down the way it had earlier at the Oak River settlement. It buzzed all through me like the sound the mirror bugs made, clearing my head. I turned toward the settlement, and the charm Wash gave me swung on its leather cord and thumped gently against my chest.

A familiar floaty feeling came over me, very like the combination of the Hijero–Cathayan technique and the Aphrikan world-sensing that I'd felt the night I'd tried to study the spells on the charm. Only this time, I wasn't sensing the spells on the charm. This time, I was feeling the beetles and the mirror bugs and the settlement spells.

I could see the spells Lan was pouring his magic into, and the way he was reaching out for me. I could see the way the beetles pulled at the magic all around them, even the magic of the mirror bugs. And I could see the little twist in the magic of the mirror bugs that kept the beetles from taking it along with all the other magic. It was a lot like the slippery twist in the magic of the charm Wash had given me, only not so old or complicated.

I stared into the cloud of mirror bugs, trying to hold on to everything I was sensing. If there was a way to include that twist in the settlement spells, the twist that kept the beetles from absorbing the mirror bugs' magic, then maybe the beetles wouldn't be able to absorb magic from the settlement spells, either. But I didn't know enough magic to do that, and anyway I couldn't get at the settlement spells. Papa and Professor Jeffries would know, but I couldn't get to them, either. I couldn't even get to Lan.

But I could get at the mirror bugs.

I smiled, and reached out.

APHRIKAN MAGIC DOESN'T TAKE A LOT OF POWER, AND IT DOESN'T take a lot of ingredients. You don't have to memorize gestures or chants. You just look at whatever you want to cast the spell on, in as many ways as you can think of, until you have an understanding of it, and then you sort of nudge whatever magic is already there, so it moves the way you want it to.

What Aphrikan magic takes is timing. Also practice, which is how you learn to get the seeing and the timing right. I'd been studying and practicing Aphrikan magic for nearly eight years, and for the last five, it had been the only magic I could get to work for me. Eight years wasn't enough to do anything that would take a lot of power or make a big change in something, but it was plenty enough time to get good at things that just needed a little bit of a push to make them happen anyway.

Straightening out the little twist in the mirror bugs' magic, the one that kept the beetles from absorbing magic from the mirror bugs, didn't take much more than a nudge.

The carpet of beetles seethed. The cloud of mirror bugs

trembled and began to die as the crawling beetles absorbed more and more of their magic. It spread fast, like setting fire to the corner of a sheet of paper — first there's just a small flame in the corner, then it spreads up one edge, and then suddenly the whole page is aflame, turning black and curling, and you have to drop it or singe your fingers.

Mirror bugs dropped out of the sky like silver rain. New mirror bugs rained upward as the crawling beetles popped and took off, then fell in turn as the beetles farther out absorbed *their* magic. It didn't take long for the cycle to spread outward from the settlement in an expanding ring. All I had to do was keep holding that little twist straight, so that the beetles could absorb magic from the mirror bugs.

Beside me, William yelled in surprise. "Eff! What are you doing?"

"Killing bugs," I said. I couldn't explain more without losing my concentration.

At first it was easy. The magic in natural things doesn't come one-thing-at-a-time, like it does with people. Oh, each mirror bug had its own little bit of mirror bug magic, but the magic itself was still all one thing, the way a river is all one thing even though it's made up of lots of buckets and cups and drops of water. Normally, that overall mirror bug magic would be stretched thin and hard to feel, but with so many mirror bugs all in one place, it was concentrated and easy to sense.

But as the mirror bugs close to the settlement died and were replaced by new mirror bugs farther out, it got harder to hold on to their magic. I had to reach farther and farther, and in all directions at once. It was the hardest thing I'd ever done, like trying to hold a full bucket of water head-high at arm's length with nothing to brace against, but I knew I had to keep at it. I had to be sure that all the beetles heading for the settlement died, or the whole mess would start up again as soon as the next wave of them arrived. I wasn't sure I could do this a second time. I wasn't sure it would *work* a second time.

So I hung on, feeding my spell with determination and anger and all the magic I had bottled up inside me. Soon the ring of changing beetles and mirror bugs was nearly a quarter mile from the settlement. Outside the ring, beetles crawled steadily forward to meet it. Inside, the ground was covered in dead mirror bugs. They were heaped over a foot high around the walls of the settlement, but where I stood, they were only an inch or so deep. I could feel my hold on the mirror bug magic starting to slip, and I knew I wouldn't be able to keep the spell going much longer.

And then I heard Wash's voice, and William's, talking next to me. A minute later, a hand touched my shoulder. "Miss Rothmer, have you ever done a spell hand-off?" Wash asked.

I nodded.

"I see what you're doing. Pass it to me," Wash said.

I'd never handed off a spell like this one before, but I didn't have time to worry that it might not work. By the time it came to me that I might not be able to do it, I'd already done it. Wash had the spell, and I was just standing next to him, feeling shaky and gasping like I'd been running.

Wash's eyes narrowed. "Mr. Graham," he said, and I felt William reach out and take part of the spell from Wash. Then Wash said, "Miss Rothmer, this would be a sight easier if the settlement could drop those protective spells for a bit."

I nodded and ran for the gates of the settlement, crunching and sliding on dead mirror bugs with every step. I'd gotten about halfway there when the gates opened cautiously and someone peered out. I shouted up to the bewildered stranger to tell Lan to stop the protective spells, but he just stood there. Then from behind him I heard Papa's voice yelling, "Eff? Eff, what are —"

"Tell Lan to shut off the protective spells!" I shouted again. "Wash says!" I was dizzy and nearly out of breath, and I didn't know what I was going to do if they didn't listen. I couldn't shout an explanation up the rest of the hill.

But Papa took one look at the dead mirror bugs and Wash and William concentrating like mad, and started yelling. A few seconds later, I felt the protective spell around the settlement collapse. As soon as it did, the ring of mirror bugs started moving outward faster and faster, and in less than five minutes it was all over.

With those extra-strong settlement spells gone, the beetles quit crawling toward the settlement and started milling around at random, the way they normally would. All they had left to pull magic from were the mirror bugs, and it seems that without that little twist in the mirror bug magic, the beetles were really, really good at sucking out mirror bug magic. It stands to reason, I suppose. They were different stages of the same creature, after all.

Wash and William held the untwisting spell until the chain reaction of beetles to mirror bugs petered out about two miles from the settlement. They figured out the distance later, by where they ran out of dead mirror bugs all over the ground.

All of us — me and Lan and Wash and William and Papa and Professor Jeffries and the settlement magician and a bunch of settlers who knew enough magic to have gotten roped into helping when the mirror bugs showed up — were pretty well exhausted. The settlement folks treated us real well, and didn't even make a fuss about getting their protective spells back up. Mr. Harrison did, though, until Papa made him be quiet.

The first thing Papa did when everyone started feeling a bit better was to get all of us together to piece together exactly what had happened and write an account of it before anyone forgot anything important.

What started it all off was the settlement magician's experiments. He'd had some ideas about increasing the power of the settlement spells, so that one magician could hold them over a larger area, but he hadn't worked the theory out right. Instead of expanding the protective spells, he'd made them give out.

That was when the settlement sent for Papa and Professor Jeffries. They'd taken one look at the magician's ideas and gotten all excited, because whatever he'd come up with was a brand-new way of working. Papa and the professor worked out where he'd gone wrong, and when they restored the spells, they used the new method.

The trouble was that the new settlement spell was so much more powerful than the old one that all the beetles in the ground around the settlement popped into mirror bugs right away, and all the beetles that were farther away started crawling toward the settlement in order to get close enough to suck up enough magic so they could pop into mirror bugs, too. By the time anyone realized what was happening, there were already so many mirror bugs and beetles around the settlement that they'd have sucked the magic and the life out of everyone inside as soon as the protective spells failed.

So they had to keep the protective spells going, but the protective spells were what was drawing the beetles and mirror bugs in and causing the problem. And of course, the more beetles and mirror bugs showed up, the harder it was to keep the protective spells going. Papa got Lan and the settlement magician and anyone who knew any magic at all to help hold the protective spells, while he and Professor Jeffries tried to find a way to lower the power in the settlement spell (so it wouldn't attract the beetles anymore) without actually having to drop it and recast it.

Lan had decided all on his own to try to reach me. Papa

wasn't any too pleased when he heard that, though he had to admit it had turned out well. Lan's idea was that if someone outside the settlement could squash or burn enough of the bugs and beetles, it would be safe to lower the protective spells. He hadn't really had a clear idea just how many of them there were.

Then Wash and William and I told our part, and Wash explained how the twist in the mirror bug magic worked. Papa and the professor got excited all over again, and started in right away to calculate how to build it into the settlement spells.

Meantime, Lan just sat and looked at me. Finally he said, "*You* found out all this about how the bugs work?"

I nodded.

"How?"

"I told you," I said. "It was world-sensing and the concentration technique and being mad as anything, all mixed together. Near as I can figure, anyway."

Lan grunted. Right about then, the settlement magician asked me what I meant, and I got all tangled up in explaining because he didn't know anything about Aphrikan or Hijero–Cathayan magic at all. I didn't start to understand what had Lan bothered until later, when we all got out into the settlement.

Turns out, the settlement folk had decided that I was the heroine who'd saved the day. Oh, they were plenty pleased with Wash and William and Lan, but I was the one they all wanted to see and talk to and praise. It got real embarrassing in less time than you might think. On top of that, it put Lan into a terrible temper. Up until then, he'd always been the one to be looked up to and admired for magic and spells, and he didn't much like playing second fiddle. A couple of times, I tried telling people what a bang-up job he'd done, holding off the mirror bugs, but it was no help. Everyone admitted he'd done a good job, then went right back to making a fuss over me.

Papa didn't really notice what was going on. He was too busy working out new settlement spells that wouldn't attract the beetles or make them pop into mirror bugs. Meantime, Wash and Professor Jeffries worked up a neat little trap that would do just what I'd done to the mirror bugs around the settlement, only on a smaller and less dangerous scale. They started with a power spell to draw the beetles in and start them popping into mirror bugs, and then switched it into a spell that untwisted the mirror bug magic to start the chain reaction. It took them a couple of days to get the power level right, but in the end they had a tidy little spell that would clear the beetles out of a couple of fields at a time in about half an hour. They planned to use higher power levels on the hills and bluffs and in the woodlands where there weren't any people.

As soon as Papa had the new settlement spells designed, Wash left. He didn't want to waste any time getting the spells and the beetle traps out to the other settlements. I did finally get a chance to talk to him before he left, though not for long.

"I wanted to give this back," I told him, holding out the wooden pendant. "And thank you for letting me use it."

Wash didn't move to take it. He just looked at me with a little smile on his face. "Now, why would you want to do that, Miss Rothmer?"

"It's too valuable for you to just be giving it away," I said. "You need it when you're out riding circuit, don't you? And — and I think I don't need it anymore."

His smile broadened, but he still didn't move to take back the charm. "I'm right pleased to hear that, Miss Rothmer, but that pendant only moves one way. Teacher to student."

I could feel my eyes getting wide. "Teacher?"

"That's what the conjureman who taught me said when he gave it to me, though truth be told he had even less time to spend with me than I've spent with you. It's not the time that matters." He nodded at the pendant. "You keep that, Miss Rothmer, until you find the right one to pass it to. You'll know. Meantime, you keep on studying it, and see what you can learn."

"I —" My hand closed around the pendant. Slowly, I nodded. "I will. And I'm right honored, Mr. Morris."

"Wash," he corrected me.

I stared at him for a minute, then grinned. "If you're Wash, then I'm Eff. If I'm your student."

Wash looked startled. I expected him to grin back after a minute, but instead he nodded solemnly. "Eff."

I looked at him a minute more, then hung the pendant around my neck again, and went along to see him off. I didn't feel as sad as I'd expected at his leaving. I was sure I'd see him again sometime, and in the meanwhile there'd be the notes he sent to Professor Jeffries.

I didn't feel sad at all when Mr. Harrison left. About two days after we'd cleared out the mirror bugs, he found a group heading back toward the river and talked them into taking him with them. None of us were sorry to see him go, though William and Lan wondered aloud whether he'd have trouble waiting for Papa and the professor when the rest of us got back. There wasn't anything to be done about it, though, and in the end, he was the one who had the trouble. About a month after we all got back to Mill City, word came from the Frontier Management Department in Washington that they wanted Mr. Harrison to come East to answer some questions, and that was the last we saw of him.

Seems that the settlers and settlements had been complaining about the way he managed things for quite some time, and that trip he took with us was the last straw for a lot of them. What really did it, though, was the way he'd acted at Oak River.

It seems the Rationalists were pretty well-thought-of in Washington, and when Mr. Lewis told them some of the things Mr. Harrison had said and done, they demanded that the Frontier Management Department do something about him, and not just a reprimand, either.

So Mr. Harrison lost his job, and it was a while before they sent anybody new to manage the Settlement Office. Papa looked pleased when he heard, but he never said anything. Professor Jeffries harumphed and said that it'd likely be a lot easier to get the new settlement spells spread around without Harrison interfering. Lan and William whooped like loons, and I was pretty happy about it myself. But that was a lot later.

Between the new settlement spells and the trap that Wash and the professor worked out, a lot of the settlements got their fields free of beetles by summer's end. That meant no grubs the next spring, so things could get back to normal for the settlers. Better than normal, some ways; the grubs and beetles had cleared a lot of land that would have taken the settlers years to do on their own, and they'd gotten rid of a lot of weeds, too, so crops that year were extra good. But that was later, too.

What with one thing and another, we stayed at the settlement for nearly a week after Mr. Harrison left. By the time we started back to Mill City, I was glad to get away. Lan was still grumpy, and I'd about had my fill of strangers coming up to me on the street to gush about how I'd saved them all. A simple "thank you" would have been plenty.

Leaving didn't help as much as I'd thought. The settlement had sent messengers to all the nearby settlements as soon as they could, to spread the word about the beetles and the mirror bugs soaking up magic. Of course, they'd told the whole story, including the part about me being a heroine. And those

343

settlements sent the word on to others. So all the way home, every settlement we passed wanted Papa to stop and teach the new spells to their settlement magicians, and while Papa was teaching, all the settlers fussed over me.

William thought it was funny.

"It's about time you got some attention," he told me. "And you deserve it."

"You and Lan deserve just as much," I said. "And I'd rather you had it than me. I don't like it."

"It's good for you," he said heartlessly. Then he grinned. "And it's good for Lan, too."

I sniffed. "Why does everything that's good for you have to be unpleasant?"

William just laughed.

"At least it's almost over," I said as all of us rode through West Landing toward the ferry at last. "Everything will get back to normal when we get home."

"You think so?" William said. He pushed his glasses up on his nose and gave me a sidelong look, the one that meant he was so sure you were wrong that he could just wait and let you find out for yourself the hard way.

I looked at him for a minute and then grinned. I had the feeling that "normal" had changed some after all that had happened in the past month, but I wasn't going to let on even that much. It would just make him smug.

"I'm sure of it," I said firmly.